Praise for Betty Corrello

"This is a hilarious and sweep... ...story about a comedian forced to return to her Jersey Shore hometown and confront everything she left behind ten summers before. A plucky heroine remaking herself. A beach setting. The meaning of home. Humor. Romance. This one ticks all the boxes."
—Mary Kay Andrews, *New York Times* bestselling author

"Fun and fresh. . . . Wry observational humor and a dose of romance strike a good balance with some tough family dynamics."
—*Kirkus Reviews*

"This novel will provide the LOLs and feels for you this summer."
—*Cosmopolitan*

"I'm in love with Corrello's voice. Vivid, fresh, and wholly singular, hers is a voice that's been missing from the rom-com pantheon. . . . Please welcome to the stage . . . Betty Corrello!"
—Julia Whelan, author of *Thank You for Listening*

"A vibrant sunbeam of a book—I simply inhaled it. Betty Corrello's writing is both achingly vulnerable and wildly funny."
—Rachel Lynn Solomon, author of *Business or Pleasure*

"Funny and keenly crafted, *Summertime Punchline* is packed with messy people, perfect chemistry, and a satisfying amount of heartfelt forgiveness. I tore through it; you will too."
—Annabel Monaghan, author of *Nora Goes Off Script*

"Humor, heart, and steam collide in this charming story about how people and places change and grow whether we're there to witness it or not. Betty Corrello's debut is the rom-com equivalent of a tight five—everything hits exactly how you want it to."

—Sarah Adler, author of *Happy Medium* and *Mrs. Nash's Ashes*

"A charmingly heartfelt and genuinely funny second-chance romance. *Summertime Punchline* is a wonderfully witty love letter to stand-up comedy, true love, and there being no place like home. Betty Corrello is a hugely exciting new voice in rom-com. I absolutely loved this book!"

—Georgia Clark, author of *It Had to Be You*

"Betty Corrello writes big-hearted, hot romance and perfectly crafted jokes that kick your ass; reading this book was like taking a beach vacation with an extremely hot single dad and the funniest person you know."

—Lex Croucher, *New York Times* bestselling author

"Betty Corrello's hilarious and sincere debut completely swept me away. The beautifully messy heroine narrates with a dry wit that gives way to a surprisingly earnest and tender core. I laughed, I swooned, I dabbed my eyes. Corrello is a voice to watch."

—Rachel Runya Katz, author of *Thank You for Sharing*

32 Days in May

Also by Betty Corrello

Summertime Punchline

32
Days
in May

A Novel

Betty Corrello

AVON

An Imprint of HarperCollinsPublishers

32 DAYS IN MAY. Copyright © 2025 by Betty Corrello. All rights reserved. Printed in the United States of America. No part of this book may be used or reproduced in any manner whatsoever without written permission except in the case of brief quotations embodied in critical articles and reviews. For information, address HarperCollins Publishers, 195 Broadway, New York, NY 10007.

HarperCollins books may be purchased for educational, business, or sales promotional use. For information, please email the Special Markets Department at SPsales@harpercollins.com.

Avon, Avon & logo, and Avon Books & logo are registered trademarks of HarperCollins Publishers in the United States of America and other countries.

FIRST EDITION

Interior text design by Diahann Sturge-Campbell

Title page illustration © Alex Rockheart/Shutterstock

Library of Congress Cataloging-in-Publication Data has been applied for.

ISBN 978-0-06-342647-4

25 26 27 28 29 LBC 5 4 3 2 1

This book is dedicated to anyone struggling to catch their breath, standing tall under the weight of an invisible burden. I hope my words bring you comfort.
You are not alone.

32 Days in May

Dear Reader,

32 Days in May is the story of one woman's experience being diagnosed with systemic lupus erythematosus, or SLE, but most commonly known as just *lupus*. The events leading up to Nadia's diagnosis are a fictional representation of what so many people with autoimmune diseases experience—an overwhelming sensation that their life as they knew it is completely over. This is, of course, not true. You, Nadia, and I have so, so much to live for.

Feelings of hopelessness, shame, anxiety, life-threatening depression, and even suicidal ideation are extremely common in folks who have been diagnosed with SLE. In fact, approximately 40 percent of patients with SLE develop depression at some point.[*] Please know that you are not alone and there is a path to feeling better. Help is available today.

If frank discussion of depression, anxiety, suicide, or living with a chronic illness is triggering for you, please proceed with great care for yourself. Take care of your heart.

With so much love,
Betty Corello

National Suicide and Crisis Hotlines:
USA & Canada: Dial 988
UK: Dial 1 16 1231

---

[*] L. Brundin, S. Erhardt, E.Y. Bryleva, E.D. Achtyes, T.T. Postolache, "The role of inflammation in suicidal behaviour," *Acta Psychiatrica Scandinavica*, 2015 Sep; 132(3):192-203. https://www.ncbi.nlm.nih.gov/pmc/articles/PMC4531386/#:~:text=Increased%20rates%20of%20suicidality%20are,during%20their%20illness%2094%2C%2095.

Prologue

Months Ago

If ever there were a physical manifestation of depression, it would be the Jersey Shore in the middle of January.

Everything is gray.

The water. The sky. The houses. My skin.

I think of my therapist's last words before we said goodbye.

You are worth fighting for, Nadia. And if this is how you win the war—then so be it.

In my pocket is a lilac Post-it note from her desk. In her sweet, Catholic school cursive, Audrey had written: *you are no one <3*

It was the first thing that had made me laugh in weeks. Maybe even since November.

How pathetic am I? I'd said when she handed it to me.

And then she'd said those last words before pulling me into a hug.

For years, I'd tried to be *someone*. Someone beautiful; someone interesting; someone you remembered from parties; someone you could tell a story about.

Now, my mother drives my car while I try to sleep in the passenger seat. She puts on an Italian song we've listened to on every drive to the beach for as long as I can remember. The sentimentality of this gesture makes my body recoil with anger. And the lyrics . . . the lyrics make me livid.

Too much trust ruins love. Now you're the mystery to me.

I find this to be so true, it makes me sick.

I'd tried to be memorable by making myself scarce. I'd tried to be unforgettable by being impenetrable. I'd tried and tried and tried. I didn't even get a chance to give up. My body did that for me.

"Do you have all your medicine?" she asks for the hundredth time.

"Yes."

"Did you take it already?"

"Yes."

"Do you feel better?"

I grit my teeth. "No."

We're at the last light before the bridge into Evergreen.

I count the seconds until it turns green.

***

March 5

I'm smoking a cigarette, leaning against the side of the house. I shouldn't be doing this, but sometimes a cigarette is the only way to stop the panic. Everything about smoking disgusts me—inflames my self-loathing and my GERD.

A tall figure with close-cropped russet hair makes their way down the sidewalk. *Fuck.* Downstairs neighbor. I'm trying to turn and book it back up the wooden steps that lead to my second-floor entrance when our eyes catch.

They look exhausted; the knees of their jeans are worn and

caked with dirt, a pair of filthy gloves tucked into the breast pocket of their flannel jacket. The tip of their nose is bright red.

"Hey," they call out. "You're Pep's daughter, right?"

Dammit. "Hey," I call back. My voice is high and pinched. "Yeah. Sorry for the—" I hold up my cigarette. "I'll get out of your way."

They wave me off, pausing at the bottom of the steps that lead to the first-floor door. "Your dad called me." *What the hell?* They catch the look in my eye and quickly add, "I think he was afraid we'd get spooked if we heard you moving around upstairs. But he also said you need a job."

My mouth falls open. That's low, even for Pep. I can almost hear his raspy, accented voice. *She thinks she's depressed! She thinks she's sick! Back in Italy no one ever depressed or sick! She just needs a job!*

"Of course he did."

They do a quiet little laugh. An acknowledgment of how ridiculous my father is, and I soften. "Yeah, I figured you didn't know about that. Anyway, I run a produce stand, and I always need help. I leave every morning around five A.M.—" I hold back a string of expletives. "Just come down and knock if you wanna join."

Yeah, right. "Cool—thanks." I sound stiff. *I sound like my dad.* I clear my throat and add, "I appreciate it."

They nod curtly. "I'm Soph, by the way. If you ever need anything, don't hesitate to knock."

***

April 1

I'm drinking my afternoon coffee on the balcony when, for the first time in months, I *want* to write. The sensation starts in my chest—a warm, comfortable light that blooms slowly into excitement or, maybe, delight, growing until it presses at the base of my throat.

I run inside, grab a pen and a notepad from the junk drawer before inspiration slips away.

Pen to paper, I begin:

things i never knew before lupus:

1. *we should be terrified of our bodies. you realize how little control you have over yourself; how all you can really do is react. if i'm afraid, i can look away. if i have a headache, i can take medicine. if someone breaks my heart, i can hold a grudge until i die. but i will never be able to stop the pain before it starts.*

I set down my pen and admire the ink pressed into the page. I like these words. These words are different from everything else I've written since November. Maybe, they're the beginning of a story.

When I look up, I see something strange, a blip interrupting the endless gray-blue horizon. Tangled in the low-hanging cable lines that stretch along the wide, empty streets parallel to the ocean.

Twisting and reaching for the dull, flat sky is a single, straggly tree branch. At the tip, there is a blink of pink. So small that without the stillness of its milieu, I would have missed it.

A cherry blossom.

Monday, May 1

Now

I repeat my mantra, out loud, to steady myself.

Deep breath.

"I am no one."

I lift the scissors and bury them into my hair.

Wild and recklessly curly. An implacable shade of light brown or perhaps dark, wooden blond. Wonderful and strange. When I was a baby, people would stop my mom and ask, *Did she come out like that?* My ever-growing mass of tightly wound corkscrew curls told the world: *she is someone.*

My hair has been deceiving me for years. Like most beautiful things, people, and places, it is a mirage.

But not anymore.

Now, it's coating my bathroom sink. Mucking up the plumbing. Twenty years from now someone's boyfriend will snake this drain and gag at the moldy, ancient clump that's choked back up.

What the fuck happened? they'll wonder.

I stare at my partially sheared head. A golden dust covers my cheekbones and the curve of my top lip. I didn't have a razor strong enough to survive the task of making me feel alive, so kitchen scissors had to do.

But, you see, I've encountered a real problem.

I can't reach the back of my head.

And, out of a real fear of being hog-tied and tossed away into a padded room, I, in a moment of true lucidity, know I cannot phone a friend.

Instead, I head out into the world with one-quarter of my hair still attached to my head. It hangs out of the back of my baseball cap like a beaver tail.

The hair salon I go into, at random, is staffed by a bunch of young, tattooed women also wearing hats. They stare on in horror.

The hairdresser does her best, God bless her.

She smooths and styles my now pixie-cut curls with mousse and high spirits.

"Oh my *God*. Babe, you look like Drew Barrymore."

I blink back a single, fat tear.

She is lying. I look like John C. Reilly.

Tuesday, May 2

My body celebrates my new hair-free lifestyle with a little torture.

Everything itches, burns, aches.

I was supposed to head to work with Soph, to sow watermelon seeds in the hothouse. Instead, I lie supine on the living room floor.

My *body* is exhausted but my *mind* is frantic, craving adventure.

What if I took the bus to Atlantic City? What if I got my bike out from the shed and rode it down to Brambleberry and went thrifting? I brought my sneakers—what if I just tried running like I used to?

It's nice to *want* to do stuff again. The world is my oyster, et cetera.

I fall asleep on the floor and wake up to rain on the balcony sliding doors.

Soon after sunset, my phone dings twice. It's my sister, Liv. She's sent me another job posting. Director of Growth Marketing and EMEA Advertisement for Big Evil Emporium, LLC.

Six figures!!!!!! she's written to accompany the link.

I know now something I would have never been able to admit before: I would sooner eat dynamite than be the director of *anything*.

Wednesday, May 3

Doctor's appointment.

I have to drive on to the mainland from Evergreen. I'm currently living in my parents' Shore house. Generational wealth in the form of a duplex next to a sandwich shop. Privilege in the form of a robust savings account accumulated after eight years in advertising. I'm unemployed, unmoored, and next to a body of water. I'm *basically* a Kennedy.

The doctor's office is freezing.

I pull my cardigan on and make a comment to the empty room about how I shouldn't have worn sandals, then I feel ancient. Gone are the days of being goose-pimpled and silent. Thirty hits and you're chasing down every manager, leaving one-star reviews on Yelp, begging the world to care about you the same way they did when you were twenty-two and fine with freezing your nipples off.

"Nadia, my dear. How's the hydroxychloroquine?"

"It's not *doing* anything."

"It can take some time to kick in." Dr. Antoniou folds his large hands and rests them on an equally large knee. "I can increase your dose. But you *are* looking a lot better."

I scoff to keep from blushing. Sebastian is handsome and Greek, both visually and emotionally. He loves his family. There are photos of his beautiful Mediterranean wife plastered all over the place. She has long, artisanal hair extensions and the most luminous fake tan. Together, they're bronzed and perfect. I imagine their chiseled, strong bodies clanging together while they fuck. Nothing but their hitched breath and the knocking of marble against marble.

"Can you imagine if I took *some time* to do anything? Four weeks to kick in at my job? Six months to kick in and pay my phone bill?" I swing my freezing feet back and forth from where I'm pouting on the table, the world's most enormous baby.

"That's a very funny observation."

Thanks, I'm a writer.

I want to say it *so* badly. But I've actually forsaken that title. Have I written anything of note in the last week? The last month?

Okay, wait. On Sunday I texted *stay clam* to Soph instead of *stay calm* and we laughed and laughed, for at least three minutes.

I used to write everyone's favorite commercials. It was a bit formulaic but what isn't? It went something like: peculiar animal with funny name + oblivious white guy. I used to write things like *Int. Day. Beach Bungalow. WIFE walks in on NAKED HUSBAND* and get the types of laughs Joan Rivers could only dream of.

Am I looking better? He can't just say that, can he? God, I want to feel better. Yesterday, I managed to bike three blocks (one and a half in each direction) to pick up sushi for dinner. Afterward, I had an epic energy crash. Today, I woke up feeling like I'd gone a few rounds through one of those old-school washing machines. Ridden hard, put away wet.

I squeeze my eyes shut. "Let's just do it. Let's increase my dose. What's the worst that can happen?"

"I'm sorry. I know you hate being on so many medications." He flashes me a mournful, sweet smile. Dr. Sebastian Antoniou puts the *bed* in *bedside manner.*

"How's your urine?" he asks with a gentle sincerity I find simultaneously arousing and degrading.

"Normal," I say, defensive. Then I shrug. "Sort of a . . . mustard yellow?"

"Any foam or froth?"

What am I, a cappuccino machine? "Everything's better. I told you," I lie. I love to lie. It's the only rush I get these days. "I think it—the, uh, foam and you know . . . blood . . . was just a onetime thing."

Dr. Antoniou works a hand over his chin. "I *know* that's what you want. And I know your situation is a rough one. Your dad and I"—I always forget that my father and Dr. Antoniou both frequent the same country club, where Sebastian, no doubt, enjoys the tennis court and pool while my father stuffs as much of the free breakfast buffet into the pockets of his supermarket jeans as possible, then drains the bunghole of cucumber water at record-breaking speed—"have discussed your work ethic. Your *passion.* He calls you his *bull.*" Dr. Antoniou clenches one of his enormous hands in a fist and holds it up between our faces.

"*Jeez.* Dramatic."

Doc laughs and nods. "Given your symptoms and that your urinary protein levels were elevated, we'll need to seriously monitor your kidneys for the next six months. Lupus nephritis is a frequent progression of systemic lupus erythematosus, and we do *not* want that for you, okay? We need to protect your internal organs as much as we can. If we don't keep this disease under our thumb, you're going to start to feel it"—Sebastian raises an inky brow at me—"*more* than you already do." He taps an uncapped pen against his clipboard, waiting for me to say something.

I don't. What's there to say?

"I'll order another round of labs for you." *Scribble, scribble.* "By the way, my cousin's coming into town for a month."

"From Eretria?" I'm desperate for a topic change. Enough of the piss talk. Enough of the organ talk. Ask me about the goddamn weather for once, won't you?

Dr. Antoniou's face lights up. He loves that I've remembered Greece, something Americans so often forget to do. "No. He lives in New York. Is it okay if I give him your number? Talia and I are headed out of town for a little while, and you know all the cool, hip spots in Evergreen."

"It's like, five streets and a boardwalk."

Dr. Antoniou crosses the room and places a heavy hand on my shoulder. Only for a moment before pulling away. "You really need to make an effort to get out more."

There it is.

Out. Everyone's obsessed with *out*.

"Or what? I'll get sick?"

"Nadia." He says my name so sweetly I almost fall in love. "Self-care is healthcare." *Jesus.* I grimace. *Never mind.* "Lupus is not a death sentence. As long as you wear a hat and your SPF—don't roll your eyes at me. You Italians think you're invincible!" Classic Southern European diaspora banter. I laugh to show I'm good-natured, but instead I show that it is possible to sound humorless and vacant, even while your mouth is producing a *ha ha ha* sound.

"Fine." I hop down off the table, angling to make a quick exit through the door Antoniou has propped open with a long, leather-clad foot. "I'd be happy to. Just don't tell him about . . ." I gesture vaguely at my body.

Sebastian laughs, the hardest he has yet. "*That* would be a HIPAA violation. As far as he'll know, you are one hundred percent healthy. Oh, and . . ." He waves a hand around his head. "*Love* the haircut."

A nurse leads me to another room, where he takes an ungodly amount of blood from my left arm. I make a joke about him being an extremely hungry vampire.

Neither of us laughs.

"Jimmy Timmon's been committed."

This is how my sister responds to *Hello?*

I set my knife down on the kitchen counter.

I've been cutting up apples for a pie I promised Allie for her birthday; she turned thirty nearly two weeks ago, so timing-wise, I'm actually doing very well. I only answered my older sister's phone call because I was feeling *too* good about myself. "*Olivia.* I don't think you can *say* that anymore."

Liv is completely unfazed by my reaction. "His mom's heartbroken. She came in to pick up two pounds of braciole and she could barely hold it, her hands were shaking so badly. *Terrible.*"

Before my diagnosis, Liv only ever called me when she was absolutely desperate for some entertainment. If her fiancé, Mike, was out of town and our mom unreachable, I was her last resort. Now, we talk on the phone so frequently I can picture *exactly* what she's doing as she yammers. I can picture her car keys jangling and swinging from her wrist and the ice in her latte clanking as she crosses the four-way intersection from our parents' butcher shop to the opposite corner where she parks her car illegally, every day. I can almost smell the sunshine on the black-topped Philly street, can almost imagine how the cherry blossoms cushion each of her steps, their last petals shed and having given way to wide, shining leaves.

"No fucking shit!" I pick up my knife again, going back to hacking up a particularly large Pink Lady. "That's her kid!"

Jimmy grew up around the corner from us, on a side street that always smelled like sulfur and dryer sheets. He'd been a scrawny, irritating kid with knobby knees and crooked teeth, cruising around on his bike or on the back of someone else's, standing on their back pegs like a captain at his hull. Most of us grew up, moved away, moved on. But Jimmy hung around, still cruising on his bicycle. *A living ghost.*

A shiver runs down my spine.

"Sad stuff." Liv sighs, but this feels like the beginning of a longer sentence she's still working her way up to. Silence settles over the phone line until I can't even hear the wind anymore.

"Thanks for letting me know," I say to fill the space, dragging out the *oh* in *know* so it sounds like a question.

"Yeah, well, I wanted to tell you, just in case you had any ideas . . . about . . . you know . . ."

"Oh my God. Are you serious right now? How many times do I have to tell you—"

"Hey," she cuts me off sharply. "Don't sass me, sister. *I'm* the eldest daughter. *I'm* the parentified one here. Mom and Dad are worried sick, and that means I have to—"

"What, threaten me with a grippy sock vacation?" I let out a biting, incredulous laugh. "Is this Jimmy news really your best attempt at talking to me about mental health?"

"Yeah, and it scared you, didn't it? Shocked you?"

Kinda. "You're sick, bitch," I say.

"I don't know what I'm supposed to do!" she cries in response. She sounds so much like Mom, I actually have to stifle a laugh. "They're on my ass, Nadia. They have no idea how to deal with this whole lupus thing—"

"It's not a *thing* that needs to be *dealt* with. It's just my life now."

"It's a serious disease."

I press the back of my hand—warm and clammy from the effort of chopping—into the space between my eyes. "Believe me, I've noticed."

"You lost your *job.*" The way she says this makes me want to barf. We've been having this exact conversation for six months, and each time it makes me hate who I used to be a little more. Cinderella lost her shoe; Virginia Woolf lost her mind; Nadia lost her job.

"Maybe it was a job I wanted to lose! Maybe I'm better off!"

Quietly, my sister grumbles, "You don't believe that."

"What difference does it make? This is my life, whether or not you and Mom and Dad think it's pathetic or weird. This is what I'm doing."

"But you're not doing any—"

"I'm fine." I cut her off before she can finish the word, before she can fully and totally accuse me of stasis. "I promise you, I'm not in crisis anymore. I'm just . . ." I search for the word. I've been searching for it for months, actually. One single word to describe what it is I'm doing. "I'm cloistering." This . . . is the best I can do.

"Cloistering?" Liv repeats carefully.

"Yeah, like a nun. I'm turning inward, searching for meaning in the meaningless. I'm finding power in stillness—"

"Jesus Christ."

"Exactly. That guy. All his stuff. He loved to be alone and wander around. In deserts. What a pill. At least I'm at the beach." I clear my throat. "I'm totally fine."

"Okay." Liv sighs again. "You promise?"

No, I don't. I am tissue paper in a windstorm, but she can't know that. She'll start listing other people we know who have blown away. Other people who made promises they couldn't keep.

I set down the knife. "Yes, Liv. I promise."

Thursday, May 4

W hy?" Allie is sitting cross-legged at the kitchen table working on a Diamond Art portrait of an alpaca farm. She does this every day before work to help steady her nerves before an entire day of being, voluntarily, locked in a room with teenagers. She calls it meditative, but I fear it may be compulsive.

"I told you why." I sit across from her. I've invited myself into Soph and Allie's half of the duplex. I do this whenever I wake up at a respectable time. They're allowed approximately three hours of daily alone time before I start to feel like they're conspiring against me, plotting to replace me with another forlorn straight woman.

When my parents bought their half of the wood-shingled bungalow, the first floor was occupied by a sycophantic palm reader addicted to diet pills. When Tamra passed, the Fabiola family was left with a gaping hole in our hearts. Who now would tell my sister and me we were too fat for our tankinis? Who now would inform our little brother that he had Ted Bundy's unibrow? A few years ago, Soph and Allie moved in. A few months ago, I attached myself to them like a barnacle. They're better neighbors than we—or Tamra—could have ever predicted. We share a wraparound porch, a carport, five beach chairs, and a shed. It's an intimate situation.

"It was too much effort. Wash days were exhausting." *And* my hair was an emotional and physical ball and chain, draining me of my last vestiges of sanity. *Plus* it was thinning and every shower I came away with a palm-size hairball that left me cosmically bummed.

Soph sets a mug of darkly brewed coffee in front of me. They make coffee so strong, it temporarily allows me to feel human again.

"Do your parents know?" Allie asks. She grew up in one of those freaky Protestant families where moms don't let their daughters cut their hair before their first blood. There's a lot of hand-wringing and crying over little girls being all grown up, as if it's never happened before.

"Why"—I pause to sip—"would I tell my parents?"

"Any word from Hot Doctor's Hot Cousin?" Soph interjects, clearly bored with all the hair talk.

"We don't know if he's hot yet," I warn them. "Maybe Hot Doctor got all the hot and Hot Cousin was left with the genes that make you mean about board games."

Soph and Allie grumble in unison. This risk is not unique to heterosexuality.

We clear the table of coffee cups and breakfast plates. Allie kisses Soph goodbye. I busy myself at the sink, awkward and unkissed.

I don't work on Thursdays, but I've been such a sack of shit lately that I force myself to help Soph, my current employer, paint a new sign for the produce stand. Busy season starts soon and we have many local septuagenarian competitors we need to bury.

I spend three hours fastidiously painting *PEACHY GREENS FRUIT & VEG. LOCALLY GROWN in MALAGA COUNTY, NJ* onto a slab of wood. Getting out of my cross-legged sitting position in the carport takes another three hours. The sun has moved across the sky, and I am still shaking the blood back down to my ankles.

ALLIE AND I are sitting around the kitchen table, enjoying a pre-dinner doom scroll, when I get a text from a 212 number.

> Hey Nadia, it's Marco Antoniou. My cousin gave me your number. Any chance you're free for dinner? :)

My jaw drops so viciously, I pull a muscle. *"Hold the fucking phone."* Soph turns from where they're caramelizing onions for a galette that will bring me as close to cumming as I've been in months.

"Marco Antoniou," I say out loud, and I almost can't believe it.

"Jennifer Aniston," Allie replies.

"Betty White," Soph adds.

"What?"

Allie shrugs. "We're naming Greek celebrities."

"What? No." I hold up my phone. *"Marco Antoniou.* He just . . . he just fucking texted me?"

"Holy shit." Allie, hunched under the weight of the work bag still around her shoulders, finally looks up from her phone. Then, she shakes herself free and appears almost instantly at my elbow. "Antoniou! How did we not piece this together? Celebs—they're *everywhere."*

Calling Marco a celebrity is incredibly generous. He's somewhere between disgraced child star and YouTuber, but also neither. Marco was on one of those network comedies that runs seven seasons without anyone noticing for, well, seven years. Then, he'd gotten a minor role in one of those Chicago shows. *Chicago: Pet Detective* or something.

After that, he'd gotten arrested for bringing a bunch of party drugs to an airport. Then, he disappeared.

No art house films to relaunch his career. No PR relationships to help reframe the bad press. Just a kid from Jersey whose luck ran out so he counted his blessings and slipped through the door when no one was looking.

Sounds familiar.

"I can't believe your hot doctor has a famous cousin," Allie marvels. "The world is *so* small."

I grimace. "He used the pervy smile."

"You *have* to meet up with him, are you insane?"

"It *could* be a different Marco," Soph reminds us—mostly Allie, who is now doing a demented little dance in place, long limbs vibrating while she does neck rolls.

"Exactly." I try to sound confident, but suddenly I'm vibrating, too. "It's gotta be a totally different Marco."

"What're you gonna say?" Allie has circled the table, back now hovering over my shoulder, buzzing like a magpie.

"I don't know. I was really looking forward to the galette—"

"I can save you a piece," Allie shrieks. It's a satanic sound and very close to my ear.

"*Fuck*, man. Fine, I guess I'll just . . . say something like, *wrong number sorry blocked*." Soph and I both dissolve into laughter while Allie melts to her knees. She crawls toward me, then grips my ankle with one of her bony, cold hands.

"You. Wouldn't. Dare."

I'M HANGING OUT with Marco Antoniou. I'm hanging out with Marco Antoniou. I'm hanging—

No. *No. We already have a mantra,* I remind myself. Words have always had a lot of power over me. *I have to be careful.*

I thunder up the wooden steps to my apartment, determined

to de–jump scare myself. My hair has still found a way to frizz, despite being trimmed down to the quick.

Water. Gel. Water. Gel.

I put on a headband and sort of look like a baby. I take it off. I put on too much eye shadow and remind myself of an iguana, huge wet eyes swirling around in opposite directions. I tell myself that my eyes are hazel, the rarest eye color. Suddenly, I doubt myself and google it. Not the rarest.

I have nothing.

I take off the eye shadow and smear on some peach-colored war paint. I'm hot and sweating and my head is starting to *pound*. I haven't taken my medicine yet. *Shit*. I take a shaky handful of chalky pills, nearly spilling them twice.

I run out onto the apartment balcony, which hangs over the front porch. "I need more coffee!" I shout down, full Stanley Kowalski.

Allie pops her head out the window below, twisting her freckled face up to look up at me. "On it!"

What am I even going to wear? I haven't had to care in months.

I yank a sundress out of my closet, then remember that the fabric tends to irritate my skin, resulting in a painful rash.

I pull out an old, loved pair of white overalls and a cropped T-shirt, also white.

I didn't plan to, but I look angelic. Blame the iguana eyes.

"You look nice," I say to my reflection. My delivery is a little *Full Metal Jacket*, but nevertheless, sincere. Maybe I'm not hot enough to be on *Chicago: Freelance Graphic Designers,* but who is? Even the cast looks confused.

I rush down the steps. Allie thrusts a mug into my chest. I lean forward and chug while she cheers me on.

It's not until I am three blocks from the boardwalk, waiting at a red light while death-gripping my steering wheel, that I realize *I never even texted him back.*

All that sweating and for what? I press a hand to my heart to try and still its ridiculous hammering. *He's just some guy,* I remind myself. *It's just one night. He's no one. He's nothing.*

Sure, I text back. Meet on the boardwalk in thirty?

"HEY!"

Marco Antoniou lifts a hand and waves, looking like he just stumbled out of an episode of *Baywatch.* Tanned and easy and warm like a summer night. He fries my corneas with a five-thousand-watt smile.

No no no no no no no no.

He's leaning against the railing, the ocean at his back, hands shoved deep into the pockets of his perfectly worn cords, wind pulling the fabric flush against his legs, so I can make out the exact shape and girth of his thighs.

Would it be rude if I just turned on my heels and booked it?

He keeps smiling and waving and I profoundly want to believe that Marco is not my type. There's too much smile. So much smile, it makes me tired just to look at. But when I open my mouth to say hi or hey, *"Sorry!"* falls out instead.

Then, the babbling starts. All the while I adjust my bucket hat, which I wear everywhere now. It serves two core functions: protecting my delicate, rash-prone face from the sun *and* being deeply off-putting to almost everyone.

That's really what unites humans regardless of race, gender, or creed: no one likes a woman in a weird hat.

"It's such a crazy, windy day, isn't it? I was going to wear a dress, but then I remembered spring is so windy and I was like, jeez—

can't do that! And *then* my housemates wanted to chat, and I just got caught up . . ."

Truthfully, I don't even know if I'm late. What I'm really trying to say is: *Sorry, I forgot to be hotter. I thought maybe I would be immune to your star power. That's why I'm wearing overalls.*

"You're totally fine, seriously," Marco says when I've finally run out of steam. He's scratching at his forearms, trying to discreetly slide a cigarette butt into his back pocket. "I got some time to, uh, take in the view."

Smoking's been illegal on the boardwalk for about a decade now. There are signs everywhere, telling us exactly that. But I guess Marco has never met a law he doesn't want to break.

I turn to look at what's behind me. The old Pirate Bay Mini Golf. I arch a brow. "And, boy, what a view."

He laughs softly and pushes the bill of his hat back with his knuckles, like a cowboy demurring to a maiden.

"Nadia, right?"

"Nadia," I confirm.

I extend a hand at the exact moment he opens his arms—muscular with a smattering of soft black hair—and pulls me in for a hug.

It's brief and more intimate than my last Pap smear. Underneath his white tee, Marco's chest muscles flex. He smells like Acqua di Parma and an ashtray. His hands stay a respectful distance above my waist. I lean up on my tiptoes and tepidly pat at the center of his back when suddenly something tickles my nose and—

We break apart and I'm not even focused on the luminescent smile or the olfactory storytelling Marco's doing, because I've noticed *it*.

Marco Antoniou has a mullet.

Not a feathered-edge ode to David Bowie or a nod to Jonathan Taylor Thomas's soft, boyish flow.

This shit is thick, hard-bodied. It chews tobacco and pours concrete. Marco's mullet is heavy layers of pitch-black hair, smoothed back from his face and sort of hidden under a Flyers hat, but I can still tell it's a *fucking mullet*.

I take off my bucket hat and stuff it into my tote bag. We can't both be deeply off-putting.

"My cousin said you've been here all winter," Marco says. I feel his eyes follow the movement of my hand as I smooth back a flyaway curl from my face, and only once I'm absolutely positive he's looked away, I steal a glance of my own.

Marco's features are exactly as striking as one would expect from a *star*. His forehead slopes heavily toward his brow; his nose is strong with a gentle hook; his jaw square and set; and when Marco smiles, his brown eyes crinkle kindly at the corners. For all his bad behavior, he looks like a cross between an ancient warrior and an all-American sweetie pie.

"Yeah," I say. "Since January."

We wander toward the far end of the boardwalk, toward the Pier Point Diner and the bike rental shop with the Technicolor marquee. "I haven't spent more than two consecutive weeks here since I moved when I was fourteen. I'm almost jealous."

"It was a temporary thing," I tell him. "I'm staying at my parents' place, taking some time away. But I think I might move down here—you know, full time."

He tilts his head and smiles, golden sun winking in his chocolate-brown eyes. "Whoa, never mind. Definitely not jealous."

Does he see it—the dark storm cloud hanging over my head? Surely he can smell the last dredges of depression on me. Why else would a single woman in her thirties move from a major metropolitan area to a freckle of an island hanging onto New Jersey by a hope and a prayer? Maybe it's my own myopia, but I can't think of a single positive reason.

Don't I ooze the frenetic energy of someone spiraling through a personal crisis? If you asked Liv, she'd say *absolutely*. I almost wish I could ask him.

"I needed some time away, too," he adds quickly before flashing me a heartless smile. Or maybe there's too much heart. Something about the way he's looking at me feels *pained*. Pulled tight and double wrapped in masking tape.

MARCO IS A natural conversationalist. He knows exactly how to pivot us away from the perilous territory of *why* he and I are both free, at the beach, on a Thursday.

Marco asks me all about Soph and Allie, the produce stand, New Jersey farming laws, how many different variations of basil we sell, whether or not I think *organic* is a scam. Is rhubarb really poisonous?

I feel, vaguely, that I am being entertained—masterfully guided through The Marco Antoniou Experience. After each question, he cocks his head to the side and listens like it's his job, like I might quiz him afterward. The rhythms of this back-and-forth that feel tenuous to me, at best, are hard-coded into his beautiful head. When I falter because I haven't made small talk in six months, he flashes me another smile and asks another question.

How many types of parsley do you carry? Which one's your favorite? You're famous, I want to remind him. *You don't have to do this.*

Marco's character on TV was a wise-cracking New Yorker, a

lothario dum-dum. He played that character for so long that the entire world assumed Marco and he were one in the same. Never mind the fact that Marco isn't even *from* New York. He's from Evergreen. Of all places on Earth, he's from this strange little beach town.

And Marco doesn't seem like a dum-dum. He seems fairly thoughtful. When I trip on a loose plank, he grabs ahold of my arm without a second of hesitation. Then, he mutters about how they absolutely *need* to fix that. "You could have broken your ankle," he tuts. For the moments his fingers curl around my biceps to steady me, a montage flashes before my eyes: I do break my ankle, actually. And Marco has to lift me into his strong, capable, famous arms and rush me off to the hospital. As I lie there, monitors beeping around me, he strokes my hair away from my face. *You're so brave, Nadia.*

I let out a beautiful, ragged cough. *I'm sorry . . . I was . . . so . . .* cough *. . . awkward on the boardwalk. I'm . . . kind of . . . poorly . . .* cough *. . . socialized . . . like a Chihuahua . . .*

He laughs and says, *No. You're perfect.* Then, we get married.

"All good?" Marco's voice punches through my fantasy, a fist through drywall.

I dust at the knees of my extremely white overalls, trying to avoid revealing eye contact. Celebrities can read minds, right?

"Good as gravy!" I croak.

Horrible.

THE BOARDWALK IS mostly empty now, except for a group of young moms pushing strollers at a brisk pace and some teens congregating on the benches across from the Bel Sol condos. One of them kicks a soccer ball and it goes flying up onto the roof and everyone breaks out into a huge burst of laughter, a sound that feels altogether too much for Evergreen in the springtime.

Marco smiles, too, laughter rolling through his chest as he moves a hand back and forth over his heart. Like he has to physically work the joy out of his chest.

I used to laugh so hard. I could laugh until I nearly peed my pants. Laughter would incapacitate me, knock me over. Sometimes I'd even laugh in my sleep. When did I stop laughing like that?

Loosen up, Fabiola. I shake out my shoulders and force my mouth into a tight, unconvincing smile.

Beyond the Bel Sol, the boardwalk turns into a long jetty that extends almost the length of a football field out into the ocean. At the end, the blue-black silhouettes of three men and their fishing lines sway in the wind.

I fold my arms over my chest and lean over the railing. "So, what else did Dr. Antoniou tell you about me?"

"That you're a writer. That's about it." Marco does the same, and the soft folds of his mullet ruffle like lotus petals in the ocean breeze. "Do you miss Philly?"

The question shocks me, and I inhale sharply. "Philly?"

"Yeah, I mean, you're from there, right?"

"Sebastian *also* told you that, then," I say, an edge of anxiety in my voice. *Please, please let that be all.*

Marco drops his head in mock shame, shoulders bouncing with deep, smooth laughter. "Alright, yes, he also told me that. But only because I asked."

My smile, maybe a little less forced, comes back again. Bigger. I feel the wind on my teeth. "Nah, I don't think I do. Philly will always be there. Evergreen's what I need right now."

Marco makes an appraising noise in the back of his throat, his gaze finding mine under the heavy umbrella of his brows. "You sound like a politician."

I snap my eyes away from his; heat prickles in my cheeks. I'm still smiling. "I'm going to take that as a compliment."

There's a natural lull in our conversation and maybe a lesser man would use this moment to say, *Well, this has been great—see you never!* But instead, Marco clears his throat and says, "You hungry?"

I'm starving, my stomach is symphonic, but I say something tragic like, "I could eat."

ACROSS TOWN, IN an old cottage on the bay, Ernie's Crab Shack offers its "World Famous Shrimp Basket for Two" and a raucous patio with enough seating for a large family reunion or a very small Italian wedding. They seat us outside at the tiniest table ever created in the middle of two enormous parties: a bachelorette weekend (or maybe a group of penis straw salespeople?) and a group of young parents and their writhing children. We're in a sea of noise. The air buckles, overburdened with vibrations.

Marco studies the menu while biting at his bottom lip. I try not to focus on how dark his eyes are, how smooth his skin is, while, under the table, the rubber tips of our shoes touch.

"Jeez, lot of options."

As soon as the words leave my lips, I want to disappear. Just, poof. Into the ocean. *Lot of options?* I could have said anything—anything at all—and what I do is make the most milquetoast observation possible.

"I have a strategy for ordering at places like this," Marco says with a bro-ish head nod toward the menu in my hands. He fiddles with his lighter, rotating it back and forth between his fingers. He's been antsy ever since we sat down, seemingly out of his element in the middle of such a crowded space. I can feel how badly he wants to get up and walk out. He doesn't like crowds. Or maybe he doesn't like *this* crowd. "No page twos."

"No page twos?"

"You heard me. You can only pick from the first page of the menu." He reaches across the table and yanks the paper menu out of my hand, flipping it over then replacing it faster than I can protest. "Humans love boundaries."

Why does this simple statement turn me on *so* much?

Regardless, his trick works. No page two has me ordering fish tacos with the confidence of a sitting president. Our waitress bounces over on her toes, eyes constantly moving around the patio, checking for empty glasses that need filling and empty plates that need clearing. Her hairline glistens with remnants of high-noon sweat. Then, her eyes flit to Marco and she stills. It all happens so quickly and yet slow enough to send every muscle in my body into a cringe.

"Weird question—" she starts. Marco's fingers freeze on his lighter. She loses her nerve. "Um, did you say no bun on the veggie burger?"

Marco stuns her with his smile. It's sideways, sloping, devastating, and makes my throat dry. "That's right. No bun."

"Drinks?" she breathes.

He orders a beer and a shot of whiskey.

Oh? I stare at Marco, eyes wide.

He stares back, mirroring my expression. "Nadia? Anything to drink?"

"Just water for me," I say, but it doesn't matter—our waitress is already running at full speed toward the kitchen.

And I don't blame her. This is probably the craziest thing that's ever happened at Ernie's Crab Shack, barring a few debaucherous bachelor parties featuring some vacationing sex pests. The front-of-house staff is about to come *alive* with intrigue.

And Marco knows it. He's tearing at his bottom lip, jiggling his knee so hard I can feel the table bouncing. His gaze has a vise grip on something over my shoulder, past the docked boats and all the couples taking pictures on the edge of the jetty. He's staring, potentially, directly into the sun.

"I'm sorry she recognized you. It's annoying, I'm sure."

There's a microscopic quiver in the corner of his mouth as he ignites his lighter. "Yeah, no. *I'm* sorry. I've always really hated that."

"Don't apologize, I don't mind at all. We can leave—"

He pulls his eyes away from the sky and looks at me. My stomach rocks side to side—he looks *hurt*, nearly torn open. "Did you recognize me?" This question is different from all the other questions he's asked me tonight. Marco actually *wants* to know the answer.

"Well, sure." I shrug, unfolding the napkin-wrapped bundle of silverware in front of me, doing my best impression of someone capable of relaxing. "I guess I did, in a way."

"You watched *Dude's Ranch*?"

That's what his show was called! *Dude's Ranch*. Two estranged brothers come together to save their father's ranch and like, raise a baby or something. I can picture the promotional artwork perfectly. Marco in a denim jacket, smile on full display. His character was the fish out of water—a Sonny LoSpecchio type from Queens or maybe the Bronx. You were supposed to look at him and think, This pretty boy? Doing a real man's job? In the real man's America? Now, *that's* hilarious.

I scoff, a hiccup of incredulity. "You wish."

He smirks. "You're too sophisticated."

Yes, I want to say, but instead I play nice. "We weren't really a cable TV family. And I was a little too old."

"What kind of family were you, then? Puzzles around the fireplace? Dad reading the newspaper?"

"Oh God, no." I laugh, shaking my head. "My parents own a butcher shop, they basically work twenty-four/seven. And we had to help as soon as our wrists were strong enough to wield a cleaver."

Marco's expression collapses from one of sardonic teasing to a look of genuine interest—perhaps even respect. "You're joking."

"No, I'm not." I take a sip of water, basking in the feeling of finally breaking through the impenetrable haze of niceness hanging around us. "Give me a butter knife, and I could carve you up."

"Fuck," he grunts, lifting his water to his lips. Condensation slides down the glass, rolling down his wrist. He places his lips against the cold material and I look away. "A butcher's daughter hiding out in Evergreen. *That* sounds like a good TV show."

Before I have a chance to respond, a different, equally bouncy waitress appears. Her smile is wide, blue eyes hazy with excitement. She's been sent by her buddy to scope us out, no doubt.

Marco stiffens as she approaches with eager, wide eyes, spine going ramrod straight. He tries to play it off by stretching his arms over his head, locking his fingers together, and turning from side to side. But I know he wants to jump out of his skin.

"Here are your drinks!" she trills. This is directed at Marco and only Marco. He doesn't even let the shot glass hit the table. He takes it from her and tosses the syrupy, amber liquid back in one smooth gulp—like a cartoon character eating a fish in one bite.

My mouth jumps into another *oh* shape. Oh, *shit*. Oh, *no*. Oh, *is this what we're doing?*

I watch him chase down the whiskey shot with two enormous gulps of beer. His entire throat shifts with the effort of getting as much liquid down as possible, and genuine shock ripples through me. Years ago, it had been well-documented that Marco had a certain *zest* for life. Drugs and women and fast cars. All the usual, predictable ways rich men avoided therapy. I guess I'd just assumed a man with a bad haircut living by the beach was healed.

Ironic. I should know, better than anyone, how wholly untrue that could be.

Or maybe this—this date, this hangout, this whatever—is so very awful that he decided, after settling into his rusted patio chair, that he needed a consciousness shift ASAP.

I should just leave. I should just get up and go, release him from his duties. But I can't.

I feel so strange—awake and giddy and electric. Horny, but not for sex. Horny for whatever is happening inside his mind.

I'm *jealous*.

There's a barely contained recklessness to Marco, itching to break loose. I want what he's having.

Before the waitress can run off, I press the tips of my fingers to her arm and order us a pitcher of margaritas.

"Two glasses," I add sweetly, without even a glance Marco's way. "Please."

"Salt or sugar on the rim?"

"Salt," we reply in unison.

And when she walks away, we do not look at each other.

What the hell am I doing? I can't drink. I haven't drunk in months. Not since—

I shudder at the memory, and now I want to drink even more. I shouldn't—I take a lot of medicine and—

Marco's lighting up a cigarette. In the middle of the outdoor patio, the beautiful man now has a cigarette perched between his lips and he's holding his lighter, aflame and flickering in the wind, to the end. "So, what *did* you watch?" A stream of gray smoke shoots from his nose. "Criterion Collection?"

I point at the cigarette. "*Really?* You're not above the law just because you've been on TV."

He ignores this comment and keeps pushing. "Come on, you're a writer, right? You have to have a favorite TV show or a favorite movie."

Duh, I have a favorite movie but I'm not telling *him*. It would be too devastating and personal to tell anyone, let alone Marco Antoniou, that *Snowpiercer* makes me open-mouth sob every time I watch it. "Everyone has a favorite movie. Even people who don't like movies have a favorite movie."

"Then tell me." Under the table he actually *kicks* me a little bit.

My eyes widen. I kick back. He smirks, bright white canines catching the setting sun. He gives me a look of practiced desire. His body language shifts and everything about him is saying, *Come on, baby, have a little fun.* The chaos demon locked away inside his brain has broken loose and gained control of the ship.

Marco thinks he can *work* me, doesn't he? He looks at me and sees another sorta-cute local girl armed with a tristate, tough-girl attitude he knows all too well, well enough to kick right through.

But he has no idea what he's up against. Deep in the crevices of my mind, my own chaos demon rattles her chains.

"Fine." I tap my fingernails on the tabletop. "Put out that stupid cigarette, and I'll tell you."

The corners of his mouth flick down in a look of world-weary appreciation. "Fine." Then, he drains his water down to a quarter of an inch and drops the cigarette into his glass. "Happy?"

I grit my teeth. "*Sweet November*. It's not *technically* a good movie, so don't even bother looking up how many stars it has. But it's—I don't know, I can't stop watching it."

"Keanu Reeves, right? He's in it?" Marco lifts his beer to his lips. "I was almost cast as his body double once."

"No way. Really?" I laugh. "He's way taller than you."

"He is not *way* taller."

"At least five inches. What are you—like, five-nine on the dating apps?"

Suddenly, he narrows his eyes at me. "I'm five-ten, kid."

I grin. He hates that he just had to tell me his real height, not whatever's listed on IMDb.

Our waitress returns with the pitcher, and we fill our glasses in a reverent silence. We both know this is not how tonight was supposed to go. When I set down the pitcher, Marco's leaning forward, big bovine eyes burrowing into me. "I gotta be honest with you, Nadia."

I take a sip, then brush some particularly stubborn granules of salt from my lips. Has he been saying my name like *that* this whole time? "Okay, sure."

"I'm sure you're a really nice person—" *No way.* Dumped before dinner? A new personal low, even for *moi*. I lean forward, too, shoulders curving toward Marco, the last splashes of big, bright afternoon sun falling over my shoulder blades. My chaos demon flaps her wings and insane joy floods my chest, and I almost feel a flicker of my old self. The Nadia who lived for the plot. "But I'm on a little bit of a mission tonight," Marco continues. "And it's not a noble one."

I take a stiff sip of margarita before immediately chasing it with another, more relaxed gulp. "Say more."

Marco breathes in deeply, locking his eyes on mine. "I'm trying to get fucked up and forget how much of a disaster my life has been lately. And I know that's not something to be proud of and maybe it's the most unattractive thing a man can do, but it's—"

"Counterintuitive," I cut him off, heart racing. I can feel blood thrumming in my wrists. This is an old dance, but I still remember the steps. "If we get fucked up, won't we just feel worse tomorrow?"

He quirks a brow. The sun snags on a freckle of lightness in his eye. "We?"

I lean back and fold my arms over my chest. I take him in. *All* of him. He's handsome but disheveled; I can see where he missed a spot shaving, right on his cheek. The haircut: obviously an issue. His skin looks a little waxy, like he's spent the last few days sitting in the dark. Full lips bitten raw. Eyebrows pulled into a frown, even as his smile softens under my gaze. His white T-shirt is perfect—too perfect. In fact, it still has the fold lines in it. Pulled straight from the package, put directly onto his body.

His words on the boardwalk come back to me. *He needed some time away, too.* Away from what?

"What did your cousin *really* tell you, when he gave you my number? Because he told me I need to *get out more*. And I bet if I hadn't death-stared a hole into his head, he probably would have elaborated."

A hiss of air shoots through Marco's teeth. Then, his mouth twists sideways. "Well, Sebastian showed up at my house, told me I look like a divorcé who only eats yogurt, ripped the blinds open, and forced me to shave my beard."

I *have* to wince. "Specific."

"Yeah, it really hurt my feelings and—" He pauses to swipe a hand over his articulated jawline, dotted with a day's worth of stubble. "I think it worked. Do I look like I eat solids?"

"You've definitely microwaved a Hungry-Man dinner."

Marco laughs. "Great. Progress. Cheers." He slugs back half his drink.

"I'm kidding, I'm kidding," I say as a means to keep him from drowning himself in tequila. "I get it. My older sister is like—" I pantomime, as best I can, how far Liv is up my ass. "She thinks I'm constantly on the edge of a psychological implosion. I know she cares, in theory—"

"But you just feel like everyone thinks you're incompetent," he says, completing my thought.

I lift my glass. "Bingo."

"I almost wish I was a divorcé. Then I could point at that trauma and say—*I'm allowed to be like this.*" He pulls off his hat and runs his fingers through his hair, eyes cast out to the water. "But instead, I'm just like, *This is who I am.*"

I wish I could tell him: *That's what you think. But even when it all makes sense, people still just want you to get better. They want you to stop the pain before you know it's coming.* But telling Marco about my depression would mean also telling him about my lupus diagnosis. And telling him about lupus would mean forfeiting this drink and any chance of tonight feeling . . . *normal.* Or, fuck, I don't know—*fun.*

"Fuck them," I blurt out. "And fuck that. Normal people need to stop punishing the rest of us for being fucked up. We're already doing that. And we're really good at it."

Marco actually throws his head back and laughs. A real, joyful bellow.

BAD INFLUENCES COME in all shapes and sizes. Sometimes they wear all white and then sort of look like one of Anne Geddes's babies.

I suggest that we start a drinking game, and Marco *really* takes to it. The rules come hard and fast as Ernie's transforms from family-friendly restaurant into a swingers-focused discotheque.

Drink every time a middle-aged woman in a tube top accidentally rests her boobs on Marco's shoulders. Drink every time a Boomer stares at the floral tattoo that wraps around my left biceps. Drink every time someone starts to ask, *Hey, are you the* . . . then loses their nut.

Drink every time we almost say the same thing at the same time, which keeps happening.

We both love to point at the sky and shout the name of the song that's just come on. *Except* when some asshole gets their paws on the TouchTunes and puts on "Sweet Caroline."

"Forget Britney, *this* is what they should have played at Somali pirates," I shout over the caw of drunken *BAH-BAH-BAHHHHH*s.

"Even they don't deserve this," Marco shouts back, pushing up out of his chair. He holds a hand out to me. "Come on, let's get the fuck out of here."

"Don't we have to pay?"

He lifts his chin in the direction of a stack of bills on the table. "Already taken care of."

Right, I think. *You're rich.*

I take his hand and Marco immediately tangles his fingers with mine. As we move, he tucks my body behind him in a protective posture that sends a trill off in my stomach.

We're so close, I can smell his cologne again, can feel the calluses on the palms of his hands against mine, the pad of his thumb pressing into the top of my hand. His grip sends a steady stream of heat through my arm; a heat that curls in my stomach, causing my breath to hitch. I haven't been touched in how long? *God.* I haven't felt another person in months.

Marco maneuvers us through the throng of bodies overwhelming the patio—sweating, swaying, and pressing closer and closer. Then, suddenly, the song changes and the crowd erupts.

We *all* erupt. Marco and I throw our conjoined hands into the air.

It's *the* song—Philly's song. Our anthem from the last time the Eagles went to the Super Bowl—and *won.* It's an extremely random, nearly forgotten hyper-pop dance anthem with the kind of bass line that makes *not* dancing impossible. The entire crowd begins writhing—on beat, off beat. The wooden planks under our feet audibly creak and groan as people jump and lunge.

Marco turns around, eyes gleaming, smile wide, ready to say something—when someone knocks into him. His body lurches toward mine, but there's no place for us to go. I loop my arm around his neck at the same moment his other hand, the one not already clasped in mine, jumps to my lower back. Now we're completely tangled.

He tucks his head down, lips close to mine and, at the same time, we shout, "We have to dance."

Marco tightens his hold on me, and I tighten mine on him. For the first time in months, I don't think twice.

Friday, May 5

We keep dancing. The crowd grows, then thins. I sweat through my shirt while Marco spins me around then pulls me back into his chest, over and over. We dance until Ernie himself kicks us out. Then we wander out into the chilly, humid night and I insist we race down to the beach.

"What, you afraid of losing to a lady in overalls?" I tease until Marco finally rolls his eyes in exasperation and unlaces his shoes. I kick off my sandals and we line up next to each other in the middle of the wide, empty street, bare feet on the still-hot asphalt.

"I'm fucking fast," I warn him again. *Present tense.*

"Yeah, right, kid." Marco swings his hat around backward, lowering his back knee to a lunge. "Prepare to get smoked."

I flip him the bird. "Count us in, then. Stop dillydallying."

He's laughing. *I make him laugh a lot.* "Then stop distracting me! Alright. Okay. Three, two—"

"One!" I scream and I take off, full speed, toward the abrupt, sandy end of the road. The beach is over the dunes and behind a line of reeds. I can almost taste the ocean. I'm flying, my feet picking up and grinding in sand and rocks and gravel with each thundering step.

I haven't run in months.

The night feels like silk, briny and sweet and featherlight around my body. I lift my arms and throw back my head. I don't even hear the jangle of Marco's keys behind me anymore. *I'm winning.*

My feet hit the sand and I double over, breathless and drunk and dizzy. I'm *also* laughing; I hadn't noticed I was laughing. Inertia carries me, head over feet, straight into the reeds. I let out a little yelp, then make an *OOFT!* sound when my shoulder connects with the sand.

"Nadia!"

"I'm 'kay!" I shout, rolling over to face the sky.

"Nadia!" This time his voice is above me.

"I'm oh-*kay*!"

Marco's head pops into my line of sight. He's standing over me—one foot on either side of my hips—eyebrows knit in concern, chest heaving with the effort of running.

"Nadia, *holy shit.*"

I'm still trying to catch my own breath. I point up at him, closing only my left eye to keep his head from bobbing and weaving in front of me.

"What is it? Are you okay?" He steps around me and brings a knee down to the sand, a hand to my forehead, the pads of his fingers sweeping down my cheek. His touch is warm, maybe a little clammy.

"I—"

"You're hurt."

I shake my head. "I won," I croak.

His shoulders sag with instant relief. "Jesus Christ, Nadia. *Yeah,* you won."

MARCO INSISTS THERE'S a scratch on my forehead that *must* be disinfected, and no, spit is not good enough. He yanks me to my feet and keeps a steadying hand on my lower back as we walk the block and a half to his uncle's place, zigzagging and bumping into each other.

"What about my car?" I whine, tossing a pouty look over my shoulder.

"You"—Marco loops his arms around my waist, securing me to his side. He smells like sweet sweat and ocean air—"aren't driving anywhere tonight."

While we walk, he keeps his arm around my hips. I push my fingers through the party part of his mullet. He leans his head back into my hand, eyes fluttering shut when my fingernails meet his scalp.

His uncle's house is an uber-modern, split-level behemoth made of glass and concrete. Marco lets us in through the garage.

"I didn't even know they had houses like this in Evergreen," I whisper.

"Rich assholes are an invasive species."

He leads me to the *bathroom* in the garage—a bathroom in the *garage*! I bite my lip to keep from revealing just how gauche I really am while Marco digs around in the cabinet underneath the sink, hunting for antiseptic and a Band-Aid.

"Seriously, I'm fine," I tell him. "I'm not even drunk anymore."

Marco pops up out of a squat, eyebrow cocked. "I'm not sending you home with blood on your forehead."

I sit on the closed lid of the toilet, face turned up toward him. I close my eyes and let the room swim around me, grounded by the pressure of Marco's fingertips against my jaw. His shoes squeak on the tiled floor as he adjusts his position. When he speaks, his voice is closer.

"I'm a bad influence on you, kid."

The alcohol-soaked towelette makes contact with a tender patch between my eyebrows and I recoil at the cold. "*Of course* you want all the credit for tonight."

"Stop squirming."

"We're in this together. We're both misbehaving—*ow*!" I throw my eyes open.

Marco is looking down his nose at me, his thumb pressed into the slight dimple at the center of my chin. A bemused smile flickering on his lips. Slowly, he lowers his mouth until I feel the steady pulse of his breath. My breathing, on the other hand, is quick and ragged.

Then, he turns, the tender skin of his lips grazing my ear. "I'm going to kiss you," he whispers.

I swallow. "Okay. Kiss me."

His fingers flex their hold on me as he turns my mouth to his. The first time our lips meet, it's so light, I wouldn't have noticed if it wasn't for the electric pulse between my thighs. The second time, I'm inching forward, dislodging my hands from underneath my legs, reaching for his belt loops. The third time, I'm almost panting.

His fingers migrate; they find the nape of my neck; they burrow into my hairline. He presses his forehead into mine. "Nadia," he whispers my name, and I know it's part of a longer thought. I can tell by the way he hangs on to the vowels.

"What?" I drag my hands up over his arms, feeling his muscles tense and relax. "Just say it."

He makes no move to pull away from me; instead, his lips travel over my cheeks, across my jaw, down my neck, all while he says, "I'm . . . not good at following up. I have a way of taking good people and good situations a-and using them up. Just sucking the fucking life out of them. A-and you're great. I think you're fucking gorgeous and funny and smart, but I'm a fucking vampire. I-I just don't want you to take it personally."

"What makes you think," I say, my voice heavy and slow. I don't pull away. I can't look at him. "I'm ever going to speak to you again?"

His fingers tighten in my hair.

Our mouths connect; this time, we're desperate. Messy. Our teeth bump together and the toilet seat groans cacophonously when I pull Marco against me, maybe with a little too much force. My head hits the wall with a dull thud and we both gasp and laugh, and while I curse, Marco's tongue slides down the side of my neck and then, my overalls are on the floor. His hands are everywhere. Under my shirt, down my thighs. Heavy breathing and sweaty T-shirts and my feet leave filthy footprints across the tile. My body throbs. It's a new throb. Tomorrow, I'll be ruined. Broken and battered. But right now, I want it to hurt.

"You can use me," I tell him. But he's so very gentle.

Friday, May 5

The moment I became too sick to keep working at Foster & Honey advertising agency is inexplicably tied to the moment I knew my life, as it had been for most of my twenties, was over.

Dance parties, dive bars, bar trivia, and biking everywhere. Sunbathing until my skin was the color of a penny and my mouth felt like the Sahara. Taking clients out to dinner, then drinks, then karaoke. Sleeping with a client, *whoops*. Lugging curb-treasure up endless flights of steps to my one-bedroom without any help.

It's a short, tragic story: I lost my job and I lost my life and I ran away.

It begins with me sleeping through my alarm.

INTERIOR - DAY - Nadia's studio apartment in Old City, Philadelphia.

The walls are exposed brick and NADIA, a voluptuous thirty-year-old with symmetrical tits and Brooke Shields eyebrows, is sleeping on a very expensive mattress on an even more expensive bed frame from some Scandinavian website. Not that Scandinavian website. A different one.

Yes, she is sleeping, but to the viewer, she appears to be dead.

Beside her, an analog alarm clock is going haywire. Screaming, rattling, nearly blowing steam.

A client kickoff meeting with a global travel insurance company she's been courting for six months is already underway. She was *supposed to be* presenting the agency's Super Bowl commercial pitch. Oh, sorry—THE BIG GAME commercial pitch. Nadia had written the three-and-a-half-minute spot set to air during the first quarter of the game. The commercial went like this . . .

> *A little girl boards her first flight alone from Boston to Shanghai to visit her grandparents for Lunar New Year. She's thirteen and brave; she has a feeling she might just be destined for greatness. But for now, she's biding her time in the wings, waiting until curtain call when she'll be unveiled to the world in all her brilliance. Maybe she'll be an astronaut—or an EGOT winner.*
>
> *But right now, she's all by herself on her fourteen-hour flight, and this little girl is starting to feel her smallness. Her youngness.*
>
> *But saFeLY is there for her. Her bags are insured. Her parents can track her flight. A flight attendant brings her an extra ice-cream mochi. Ice cream still solves many of her problems. One day it won't; life will become more and more complicated. But right now, everything is very simple. This little girl is safe.*
>
> *Fade to end card: saFeLY. Life is hard. Travel shouldn't be.*

Yes, this is the script Nadia should be reading to a room full of rapt marketing executives. Instead, Nadia is asleep.

I'd spent hours and hours perfecting that script, polishing each line of dialogue, working with our art director to assemble the perfect mood-board, even curating a playlist made up of Chinese indie rock bands to run in the background while my copywriters performed the script.

I didn't know I had lupus. I didn't know it was even a possibility that I could have a disease like lupus, because nothing materially bad had ever really happened to me. I mean that. Sure, I'd had my heart broken. I'd gone through phases of intense personal grief. I'd hated myself, wondered if I was worth anything. I'd pinched the fat on my thigh till it bruised, wondering why I wasn't naturally slender and waifish.

But all of that felt like part of the Faustian bargain that is living.

Plus, I was ambitious and hungry and I *could*. That was the best part: when I wanted to, I could just go and do and be. My insecurities and times of sadness had felt like seasons, not sentences.

How I had taken that for granted.

The rashes, deep red swatches that spread from my ears down my cheekbones, were from stress. The headaches were from dehydration and PMS. My brain was distracted and oversaturated, not foggy, and my sluggishness could be more than explained by sixty-hour workweeks. I was grinding myself down—not just on this project but *every* project.

And when I wasn't working on writing the perfect script, I was very busy fucking my boss, a demanding and temperamental art director named Kai who looked like a wish.com Oscar Isaac. Our relationship was imploding. Kai was a collector—of objects, experiences, people—and I had a feeling I was keeping him from expanding his palate. Dating him was exhausting and inescapable.

Kind of like my job.

But I was *fine*.

This was what adults did. This was what work was.

I just needed some time off, a beach vacation where I got to totally disconnect.

The horror that enveloped me when I realized I had overslept for the most important meeting of my career was second only to the migraine that kept me pinned to my bathroom floor for the next forty-eight hours.

"It will never, ever happen again," I swore, cheek pressed against the cold tile, blinds shuttered against the milky November sunlight. Between phone calls, I would retch into the toilet and force down sips of Coke. "No excuse, I know. But I promise . . ."

There was a lot of *we don't want to do this, but we have to do this*.

saFLeY hadn't noticed I was missing from the meeting; my team had been able to cover perfectly fine without me. Our account manager presented the deck without any issue, aided by copywriters I'd tasked with memorizing and performing the script for the client as if they were at a table read. That was the real issue. I'd gone ahead and handed over proof that I was nothing more than an expensive, unreliable overhead cost that the boss was sick of seeing around the office. All my shine had been rubbed away.

"Take this time to find yourself, Nadia," Kai had said, leaning across his desk to offer me his hand one last time. He had one of the only offices in the Foster & Honey building, an old converted warehouse in Fishtown. Exposed pipes and concrete walls, imported espresso machines and bean bag chairs, all provided the perfect cover for tattooed, vegan narcissists.

I didn't take his hand. "I know who I am."

It was the last moment I would feel confident for months.

I pushed my company laptop across the desk, dropped my badge on top, and ordered myself an Uber home. Then, I slept for thirteen hours.

Former coworkers reached out. They wanted one last dinner that turned into karaoke and tequila shots and eventually breakfast sandwiches. But even after my headache eventually passed, I'd noticed my hands were shaking and my bones hurt. They hurt *so* deeply I could imagine the marrow inside them calcifying, turning to useless dust. I didn't reply, and those coworkers never reached out again.

I was tired down to my very nerves, which sent haphazard electric zaps up through my knees, into my lower back. Tiny, little cries for help.

Probably just the flu, I told myself over and over. Worst flu of my life.

I WAKE UP feeling like I've been bludgeoned. The evidence of last night is strewn across my bedroom. A trail of sand details a path from the door to my abandoned, filthy overalls to the bed.

My mouth feels like it's caulked shut. The effort of trying to move my lips makes my skull throb.

Am I naked? I feel around under the sheets. *Yes, I am naked.*

How did I get home?

A memory arrives in my brain with the pain and power of sudden noise; like cymbals crashing together.

Marco called an Uber. Took it with me. Walked home.

What a gentleman.

Did we fuck?

No. We tried. Heaven knows, we tried.

My joints won't work, so I literally roll out of bed, taking a sheet with me. I keep rolling until I reach the kitchen.

My phone vibrates on the countertop.

Soph. *Fuck.*

"I know," I say as soon as I pick up. "I'm late and you're calling—" I pause to let out a painful, dry cough. "To fire me."

"You're fine, actually." Soph sounds so fucking chipper, I have to hold the phone away from my head. "Farmers market starts in an hour. I'm here early, trying to get us a better spot, but the goat lotion people are fascists. Can you bring me the crate of chard I left in the driveway? Before Frank DiBiase gets to it." *Frank.* Notorious little klepto.

I pull my phone away from my face and stare at the time on my lock screen. After way too long, it registers. I actually woke up *early.*

"Roger that," I croak.

After we hang up, I spend ten minutes lying on the freezing-cold kitchen floor, sorting through all the various sensations coursing through my body, so copious they threaten to send me into a full meltdown.

Nausea. Okay, a lot of nausea. I really need to eat something.

Headache. Duh. But also, an extra-dull ache radiates from the back of my head. *The wall.* I cringe at the memory, then groan because even cringing hurts.

Shoulder throb. I'd flipped or fallen or maybe yeeted myself a great distance. I remember that much. Won't be able to lift my right arm for a while, that's for sure.

Feet. Destroyed. Wrecked. Useless.

Knees. Forget about it. Might as well have them removed.

With my inventory over, I crawl to the bathroom and run the hottest bath I can tolerate. I have exactly forty minutes to undo hours of damage.

WITH MY CAR nowhere in sight, I'm forced to bike to work. It is *very* hard to maintain your balance when you're pedaling approximately twice per minute.

The vibrancy of my sunny-yellow bike makes me feel like my eyes are being etched with a diamond-tipped drill. The real sun is also an absolute assault. With every tire rotation, I whimper. Two blocks in, I lie down on a public bench.

There's fight, flight, and whatever the fuck this is.

"Your chard, my liege," I announce with all the fanfare of a rotten apple as I drop the two overflowing bags of leafy greens onto the table where Soph has already set out cartons of perfectly ripe kiwis, meticulously cared for kale, and fragrant bundles of Italian parsley.

St. Agnes's Friday morning farmers market brings out the best of Evergreen's underemployed and retired weirdos. Jeanine Spellman, who picks her nose and then touches every single grape she sees. Steve Donoghue holding down his anti-circumcision booth, week after week, always with a fresh stack of pamphlets on deck. And Carla Catalina, who loves to just be . . . Carla Catalina.

Soph has one of the smaller booths—a tented table right next to the broad stone steps that lead to the church's lacquered oak double doors, directly across from where the food trucks park. The new sign I painted leans up against the table accompanied by the sandwich board I've taken to scrawling with a recipe featuring whatever produce we have an overabundance of.

Last Friday, I shared my sacred tomato jam recipe. Darlene Colli made it for the VA potluck and left with four different phone numbers.

Today, the board is empty save for a few pathetic ovals that—*I think*—are supposed to be zucchini. My first and only clue being that Soph has half-heartedly scribbled *Z u c c H i N I* in a shaky script underneath.

"You're a hero," Soph declares, mopping their dewy, sunburnt brow with a gloved hand. Then, they pause to take me in—my oversize T-shirt, grubby Nikes, and the unbuckled bike helmet still on my head. "You biked here? Damn. Good job."

"Yeah, well." I limp my way over to my usual spot beside Soph. "Save my Purple Heart. I probably won't make it through this shift."

Soph laughs and hands me my apron and a pair of gloves. "Hey. Catalina, incoming. One o'clock." Sure enough, there she is, trolling around the blond couple from Cape May who run an organic honey stand, undoubtedly grilling the lanky husband with questions like, *Don't ya knees hurt from standing so tall all the dang time?*

"She's on one today," I observe, my voice coming out thick with exhaustion and about two octaves deeper than usual. "She's going to say something about my hair."

Carla's coming toward us at full speed and we must prepare ourselves for imminent attack. The woman is absolutely tearing up the lawn with the front wheels of her walker.

"What happened, Car? Hurt your hip again?" I call out.

"Ugh, Nadia. Let me tell you something," she begins. "When I moved here in 1965 . . ." Soph grabs my hand underneath the table. *Yes,* I think. *Yes. More. More.* This *is why I get out of bed.* "People actually frickin' took care of their properties. Now? Cigarette butts, bicycles all over, *chairs* on their lawn. It was never like that before. These people are degenerates. You wanna sit outside? Don't you have any chairs in your house?"

"Did you trip over someone's lawn chair?"

"What?" She looks at me like I'm insane. "No, I broke a toe at aquagym."

My mouth actually falls open.

"I have your favorite today. White peaches." Soph swoops in, handing Carla a free sample.

"Thank you, doll. Can I still call you *doll*?" The last few Fridays we'd dedicated a not-insignificant amount of time explaining to Carla that Sophia now went by Soph and didn't really love being called *pretty lady*.

Sensing danger, Soph simply replies, "Nadia cut off all her hair." *Bitch.*

"Oh my goodness, gracious God. I *knew* you looked different. Nadia Rose Fabiola, how the hell could you do a thing like that to us?"

There's no *Reader's Digest* and I'm barely hanging on as it is. So, I sink into the conversation. I let myself get comfortable. This, after all, is probably something I should practice telling people.

I tell Carla everything. About how weak my hands are sometimes and how hard that made it to scrub my scalp through my dense, tightly curled hair. How I didn't have the energy to make it to the hair salon so someone else could wash and deep condition my locks. I told her about how it actually felt like my energy was growing out into my hair, instead of flowing down through my body. I wanted to be done, I told her, just for a little while.

She eats like, six peaches while I talk.

But she listens, watery green eyes fixed on mine, the shaky outlines of her lips parting with emotion at the details of my diagnosis. My whole life might be over, but when it was all still alive and going and filled with movement, no one ever listened to me this long. No one ever listened the way Carla does.

AFTER THE MORNING rush, Soph brings me an egg and cheese on a toasted everything bagel and thirty-two ounces of iced coffee. The cup is so big, I have to hold it with two hands. God bless America. I suck down my coffee along with five hundred milligrams of something that will save my life.

I man the register from an Adirondack chair with Soph by my side, generously lifting anything that weighs more than a number two pencil. They've seen me like this before; they get it.

"You good to stay till close?" Soph asks as they finish stacking empty crates to be dollied back to their truck.

"Definitely."

They give my head an appreciative pat. "I'll meet you at home."

The churchyard has mostly cleared, only thirty minutes left for folks to shop. Steve is packing it in early and when he takes down his last pro-foreskin poster, I catch a glance of light smarting off a very familiar cascade of hair.

Oh, fuck.

He's crossing the lawn, hands shoved into the pockets of his joggers, looking as well rested as ever. Meanwhile, I'm fairly certain my left eye has been slowly melting down my face for the last two hours.

What the fuck is he doing here?

"Any peaches left?" Marco asks as he approaches, his voice tired and raspy.

Without making any eye contact, I gesture at the remaining cartons. "All yours."

Marco doesn't reach for them. He just stands there, watching me while I pull my gloves off and take off my apron. "So," he says finally. "How's your head?"

I press my lips together. *What a way to ask.* "Um, throbbing."

He chuckles. "I tried to give you ice." *But then we got distracted trying to google* whiskey dick solution. "I watched *Sweet November* this morning."

I wince, which hurts. So, I wince again. "Yeah?"

"Yeah. I loved it." He plucks a golden peach off the top of the pile and sinks his teeth into its tender flesh and suddenly, I have to look away. "You should have warned me. I cried my eyes out. The ending destroyed me."

The night before comes back to me in a single, blazing flash from my heart to my thighs. I quickly fumble to find ways to busy myself behind the table, even though there's a plastic bag blowing by Marco's feet that I should absolutely grab. I need this table between us. "It's not really a romantic comedy. It's like a . . . romantic drama with one-dimensional queer characters for comedic relief."

He laughs again. "Yeah, that part was pretty bad. This peach is amazing." He spins the fruit around, taking another bite, this one down to the pit. Marco's wearing a different hat today, and another crisp, perfectly white T-shirt that probably cost more than my entire education (twelve years of Catholic school, plus college). "The woman—Charlize Theron—she reminded me of you." A smile flickers over his full lips before his tongue darts out to catch a droplet of peach juice ready to slide down his chin. "Her hair's like yours—short and sort of honey brown. And the way she smiles. Her attitude."

What the hell happened to "Don't take it personally if you never see me again"?

I snort, keeping my hands and eyes focused on wiping down our table and closing up. "The only thing Charlize and I have in common is two X chromosomes." I open the till and start counting out the money. *One, two, go away, seven, forty, right now, five.*

"Come on." He laughs, dry and gravelly, filled with real longing. "You know what I mean. You're both quirky—different."

I drop the cash back in the register and lock it. "She's a lot more whimsical than me. I'd never wear that many scarves."

Marco tosses his peach pit into a trash can and reaches for another. A doughnut peach. They're my favorite.

"We should do what they did."

"Get cancer and die?"

"Jesus, no. We should, you know—"

I do know. Of course *I* know. The plot of *Sweet November* is incredibly simple and there's really only one thing the two main characters *do* together. "You just said you hated the ending."

"Let me finish." He chomps his second peach, chewing much more slowly this time. "Okay, so. Us? Right. Me and you? We date for one month. For all of May. Just May. Only May. While I'm here in Evergreen."

"*Ooooh*," I coo, drawing out the *oh* as long as I can while I fold my arms over my chest. "You're still drunk."

"Actually, I am horribly sober and very hungover. In fact, I never want to see another drink ever again."

"Did you hit your head?" I demand, my voice coming out full and harsh. "Because I really feel like we left things on a *very* specific and *clear* note."

"Clear?" Marco balks. "We were completely incoherent. You did a front flip into a sand dune."

I scrunch my nose at him. "You're such a sore loser! I won fair and square."

"First of all." Now he's the one wincing. "I let you win—no, never mind. Forget it. I had fun last night."

I run my tongue over my bottom lip. "Okay." I clear my throat. "I did, too." *Way* too much fun.

"So?" Marco's watching me, eyes sparkling, mouth twitching with a little preemptive smile. Instantly, I regret admitting I had fun. I've known the man for twelve hours and already he's pulled so much out of me. "One month, that's it. You keep your life, I keep mine. In thirty days, I fuck off. No hurt feelings."

The man is not joking; he's looking at me with wide eyes and not a single ounce of irony.

"You're an insane person. And you don't know me." I have more in common with Charlize Theron's character than I'd like to admit—more in common with her than Marco would enjoy. "I could be a very dangerous psychopath. Obsessed with knives. Obsessed with *you*."

Marco rolls his eyes. "You are not obsessed with me. I know my demographic. What else do you have going on? You're working at a produce stand—"

I yank my head back. "Excuse *you*. Is this flirting? Is this you being charming?"

"Hey, I'm underemployed, too." His lips pull back and he almost blinds me with a smile. "Admit it, you're bored here."

That's the point, I want to tell him. I have to be bored. If I'm not, I'll realize just how much I'm missing out on.

Instead I feel a tiny—*minuscule*—part of myself actually considering this. Maybe it's the way he's holding the rest of his half-eaten peach gently between his index and ring finger that has me flashing back to last night, the way he tangled his fingers in my hair. Maybe it's because I can hear Liv's voice in the back of my mind. *Look, Mom and Dad are worried.* Having a boyfriend would really get her off my case. Having a semi-famous boyfriend would extremely get her off my case.

"Is this like . . ." I look around before I drop my voice. "About last night?" I don't want to embarrass Marco with a reminder of how our night ended. It's not like I was in any state to, uh, *help* the situation. I couldn't fault someone for wanting to prove themselves.

"Oh, no. No!" He snaps his eyes away, suddenly rubbing a hand along the back of his neck. I think he may even be blushing. "That's not why I want to date. I want to date you because . . . because why not?"

You have no idea. I busy myself bagging up everything left on the table, ignoring this question. "So," I say, maybe a hair too loud. "Where do you need to be in June?"

Marco snorts. "Back on planet Earth, far away from here."

Ouch. "Well, isn't that nice," I retort, handing him a bag of peaches. "Take these. Free."

"Thank you," he replies and every part of him lingers. His eyes drag over my face, his hands seemingly float to take the bag.

I yank it back. "I thought you were a vampire."

"Still am. I just happened to watch a very compelling movie."

I narrow my eyes at him. "You know, I hate that you smoke. If you want me to even consider this, you have to stop. And . . . and if you don't, I'll call every tabloid and tell them you're here to spear-hunt whales."

Marco's eyes travel over me, his mouth curving up into that smile. That damn smile. Then he lifts his sleeve to reveal his triceps. In the center of his skin is a white square.

A nicotine patch.

Marco grins, firing off all kilowatts, and he actually *looks* happy. "Already on it."

MARCO INSISTS ON walking me to my bike after I pack up my bag. He carries the produce that didn't sell—two totes of leftover lettuce and a box of nectarines—and I'm extremely grateful for the extra set of hands, considering mine are swollen and useless.

We walk in silence, a crimson sunset dripping off the vinyl-clad row homes and cloaking us in the last of the day's warmth. We pass the record store where someone has propped open the door with a box of freebie CDs. Willie Nelson's voice twists on the air followed by the smell of coffee from the doughnut shop next door. Suddenly, I feel like I've slipped through a crack in time and found myself back in my childhood. Wandering around Evergreen with my bike for hours, every street feeling like the next page of a storybook where I am the protagonist—a wayward knight; a powerful witch flying on her broom; a thief on the lam.

I spend our walk alternating between two thoughts: *Tonight is quite literally a perfect night* and *Wait, wasn't there an episode of* Dude's Ranch *where someone kisses their first cousin?*

"So," I pipe up, when the silence suddenly feels too saturated. "You have a mullet."

"Oh. Yeah, I do." Marco laughs, knocking his hat back with a knuckle and ruffling his free hand through the business part. "Isn't it awful? It was for a role."

"*Was?*"

His mouth falls completely straight, brown eyes pulling away from mine. "I don't think it's going to work out."

"I'm sorry," I say quietly. From what I know about Marco, he hasn't worked in years. Not that he needs to. Not that I am personally one to talk. "For what it's worth, that's a very impressive mullet. I'd believe you were a constable or a trucker or maybe a white Christian nationalist."

"Thanks?" He laughs again, furrowing his brow at me. "It's been a fun experiment. After having to have the same haircut for seven years, it's nice to take risks now."

"Can I know what role the mullet was for?"

"For a play. Ever heard of *Brokeback Mountain*?"

"Of course." I perk up, like a dog. "It's my favorite short story, barring a few crucial Alice Munro hits. It just crushes me." Then, I add, "I sort of like things that make me sad."

Marco nods. "Me too. I love being sad. I love having a reason to sit on my couch and cry."

"Do you like to sob or do a wide-eyed, stone-faced thing?"

"Sob. One hundred percent. You?"

"I'm stone-faced every time."

We're talking in that higher pitch, increased speed that happens when two people realize they like the same things.

"So, the stage play—"

"Right, they're doing this Broadway revival with a young director from Edinburgh. I was so excited about it—but they went with someone . . . younger, I think. Everything happens for a reason and all that." There it is again. The switch in his voice; the distance he so easily puts between himself and his life.

I point at my beach cruiser chained to a parking meter at the end of the road, in front of The Billiards.

"That's me."

Marco's mouth twitches. "Of course it is."

He helps me secure the leftover lettuce into the crate I've Mac-Gyvered onto the back of my bike. His hands are steady and strong, his forearms thick and vascular, muscles flexing with effort.

He steps back and observes his handiwork with his fists pressed into his waist. "Let me know, okay?" This question is directed at my bike's tires.

"About what?" I ask, buckling my helmet under my chin.

Marco licks his lips slowly, pivoting in front of me, as if he knows taking that exact half step will bring the setting sun into perfect alignment with his eyes, turning them from chocolate brown to crystallized amber. "Dating."

He brings a finger to my cheek; quick and vibrant warmth percolates in my chest, making my next breath snag. This, he must notice. He holds up his finger. "Eyelash."

User. Vampire.

I bat his hand away. "Yeah-fucking-right."

MARCO AND I go our separate ways with all the balls in my court. Except I know he's meandering back to the bay-side of the island, to a magazine-spread-ready home with a bathroom in the garage and a panoramic view of the sunset.

Meanwhile, I bike back to the modest, wood-shingled beach shack my siblings and I will squabble over for decades, once it's passed down to us. The fact that Marco wants to date me? It's more than opposites attract. It's farce—it's sketch comedy. It's Stuart Little getting adopted by humans.

The Fabiola beach apartment is just three bedrooms at the end of a short, dark hallway attached to a kitchen with a skylight, a sitting area, and double doors that lead to the balcony. Everything is Tuscan-inspired and dated with flesh-toned walls and an over-stuffed brocade couch. Years of moisture have caused the linoleum cabinets to peel and buckle. My dad has patched the same leak around the edge of the skylight every year since he bought this place.

But it's ours. It's so very *us*.

A photo of my parents has been secured to the front of the fridge for as long as I've been lucid enough to remember coming to Evergreen. My mom is sitting in my dad's lap in a white plastic chair. My dad's mustache is pitch black and enormous; my mom's honey curls are teased into an updo. Tiny orange numbers in the corner read: *08/15/1986*. They're two teenagers, some place in Southern Italy, thinking about what they might have to do to make their dreams come true. They don't know that one day they will have a regular home *and* a beach home. They can't even imagine what it's like to have enough money to not spend their nights awake, worrying.

Sometimes, when I'm in the mood to wallow, I stare at this photo and think about how deeply I've let them down over the last year, how badly I've disrupted their first year of retirement.

I get home, drop my bags, and make a beeline for the fridge, and as I'm preparing to eat strawberries right from the container in the blue-green glow, I catch their eyes.

My dad never smiles, but in this picture he's grinning, one hand tight on my mother's waist, the other on his knee. The way my mother tells it, they've only ever loved each other. The biggest decision most people make—whether or not to give their heart away—and they got it right on their first try.

There's a knock at the front door, then it creaks open and Allie pops her head in. She catches me staring at the fridge, in the dark. Embarrassing.

"Soph and I are gonna go out for a drink. Wanna join, babe? Talk about your date?" She has a crisp Midwestern accent and the sweetest way of handling vowels.

"Um," I say and my voice cracks. Because I haven't spoken a single word out loud since I said goodbye to Marco. I clear my throat. "No thanks. Not tonight."

She flashes me a gentle smile. "Not feeling good?"

I nod. "I should probably get some rest so tomorrow I'm in better shape."

She says goodbye and pulls the door shut.
Once again, I'm alone.

I TEXT MARCO: We date until May 31st and then that's it

> **Marco:** We said a month.

> **Nadia:** May 31st and you're done

> **Marco:** You're being difficult.

Then, he writes: Might be my second favorite thing about you
I frown at my phone. What's number one?
He writes back almost immediately. Your smile

Saturday, May 6

I wake up, roll over, and add to my *things i never knew before lupus* list:

  2. *disease is isolating. prepare to be alone. or get really good at lying.*

"You're still coming tonight, right?" Allie asks.

We're bagging green beans on the front porch while a mid-spring shower cleans the pollen off our cars. It's a hot, sweet rain that smells like wet sand and sulfur, wafting heavy off the bay at our backs. We live on the skinniest part of Evergreen, only two blocks from the bay and the beach in either direction. Locals love to remind us that we'll be the first part of the island to go. But we know they're just jealous.

It's quiet down here, far away from the boardwalk and motels and bridges in and out of town. A bird sings through the storm. Today, my mind is tired, but my body is hanging in there. Lupus has brought me an acute awareness of the way my various parts work—or don't work, really—together to make me a full human. The world is heavy around me, just like the muggy air, and I feel as if I'm moving through an odd but familiar dream. Before I knew I had lupus, I always thought I just had déjà vu. Now, I know that my mind, leaden with brain fog, was saving itself the energy of processing, leaving me in a stop-motion dream state.

"Is this the spring musical or the end-of-year concert?"

"Musical."

"Oh, fuck yeah, I'm in." Allie's an English teacher at Malaga County High School and their one-woman theater department.

She twists her hair, as blond and fine as corn silk, away from her face and lifts another handful of green beans from the crate at her feet onto the scale between us. "Half a pound."

I stick a handwritten label to the front of a plastic bag before scooping them up. "Is that redheaded kid still the lead in everything?"

"Charles Roberto Jenkins? No, unfortunately he couldn't audition this semester."

"Man, what a star. I hope he thanks you in his Tony acceptance speech."

My phone dings. I know who it is before I even look. Or, I *think* I know who it is, because I know what I've done.

> **Marco:** First date?

"It's happening," I announce, like a woman going into labor.

Allie looks up from her dirt-covered hands. "What?"

"Marco." I clear my throat around his name, embarrassment churning in my stomach. "We're dating. Tonight. We're dating."

"*What?*" She scoots to the edge of the porch swing with such force, she almost flings a Birkenstock at my forehead. "*Again?* So soon?"

"Don't get excited. This man is absolutely up to no good. I don't know *what* his end game is, but I'm highly suspicious." I can't believe what I'm about to tell her—what I'm probably going to repeatedly tell people all month. "Have you seen the movie *Sweet November*?"

Allie shakes her head, zipping her hoodie up under her chin. "We were a *Veggie Tales*–only family."

"Right. Well, it's this rom-dram I brought up to him where these two morons promise each other that they'll date for one month and one month only. Then—surprise, surprise—they end up falling in love. Now he wants us to *Sweet November* but different, which—within the context of the movie—just means I don't ghost him and die."

For the first time I've met her, Allie is stunned into silence. Eventually, she stutters, "Well, that's very, um, that's kind of . . . romantic, right?"

"Soph whittled you a whistle for your one-week anniversary," I remind her. "You know, he's so hot that it's actually like, a joke, seeing him walking around Evergreen in the middle of the day. Oh, and he definitely hates it here—"

"Poor guy, leave him alone! Someone could say the same thing about you."

"I make sense here," I fire back, holding up a handful of dirty green beans. "I'm not some douchebag fallen from grace trying to—*Jesus Christ.*" My phone starts buzzing in my lap and I almost keel over from the shock of it. "He's *calling* me." Of course, I immediately put him on speaker before shouting into the receiver, "You're relentless!"

"You've given me no choice," he replies calmly. "I only have twenty-five chances to hang out with you."

"Why are you in Evergreen?" I demand.

"I'm house-sitting for my uncle." He sounds totally unfazed—amused, even. "Why are *you* in Evergreen?"

"Irrelevant. Why do you need a fake girlfriend?"

"There's nothing fake about this. I want to date you. I need to be outta Dodge in a month. You don't seem to want something serious. Simple."

Allie's eyes have quadrupled. *"Invite him,"* she's hissing over and over, *"to* Mamma Mia! *junior. Invite him."*

I turn away from her and take Marco off speakerphone. "It *is* fake. And *Sweet November* is not my favorite movie."

My eyes settle on the Bracken house across the street. It's the only beach cottage left on a block of totally gentrified beach house behemoths. For all of the summers of my childhood, the Bracken house had been inhabited by the elderly widow Eleanor Bracken. Even in my earliest memories of Evergreen, Mrs. Bracken was ancient—a frail, sweet-voiced woman with long gray hair she clipped away from her face with a mother-of-pearl claw clip. Back then the other houses on our street had also been petite Cape Cods, though none of them had dreamy lilac shutters and a screened-in porch like the Brackens'. Now, the cottage stood alone in its sun-faded, dilapidated charm. Even my parents had made a series of slow but significant improvements to the duplex, like painting the wood-shingled façade a rich, trendy navy blue and replacing the old cement lawn ornaments with WASPy little pinwheels. Last month, Dad had the carport freshly paved.

Eleanor passed away two years ago, finally joining her beloved Victor on the other side. In my funky lava-lamp brain, this realization hits me anew. I can still picture Eleanor pruning her rosebush by the buttercream-colored front door, waving to us as she smiled up from under her sun hat. She'd been missing Victor the entire time, hadn't she? Distracting herself with the task of keeping their family home in tip-top shape. It had been a beautiful, meaningful task. But still, a distraction.

"Too late. You said it was." Marco's voice, lilting with sarcasm, snaps me out of my sudden plunge into sentimentality. *Man, I really am lonely.*

"It's not, though, I lied. It's a fucked-up movie about . . . about people making weird, selfish decisions instead of just being normal. Poor Nelson's probably still in therapy. And the little boy with no dad? No *way* he made it out unscathed."

Marco's laughing at everything I say, and I'm also losing a slow battle against my own smile. "Well, I watched the movie and I liked it. I thought it was very romantic."

"What if we did separate movies? You can *Sweet November* me, and I'll *50 First Dates* you."

Marco sighs. "Feels like that's already what's happening. *You* texted me, remember? *You* agreed." Years in California haven't taken any edge off his accent, and every vowel rolls around the entirety of his mouth before finding its way out of his mouth.

"We were . . . very naughty the other night. This . . . this is rightfully earned skepticism."

"Naughty, huh?"

"*Very* naughty."

A low laugh rumbles from him.

I wonder if Marco would care about the Bracken house—about Eleanor and Victor. I think he would; I think the way I'd tell it, he'd even cry. "Did you mean what you said? About keeping our lives separate?"

"I did. I'm not looking for anything serious," he replies softly. "But I had fun with you. Real fun. And I want to do it again."

I used to agree to tons of harebrained ideas, sometimes just for the story of it. Just so I had something interesting or funny to talk about at dinner parties or for the inspiration it might bring me down the road. This would have made a great premise for a commercial. Maybe something for a psoriasis cream. *Moderate to severe plaque psoriasis doesn't have to rule you. Take back your life. Take back spontaneity.* "Okay," I relent. "Meet me at the Daniel G. Hopper Convention Center at six-thirty."

"Ooooh," he mews. "Dinner and a show?"

"Yeah, yeah. Make sure you bring cash. And *don't* wear a hat."

We hang up, and when I turn back around, Allie is watching me, rapt.

"I can't tell if he hates you or wants to marry you."

I know exactly what I need in order to feel sort of okay.

Three liters of water.

Hydroxychloroquine.

Meloxicam.

Anti-itch lotion.

A double espresso, every three hours.

Multivitamin.

And today, the first pill of a particularly hairy set of steroids, necessitated by my night out with Mr. Antoniou.

This is what it takes to make me feel vaguely human, to keep my brain from lava-lamping and my kidneys from failing and my body from crumbling into a pile of ash. Some of these drugs work daily to make me feel significantly better; others will work over my entire lifetime as a sort of organ insurance.

I need all of them. I can miss *one* day—max. Anything more

and I feel it. My joints will ache and swell. I'll become exhausted, fatigued, rash-ridden, irritable. And depressed.

Then, who knows what else? I've learned I can't predict what my body will do next.

By six, the rain had eased from a heavy pour into a soothing drizzle and we pile into Soph's truck, wet shoes and raincoats slipping and squeaking against the leather seats and plastic floor mats.

"Nadia has a boyfriend," Allie sings as soon as she slams the passenger side door behind her. I'm in the back seat—their large, pouting daughter.

I heckle Allie. "Traitor! I hope Donna eats shit during 'Chiquitita.'"

"Why would you say that?! Donna has a full ride to Penn State!"

Soph's jaw is locked into a frightening clench. "Ladies, *please*. I just spent five hours at a soil convention."

The boardwalk is quiet and dark, except for the buzzing street lamps, and underneath our feet the planks exhale moisture with every step we take. The ocean makes itself known on the air but otherwise, she sleeps.

We walk in comfortable silence, our faces turned toward the misting sky. A rain as fine as glitter covers my face. To our left, the shops and stores are still closed for the offseason. In the distance, on our right, the convention center marquee glows blue. It's a grand building, an architectural throwback to when Evergreen was a bustling resort town over a hundred years ago. Patinated buttresses cap redbrick columns, arched windows wink in the night sky, speckled keystones and cornices outfit the roof like icing on the edge of a birthday cake. It's shockingly grand for a place like Evergreen and yet—it's an extraordinarily comforting sight.

Marco's already here, leaning against the front double doors, an Eagles hat pulled down low over his eyes, shielding him from the soft rain.

"You wore a hat," I call out across the planks. Anxiety thrums in my ears, and I can't think of anything to say that's more charming or interesting.

He looks up from his phone and a smile breaks across his mouth, traveling to his eyes with the speed of a shooting star. "Hey."

"You wore a hat," I say again so he won't hug me. I cannot be chest to chest with this man. Not right now. Not when he's pressing his lips together to keep from grinning. He takes a few lazy steps toward me, hands stuffed in his pockets. His gait is languid but swift, like a baseball player's.

"I had to. I tried to make the mullet work, but it's beyond help."

"You need a haircut," I say. "That can be our date tomorrow."

"Tomorrow, huh?" Marco smirks. He pulls a hand out of his pocket and I actually flinch, terrified he might pull the whole *eyelash* thing again. I'm back to my normal, Chihuahua-like self. He's looking at me with complete amusement.

"Don't do that with your face. We're *Sweet November*ing. We go on dates."

"I thought we were also *Groundhog Day*ing and every morning we'd have to have the same fifteen-minute argument before you agreed to see me," Marco teases. We start to make our way inside, taking refuge under the convention center's overhang.

"Don't punish me for being amenable to your terms and conditions," I warn him, but it's also a reminder to myself. *You will probably be punished for this.*

Marco *said* he was a user, a vampire. But rather than simply believe him, I did my own research.

Is he a cheater? Yes. Allegedly he cheated on a longtime girlfriend named Alix Marie while filming the *Dude's Ranch* season-seven holiday special, "Dude's Ranch: A Very Hawaii Hanukkah," on location in Maui.

Is he a gambler? Unclear, but his net worth is apparently only six million (*gulp*), which doesn't make total sense when one factors in that, at their peak, each principal cast member of *Dude's Ranch* was making three hundred thousand dollars per episode (*scream*).

Is he a drug addict, criminal, general ne'er-do-well? Insert knuckle crack here.

On March 15, 2019, Marco Felix Antoniou was arrested after arriving at LAX intoxicated, carrying enough of *the good stuff* to make TSA go *you're under arrest* and also *uhhh, you okay, buddy?*

The former sitcom star and once-heartthrob was swiftly cuffed and booked—which, apparently, he took very well. The arresting officer noted that Antoniou was incredibly respectful and even autographed a coffee cup for his thirteen-year-old daughter. He promptly attended a thirty-day in-patient rehabilitation facility in Barbados, went on probation, endured a ghoulish fortnight in the meme circuit, and then mostly disappeared.

Leading up to the whole LAX thing, there were telltale signs that maybe things weren't going particularly well for the man who played America's favorite roguish city slicker trying to save his father's ranch while having every teen girl in a sexual headlock. Marco was a TV actor on a lowly, cringe-worthy sitcom meant for stay-at-home moms and teenyboppers, and his character, Vinny Baldacco, was getting less and less screen time. When Marco crashed his motorcycle into a stop sign in Venice Beach and fled on foot, no one wondered what was really going on with the once-promising young actor.

I'm not some J-list celebrity apologist, but looking at his mug shot—eyes glassy, hairline drenched, lips chapped, skin sallow—I couldn't ignore flashes of the Marco I now knew, the kind, thoughtful man with eyes like honey and dimples deep enough to swim in.

The man who had agreed to see the junior version of *Mamma Mia!* The man who now holds the door open for me, even though I spent an entire afternoon cyber-stalking him well beyond what could be considered ethical or necessary.

Warm light and cool air pours out from the lobby, but I'm still standing there in the chilly, wet night, staring at Marco with my hands tucked into my armpits like a moron.

Marco frowns gently. "What's wrong? Are you mad I made a *Groundhog Day* joke? Is that your actual favorite movie?"

I gesture at my body. My half-zipped raincoat is so big it covers the entirety of my outfit. I look like I'm wearing a men's rain slick, Chelsea boots, hoop earrings, and nothing else. "I wore a dress. For you. For the show. I wanted to look nice."

"Oh." He tilts his head to the side. "You look great. Very hip-hop. Gwen Stefani."

"That's a generous interpretation." I step inside and pull the rain jacket over my head, smoothing out the ruffled chiffon fabric of my dress. When I look up, Marco's heavy-lidded gaze is fixed on me. When our eyes connect, he snaps his gaze away.

"You're beautiful, Nadia. Don't worry."

But I have been worrying—and once he calls me beautiful, I worry even more.

MARCO DOESN'T KNOW it, but his level of enthusiasm as an audience member is a test. I've got one iguana eye on the chorus line, high-kicking to "Lay All Your Love On Me," and the other on Marco, whose bouncing knee keeps coming dangerously close to grazing mine. If I sense anything less than sheer, unbridled joy, he's done for. Over. Kaput.

But, to my surprise, Marco spends the entire run of the musical pinned to his chair, eyes wide. He laughs loudly, claps graciously, and even leans forward, elbows pressed into his thighs and hands clasped under his chin, when Donna and Sophie finally reconcile. During the thirty-minute intermission he immediately turns to me in his seat and asks, "*What* about that Rosie?"

Afterward, he personally congratulates Donna on her performance—then, he takes a picture with her mother, who recognizes him almost immediately.

"Elder millennial moms. That's your demo," I tell him. I've been waiting for him by the trash cans near the back of the theater, raincoat draped over my arm, while a group of red-cheeked women fawned over him.

"Oh, yeah. Big-time." Marco trashes his second—third?—can of Diet Coke. "Walking home? Or did you bring your hot wheels? I'm guessing no." His gaze skates over my dress again—short, flowy, slightly too feminine to be sophisticated, and in no way built for bike riding.

"If you're talking about my bike—no, I did not bring my *hot wheels*. Soph gave me a ride."

His eyebrows jump. "Well, then, can I give you a ride home?"

"Of course you can."

Shockingly, this consent does not come from me. I turn toward the voice—Allie's over my shoulder in her black show blazer and pointy flats, looking sweaty and professional. "So nice to finally meet you, Marco."

I glare at her. *Finally?*

"Hey, sure. Likewise." His brow quirks for a moment and his eyes briefly connect with mine—*Finally?*

"Alison, I thought we were going to get dinner—"

"Well, then Marco can join us." She shrugs and grins, because she's so proud of herself, but she also flinches because she knows I'm mentally throwing knives at her. "Marco, do you like dinner?"

He's standing there with his hands in his pockets, mouth pulled into a flat, observant line. His eyelashes are so long that under the dim theater lights, they cast long shadows over his cheeks that look like the delicate, angular legs of a spider. "I love dinner," he says earnestly. His voice is deep but sweet. Suddenly, I want to kiss him again. I want to hug him and feel his chest muscles tense underneath me and then bite into his tan skin. I believe this is what they call *cute aggression.*

"No one loves dinner." The words leave my mouth before I can stop them.

Marco lifts his chin at me, bemused, and crosses his arms over his chest. "Excuse me? I absolutely love dinner. Meatloaf? Mashed potatoes? These are top-tier foods."

Now I'm angry—unthinkably angry. "Breakfast is the only meal that is even worth making an argument for. You'd take meatloaf over waffles? Over an omelet?"

"Yes," Marco says plainly.

I throw my hands up in the air and announce loud enough to turn some heads: "Well, then, I guess I'll just go fuck myself."

Allie grimaces, tossing an apologetic look Marco's way. "Sorry, she doesn't get out much."

Marco, Soph, and I wait patiently while Allie collects her well-earned congratulations from proud parents and grocery store bouquets from giddy, glassy-eyed teens before we all decide on dinner at the Pier Point Diner situated at the very end of the boardwalk. The diner's brightly lit interior is mostly empty, save for what appears to be a very chaste double date and a few waitresses in cobalt blue polo shirts, swiping crumbs off the breakfast counter and clearing out the cake display case. We all slide into a booth, Soph and Allie shoulder to shoulder, looking pink and eager in their humid coats. Marco climbs in next to me, struggling to pull off his jacket without elbowing me in the throat.

"We didn't even get a chance to tell you how amazing tonight was." I reach across the table and give Allie's wrist a squeeze. "Another impeccably directed masterpiece."

"Your best work yet," Soph joins in, giving her a hug around the waist. "Incredible job, babe."

"Really? Y'all don't have to lie, you know that. I felt like the chorus was a little low energy in the first half. I kept telling them— *if you're not having fun, the audience won't be either!*"

"They were perfect. Everyone was," Marco chimes in. He folds his hands on the table and his elbow grazes mine. "Consider me an unbiased third party. Best performance I've seen this year, maybe."

"Oh jeez." Allie smooths a hand over her cheek, strategically hiding the sudden flush blooming there. "Well, I guess I have to believe you, then."

Oh, no, even *Allie*, gay as they come, is charmed. Is no one immune to this man? Soph and I swap a quick, bemused look before our waitress drops off a stack of sticky plastic menus and four ice waters.

"So, how'd you all meet?" Marco asks, skimming past the section dedicated to regional tragedies like creamed chipped beef and disco fries. *Thank God.*

"We're neighbors," I say casually, eyeing Allie and Soph over my menu. I'm sending them paragraphs of data with just my irises. "We share a duplex." *He doesn't know I have lupus or that I lost my job or that I'm living at my parents'. Well, he kind of knows that part but anyway, please don't say anything too—*

"We moved into the downstairs apartment like, two summers ago?" Allie says. "Back then Nadia was too cosmopolitan to be our friend. She'd show up Saturday morning, run ten miles, then she'd be gone. She was way too important for little old Evergreen."

"I did *not* run ten miles. I'd run like, seven and a half."

"Seven and a half miles?" Marco lets out a low whistle. "What was your split?"

"I don't know, eight minutes?"

"Damn, you *are* fast."

Heat springs up from my neckline.

"But we all need a change of pace sometimes." Soph jumps in and saves me, a preternatural empath despite their best efforts. "Nadia makes all my chalkboard signs."

I'm actually, fully blushing now—a good sign that the conversation needs to move on. I bury my nose in my menu and announce, "You know, Marco grew up in Evergreen."

Allie perks up immediately. "Did you go to Malaga County? Are you in our hall of fame? Do you want to come talk to my first-period freshmen? They *desperately* need a mentor."

"No, unfortunately," Marco responds, weariness edging into his voice. "We moved to LA when I was fourteen—my mom and me?"

"Did you always want to be an actor?"

"I *really* wanted to play professional baseball. But I wasn't good enough. And my mom was big into . . . " He pauses for a moment, carefully selecting his next word. "Hollywood. It worked out."

Sensing we may have accidentally wandered into unpleasant territory, the table falls quiet as we turn our attention back to our menus. Soph and Allie slip into their own private world, giggling and arguing under their breath, so I lean close to Marco and say, "You're going to order the meatloaf, aren't you?"

"Well," he whispers back, nudging the corner of his menu into mine. "It comes with green beans and mashed potatoes. Not a bad deal."

"It's almost ten P.M."

He snaps his menu shut. "I love a digestive challenge. What about you?"

"I don't know . . ." I chew at my bottom lip. I don't have much of an appetite these days. "Maybe I'll just have a coffee."

"C'mon," he says gently. "You have to eat. Let's split the meatloaf."

"Mmm. Pure romance."

"You seem like you have a hard time committing," he ribs me.

"Oh?" I arch a brow at him. "So, you'll just help me out, then?"

"Mmm-hmm." He nods. "I'm a nice guy, aren't I?"

"According to who?"

We place our orders and receive only a moderate amount of horror when Marco tells the waitress, "One meatloaf, two straws."

Our food arrives and everyone falls quiet, until Allie has half a milkshake in her.

"So, you're *just* back for thirty days, huh?" she barbs, Midwesternly. Marco quirks a brow at this. The specificity, the intent of the comment, it's not lost on him—or me. I try to kick Allie under the table, but instead Soph lets out a little yelp and my ears turn pink.

He nods, pushing a spoonful of mashed potatoes toward my

half of the oblong, trough-sized dinner plate. "More or less, yeah. I'm looking after my uncle's place while he's in Greece, but I'm back and forth to New York every few days, working on some big projects. Just living in the moment."

I make a conscious effort not to roll my eyes.

"And your mom?"

"*Allie*," I hiss.

"It's okay." Marco laughs. "She's in Florida now. Retired."

"Is your dad still in Evergreen?"

This question hits my stomach like lead. Dad territory can be risky.

"Uh, kinda." Marco directs this comment toward his meatloaf, which he saws into sixteenths. "He's a real character, but I think old age has slowed him down. He called me from Montreal last month."

Sometimes I want to punt the woman into the sun. She has this naivete about how complicated and painful simple things like family can be. It's obvious, painfully so, that talking about his parents is making Marco itch. I almost want to reach under the booth and take his hand in mine, give him a squeeze. A little hand Morse code: *sorry-she-sucks*.

Instead, I reach over to take another forkful of buttered green beans from our shared plate. "Dinner food was a good call," I say. "Hey, why don't we ever sell any vegetables to the diner?"

Soph furrows their brow at their apple pie. "I don't think we could keep up with demand. They probably move the same volume of potatoes in one day that we sell in a month."

"No way," Allie says. "Even in the offseason?"

Soph nods emphatically. "The people of New Jersey love potatoes. Think about how many french fries a diner serves in a day."

Marco's gaze floats to mine, and a soft smile plays at the corners of his mouth.

After settling the check, we all wander out onto the desolate boardwalk, where an icy breeze is coming in off the ocean. If no one else was here, I'd take off my shoes and walk out onto the cold, wet sand. Get close enough to the tide to feel the freezing water whispering against my feet and walk all the way back to the bottom of the island, back home. We only have a few more weeks of cold nights before the season really starts to change, and I want to soak in every moment.

Soph wraps their arm around Allie's shoulders and they meander away, heads close together, cheek to firecracker-red cheek. I know that, theoretically, they get plenty of time alone together, but I can't help feeling bad for how much I've made myself a part of their life. I hang back, pulling my jacket tighter around me as I face the ocean, cold air stinging my eyes.

Before I can decide how I feel about it, Marco strides into my periphery, setting his elbows down onto the railing that separates us from a substantial fall down onto the sand.

"I think I'm gonna head out," he says softly. "But I'll see you tomorrow, right?"

I rake my teeth over my bottom lip. *Yes, tomorrow. And the day after. And the day after that.*

"Sure." I nod, letting my eyes meet his. "Thanks for coming tonight."

"Of course. Thank you for having me." Marco lingers, shoulders hunched against the wind. His lips open then close, until finally he says, "Let me give you a ride home." His eyes are so dark, I can almost see the shimmer of my earrings in their reflection.

"You're not sick of me?"

"Not at all."

I drop my eyes, smiling softly. "I'm sorry about Allie. I wanna blame it on all the homeschooling, but—"

"I'm a big boy, Nadia," Marco says, quiet laughter shaking his shoulders. "I can handle a few questions about my family. No feelings hurt, I promise."

"Good." A breath of relaxation falls from my lips. "I'd love a ride home." I tilt my head toward Soph and Allie, locked together in a kiss one streetlight over, their bodies having dissolved into a single shadow. "I think the lovebirds are busy."

Marco drives me home, carbs and chilly weather lulling us both into an easy, contented silence. We keep our eyes trained on the wide, empty streets of downtown Evergreen, even though the air in the car feels choked and charged with the giddy energy of *what next?* We'd see each other tomorrow, of course. And then the day after. And the day after that one, and so on and so on. After months of continuously feeling nothing, on a *good* day, I now couldn't stop wondering: What would this month bring? Would it always be like this—soft and easy? Would it hurt when we said goodbye?

When he pulls up to my parents' house, we say good night and he assures me he'll call. All of this makes my head spin, but I somehow find myself saying *okay, see ya.*

After brushing my teeth and taking my meds, I settle between my clean, cold sheets, a ball of unspent energy and fiery nerves.

"Fucking Marco," I say out loud, to my ceiling.

You wish, I think immediately.

I toss and turn, making a good, solid effort to fall asleep. But my mind won't still, I just know it won't, until I do *it.*

With a groan, I roll toward my phone and poke the screen to life. *Twice in one day?* In a matter of days, this man's turned me into a pervert of the highest order—a *fan*.

Nevertheless, I tap open Google and my fingers find the letters of his name. I'd told myself I'd never do this again. And somehow that makes it feel all the more delicious. I can't believe I'm doing—

A new article. There it is, at the top of the list, a blue link unsullied by my feverish clicking.

MARCO ANTONIOU IS DONE WITH ACTING

**Years in the limelight—and away—have taught
Marco a lesson he'll never forget: Som . . .**

The preview pane cleaves the sentence mercilessly. *What* had it taught him? *What* had he learned? Above the headline is a thumbnail photo.

I can tell the photo was taken recently because he has the mullet and he's on the beach. An Evergreen beach. I would recognize the dunes—which Marco lounges against, his weight shifted backward onto an elbow so that his linen shirt dips open perfectly, revealing a triangle of tan chest—anywhere. His hair is expertly styled, smoothed away from his face in careful waves. The party part of his mullet, the worst part, is brushed back and cast over his shoulder. Marco's gaze holds mine from the photo, eyelashes framing his chocolate-brown eyes like kohl. He's not smiling; instead, his full lips are pushed together and parted ever so slightly, like he's been caught mid-sentence.

God, he's perfect, I think.

The thought comes to me so fast, I can't even stop myself.

MARCO ANTONIOU IS DONE WITH ACTING
Years in the limelight—and away—have
taught Marco a lesson he'll never forget:
Some bad days will haunt you forever.
By Sage Liu

When Marco Antoniou agreed to do an interview, I didn't think I'd have to take two trains and a bus to reach him. But these days, the former *Dude's Ranch* star spends his time hiding out on the tiny island of Evergreen, a lesser-known Jersey Shore point fifty-five minutes east of Philadelphia and two hours south of Manhattan, where Marco usually lives. My trip down is organized directly with Marco, who prefers to manage his own schedule. He buys me a first-class Amtrak ticket to Atlantic City, and apologizes profusely for being unable to pick me up. Marco assures me that the bus ride to Evergreen will, at best, leave me feeling inspired—or, at worst, give me some time to catch up on emails. And like that, I agree.

Marco's charm has long been noted—by critics, who mostly panned *Dude's Ranch* as low-brow junk to fill the airwaves before *Thursday Night Football*, with the exception of Antoniou's performance as the winsome Vinny Baldacco; by business managers on both sides of the negotiation table, who describe him as humble and hardworking; and best of all, by his friends, who have stuck with Marco through thick and thin.

I take the train to Atlantic City and then a bus to the little shore-point island Marco refers to as his "sort of hometown": Evergreen, New Jersey.

Evergreen is a juggernaut; a tiny town of 10,000 residents that balloons to a cultural hot spot of nearly 200,000 during the summer season. Comedians and musicians travel from all over to play to a boisterous, sold-out crowd at The Billiards Backroom, and there are rumors that even pro ballers and A-listers have looked into purchasing bayside property on the hyper-secluded micro-islands that freckle the southernmost tip of Evergreen. This is to say, it's not weird that Marco is here. But it is certainly a choice.

"New York gave me my livelihood back, but when I'm here I reconnect with who I really am," he remarks while giving me a tour of his family's sleek, European villa, which includes a private dock on Malaga Bay and a row of perfectly pruned fig trees.

Marco has a tendency to do this—to sort of speak in greeting card phrases. I can't tell if he's the sweetest man on Earth or messing with me, sending off one-liners he knows will click into place perfectly for a cover story. It's this tension that keeps me on my toes.

Having grown up in the PNW, I wasn't familiar with the cultish fervor tristate locals feel for the Jersey Shore. Like many Americans, I associated the phrase with a reality TV show and the ensuing mid-aughts hedonism. But Marco assures me I am in fact in the greatest place on Earth. Evergreen is a place of paradox, he says while thumbing a ripe fig. "That's why I fit in perfectly."

From the balcony off the back of Antoniou's temporary home, you can see exactly where the bay meets the Atlantic. "This is my favorite view," he tells me, passing me a mug of what looks to be perfectly brewed black tea. Marco has been living a sober lifestyle since 2019, but he still feels awful for only being able to offer guests sparkling water or some form of caffeine. "I try to remove all temptation and then I look like a total asshole." His accent crests on the word *asshole*.

The mention of temptation feels like a natural segue into talking about the notorious, albeit very private, heart-throb's love life. Strangely, unexpectedly, when I mention the idea of love, Marco is incredibly forthcoming.

"I'm a romantic. It's the only core belief I have that I haven't managed to destroy." This is delivered with a soft laugh. "People are falling in love all over the place, all the time. Even in their darkest, most fucked-up hours. That was the most consistent part of rehab, actually. Illicit romances.

"I just don't think it's in the cards for me," he adds. This feels like a profoundly vulnerable revelation, delivered with a cigarette hanging from the center of his lips—his only remaining vice. "I think different people have different energy. For a long time, my energy was not attractive. And now, I'm old." He laughs.

"Too old for love?" I ask.

"Too old for heartbreak."

What a correction.

These days Marco stays busy with a number of investments in small businesses, most of which are run by the dear friends he made in the wake of sobriety. He's part owner of an olive grove in southern Lazio that produces award-winning oil; he's an investor in a woman-run health-care app; he provided start-up capital for a tattoo shop in Bed-Stuy. He's liable to show up at any of these places, at any time, to lend a hand wherever needed. Marco is a jack of all trades, and by his own judgment, a master of none.

"I was a fine TV actor. I can deliver a line, hit my mark, have a positive attitude. But really, I think what I'm good at is just being there for people. It's a skill, and I'm always working at it. I like the idea of being a reliable guy. You need a ride? A plus one? Someone to sit with you when things suck?"

"So, I take it this is your way of saying you won't be making a comeback to TV?"

Marco scoffs playfully. "A comeback? Are you kidding me?"

We settle into matching rocking chairs on the back deck and talk for what feels like both fifteen minutes and five hours. When the sun starts to set, Marco tells me he'll take me to his favorite barbecue place. He drives a ten-year-old Cadillac that's in near-pristine condition.

"I feel like an old-school mobster in this thing," he says with a rakish grin. Behind the wheel, Marco looks like he could easily star in a glossy remake of *The Godfather*. He's a testament to the existence of star power. Even in a navy-blue T-shirt he claims came in a pack of three, Marco looks like someone worth watching.

And he is. Marco Antoniou may never cross our screens again, but I have a feeling we haven't seen the last of him. When I ask him what's next, he details a project that is equal parts glamour and sophistication.

"This is my second act, for sure. This is my part two. Everything's different. I'm ready for everything to be different."

"So, you'll quit smoking?" I tease.

He looks at me over the top of his sunglasses and flashes a heart-stopping smile. "For the right woman, absolutely."

I throw my phone across the room.

Sunday, May 7

This isn't like you! You've *never* left your mail sitting this long. *Ever*." Pause for dramatic effect. Then, the button: "You need help, Nadia."

Liv is lecturing me again, this time from where she sits cradled in the pink satin pillow, on speakerphone.

I'm starfished on the bed in my underwear, the echoes of my night out with Marco *still* ricocheting through my bones. Overhead, the ceiling fan whirls at full tilt, rocking gently in place. The cool air is both a salve for my limbs and like a cast-iron frying pan over my head. My sister takes for granted that I may actually be depressed or be suicidal. To her, depression and anxiety are mere concepts reserved for hypotheticals you read on the internet or characters in a TV show.

"Please, God. *Enough.* I'm already fucking exhausted."

"What about holistic medicine?" She keeps going. "Isn't there an herb you can rub on yourself? I just feel like you're not trying—"

"You think I haven't tried all that stuff? I'm *on* medicine. I'm *on* steroids. It all just takes a while."

"You know, I read an article about a woman with cancer who bought a ranch, tilled the land, and *cured* herself."

"And I read an article about a man from Nantucket with a really big bucket."

She sucks her teeth at me. "*Very funny.* Just wait until Mom and Dad find out you've been making a dent in their king-size mattress."

Our parents are currently on a Mediterranean cruise for their fortieth wedding anniversary. They're two people who, as long as I've known them, have done little else besides work at the butcher shop. They're hardwired with an old-world work ethic and skepticism. The only thing they believe in fully is the Catholic Church, which is, fortunately, the basis for their marriage. I can't imagine them anywhere other than the shop; the row home where they raised me, Liv, and our little brother, Nicky; and the Shore. But right now, as I speak to my sister, they've elected to be trapped at sea, on a vessel where group activities and line dancing are strongly encouraged. I picture my dad, five-two on a good day, frowning at the shores of Crete, longing for his tomato plants and the patch of sun in the carport where he loves to sit in a lawn chair.

"Don't worry, I'm just making a dent in your queen-size mattress."

"Oh, thanks a lot," she huffs. "Typical, ruining *my* bed."

"Your room is way bigger and has the ocean view. Mine has a fucking porthole, Nicky's baseball gear, and all those jars from Dad's pickling phase."

Liv lets out a dry laugh. A door slams in the distance, and I know she's arriving at Fabiola Sausages to open in time for the post–Sunday morning Mass rush. "Remember when he was obsessed with jalapeños? You smelled so bad that entire summer."

"The funk was trapped in my hair. Thank God it's g—" *Fuck.* I stop short of the word *gone* leaving my lips. But Olivia is a hound dog. She could sniff out a poor life decision from planets away.

"Thank God it's what? What is it?"

"Nothing. I just got a haircut, that's all. Just a trim."

"Why do you sound like that?"

"Like what?"

"*Just a trim!* You sound British."

"I do not—"

She launches into an awful impression of what I guess is supposed to be me. *"Just an inch off the bottom, dearie. Tidy ho!"*

"Ew, shut up," I whine and it's the most enthusiastic I've sounded this entire phone call.

For most of our life, it had just been Liv and me; eighteen months apart, both of us girls. We'd never really been similar—in school, Liv loved clubs and organizing parties and could probably convince a flock of geese to unionize. I was quieter. I liked pressing flowers and limping around the playground, pretending I was an abandoned carpetbagger on the Oregon Trail.

"Spot of cream!" Liv's still going.

Then, when we were both pubescent, Nicky was born and weirdly, everything finally felt complete. Liv and I made more sense with this little whiny baby boy around. He needed us both, for different reasons.

It was never either of our dreams to take over the butcher shop, but Liv had a hard time making herself unavailable. Then, she dropped out of hair school and met a nice neighborhood guy with forearms like oil tankards and all bets were off. She was the heir apparent.

"Whatever," I say, instead of telling her to fuck off. The curse of being a younger sister. I physically cannot bring myself to be as mean to Liv as she is to me. Liv has had an existence, however brief, before me; I have never been without her. She was my first friend and probably will be my last.

"You need a *jay-oh-bee*, baby. A real one. If you don't get moving, Dad's gonna stick you back in the shop and that's the last thing either of us needs."

Liv isn't wrong, but she's being such a dick about it.

"I can't come back to Philly," I half whisper. "That might actually kill me." Unlike lupus, which will just make my life infinitely more irritating over a fairly normal amount of time.

"I've known you your whole life, and you're not a do-nothing person. You're hiding, Nadia. I'm just worried, believe it or not, and I'm not going to *coddle* you."

Now she's recycling talking points, but my phone vibrates and I see Marco's name and suddenly, I'm sitting up.

> **Marco:** The only place I could get a hair appointment is in Cape May. Five star place tho.

My fingers explode over the keyboard immediately and I know he sees the three hovering dots. I backspace the nonsense I've written and flop back on the bed. My heart is pounding erratically in my chest.

"Are you even listening?"

"Uh huh." I squeeze my eyes shut, trying to keep my voice even. "I hear you, Liv. I gotta go, okay? Tell Mike I say hi."

"*Ugh.* Fine. Goodbye. I'll see you Tuesday. *No* flaking."

Right. *Shit.* Tuesday she's coming into town to go bridesmaid dress shopping. *That* was why she called. The beginning of our conversation was so long ago, I can't even remember the woman I was when it began.

"See you Tuesday," I repeat, trying my best to make sure it doesn't sound like a question.

***

> **Nadia:** Cape May is an HOUR away

> **Marco:** So?

Nadia: I have a life outside of Sweet Novembering

Marco: Prove it

Damn. Well, he got me there.

Nadia: Fine, but we have to go whale watching

I pause before hitting send on this text. Whale watching off the coast has been on my bucket list for years, even before moving to Evergreen. Back when I didn't have a car. I'd talked about my dream of seeing a jumping whale endlessly to friends and guys I'd dated—especially when we found a day or two to sneak away to the Shore between the usual, unending thrum of life.

Then, suddenly, I was in Evergreen full-time, and I had a car— but nothing else. No friends (until I fully annexed Soph and Allie). No boyfriends. And frankly? No desire. What was I going to do, drive an hour to sit, exhausted and achy, on a boat alone?

What he's proposed is, essentially, a very long errand. What I'm proposing is a dream come true. *He doesn't need to know that*, I remind myself. There a lot of things Marco doesn't need to know.

I hit send.

Oh fuck yeah, he replies and we agree to meet at 1 P.M. in the Billiard's parking lot.

"THOSE KIDS WERE crazy-talented last night," Marco says, dragging a hand down over his stubbled chin.

We're taking all the back roads to Cape May, whipping past farmland and fields of reed, windows cracked, and sunshine-filled neo-jazz playing softly. It's a little unseasonably warm, but I try not to think about it. Climate anxiety used to keep me up at night, but my world has shrunk. I take the sun at face value.

My throat hurts, but I'm trying to act like I don't feel it. I'm trying instead to focus all my attention on the gentle, one-handed hold Marco has on the steering wheel. A sore throat is a bad sign. An omen for worsening symptoms, potentially even a flare-up. A shadow that's suddenly hanging over me, and I'll have to put as much effort as I can into not showing it. Especially considering how frequently Marco's eyes drift from the road over to watch me.

I should take some ibuprofen now; that way it will have started working before we get there. Then, while Marco gets his haircut, I can wolf down some yogurt and take the Big Guns. The Good Stuff.

I don't want to think about medication. A petulant little thought. I wish I could stomp my foot. Throw back my head and whine. I don't want to deal with any of this. For the first time in months, I just want to be here, completely, in this moment. *I want to have fun.*

"You okay?"

His voice snaps me out of my spiral, and I toss Marco a small smile. "Yeah, sorry. I thought maybe I forgot something at home."

"We can turn around—if you need to check for the thing you forgot . . . or maybe just get out of spending the entire day with me." He adds the last part softly, kindly. *He's giving me an out.*

"No, no. I'm good. I really . . ." What I should *not* do is finish this sentence with: *have been looking forward to this.*

Marco laughs, flexing his fingers around the steering wheel. "Don't hurt yourself."

"Whale watching is something I've always wanted to do," I say, recalibrating. "I'm excited."

"I'm excited," he parrots back in my monotone. "Why do I feel like that's glowing praise from you?"

"Because I fascinate you."

He lets out a low, deep laugh. "You're definitely one of the most interesting people I've ever met."

"No way." I pull three ibuprofens from my pill pouch. "You've like, hosted award shows with Japanese sex symbols."

Marco shrugs, twisting his hat around backward. "Hedonism is kind of boring. Once you've seen one nepo baby try to network while in a k-hole, you've seen them all."

I laugh through a sip of water, swallowing back my medicine. He doesn't even notice. "What a sinister sentence."

"Speaking of which . . ." He tightens his grip on the steering wheel for a moment, and I straighten in my seat. "The other night, when we went out and got drunk . . . " Dread crackles in my stomach. *Oh, no.* "I'm supposed to be living a completely sober lifestyle. I'm a drug addict and . . . " He pauses to lick his lips. "This conversation is going awfully."

I shake my head. "Keep going."

"I know myself and once I start down that path, it never ends well, and I never want to put myself in a situation where I'm tempted to potentially make an even worse decision. Which is exactly what I did." He drags his eyes away from the road to meet my gaze for a moment. "I'm sorry."

"Hey. No." I place a hand on his shoulder. He's like a hummingbird trapped in a greenhouse, slamming into all-glass walls over and over. My hand, gently placed on his warm shoulder, stills him. "I'm sorry. I shouldn't have . . . instigated. Or fanned the fire. Or *whatever the fuck* I was doing."

I feel the tension in his muscles dissipate. "How were you supposed to know?" He runs his tongue over his bottom lip. "By the time I was being honest with you—"

"You already had your hands down my pants." Thankfully, my joke lands and we both dissolve into laughter.

A very modest cast of pink expands upward from the collar of his shirt. "Well, that's a little humiliating."

"Hey, life is just a series of humiliations and then sometimes . . ." Sometimes what? I have no wisdom for Marco, only sympathy. "Sometimes you get to go whale watching."

His eyes dart off the road again, toward where my hands rest in my lap. He reaches over and gives my knee a squeeze. "Thanks, kid."

"You're welcome. But you have to stop calling me that. It reminds me of this mega-douche I dated. He was always using *experimental* pet names. One time he called me *little dove* in front of a waiter."

Marco grimaces. "Oh God. I'm so sorry. Never again."

"Thank you." I laugh. And then we both relax back into a more comfortable silence. Outside, the sky is a cloudless wash of cornflower blue. The low, vibrant farmlands of South Jersey whip by. After a moment, I say, "Can I ask what triggered you? To drink?"

Marco makes a small noise in the back of his throat. "I guess getting recognized. And honestly?" He lets out a dry laugh. "The boardwalk."

"The boardwalk?"

"It's all the . . . the . . ." He takes a hand off the steering wheel and gestures vaguely, rolling his wrist. "The *shit*. The bright lights, the crappy overpriced food, the hokey stores. It makes me feel like I have a plastic bag wrapped around my head. I *want* to like Evergreen. I'd even consider staying there forever if they just would burn down that goddamn boardwalk."

I huff. "I can see that. When I was a kid, I hated anything where I was told I was supposed to be happy. Even now, I still hate it. It's like . . . like, fuck you! You can't *make* me be happy. You can't *trick* me with flashing lights and clown music."

"Exactly. If you tell me I should be happy, you know what I'm gonna fucking do?"

"Be unhappy," I jump in, twisting in my seat to face him.

Marco's eyes shine, fixed on the road, with a look of satisfaction. "Right. I'm going to be unhappy just to piss you off."

"And then that'll make me *actually* happy," I say wickedly.

He lets out a growl of approval.

WHEN MARCO AND I get out of the car I notice the film camera hanging around his neck.

"Is that a prop?" I tease, lifting the camera away from his chest and turning it over in my hands. It's heavy and looks loved, with visible wear marks around its leather body.

"Sure is. Gotta look tortured and artistic. Part of the brand," he deadpans, pulling his arms through a flannel. We're the closest we've been since Thursday night, and the memories are catching up to me. Especially now that I can smell his cologne—a floral musk that dusts his neckline.

He places his hands over mine, engulfing them. Suddenly, I'm back on Ernie's dance floor, Marco's sweat-slick chest pressed against mine, his lips flush against my ear. *Wanna get out of here?*

We shift toward each other, one foot crossing lazily over the other. There's something about his body that pulls me to him— that pulled me to him the first night we met, as soon as I had enough tequila in me to shut down the never-ending rush of self-loathing running through my head. Right now, there's no tequila, but there is our *contract*. We're dating. This is okay.

Marco is the kind of guy you yearn for. The kind of guy you dream of fucking, and if our first night together was indicative of anything, it's that we're both horrible at pacing ourselves. We both have lead feet, and this experience is a race car aimed at a cliff.

But I don't want to slam headfirst into intimacy again. I've done that before, over and over, and the ending is always the same. Luckily, this time I already have our ending. I can work backward from there.

On May 31, we'll meet at the Pier Point Diner and split a stack of pancakes. I'll tell him about my diagnosis; I'll tell him about how I'm feeling *sooo* much better and I finally got a great job doing *something cool* in Philly, and I'm headed back. He'll be completely overjoyed; he'll tell me he got some part playing a grizzled dad, and he's moving to Vancouver. I'll be completely overjoyed.

Ten days before that, he'll tell me he never wants kids.

Five days before that, he'll tell me he thinks monogamy is a prison.

Two days before that, we'll have sex for the first time.

Today, we'll hold hands and see a whale.

He runs his thumb over the letter embossed on the camera's leather case, and I feel a pang of excitement deep in my stomach.

Marco's been monologizing about his camera this entire time. ". . . and then he told me it was actually manufactured in East Germany. It says it right here on the bottom, but I also have a certificate . . ."

I can do this.

IT TAKES FIFTEEN minutes for me to convince Marco he really *does not* want me there for his haircut. I just keep shouting, "I'm too judgmental! I'm too persuasive!" while he shouts back, "Who cares!"

We compromise, in the end. I sit in the waiting area reading the *Cape May Gazette* while a middle-aged man in very pointy shoes guides Marco behind a frosted-glass wall where I can distantly hear a symphony of blow-dryers whirling.

The cover stories are a recap of the Miss Teen Waves competition and an op-ed about the environmental impacts of rabid gopher extractions. It takes an entire paragraph for me to realize that one story has ended and the other has begun.

Twenty minutes later, Marco rounds the corner, smoothing a hand self-consciously over the freshly close-cropped sides of his new 'do. I let the newspaper fall to my lap.

I don't know much about men, but I do know that there are three acceptable haircuts, two unsightly, and then there is one haircut that makes anyone attracted to men go absolutely *feral*. Shorter on the sides, longer on top. Long enough that it requires constant smoothing, but not so long that it could get caught on a ceiling fan or sucked into a jet engine.

This is the haircut Marco has.

Now I can really see his face, no heavy flocks of hair or a baseball hat brim in the way. Marco's forehead is perfectly square, his eyebrows thick and placed precisely on the ridge of his brow bone, which would otherwise make him look concerned or perplexed if his eyes weren't so warm, dark, and liquid, surrounded by faint smile lines. Without the hat and hair, I can see now the articulated angle of his jaw and the way his mouth permanently pulls to the side, like he's chewing his cheek or getting ready to laugh.

The older gentleman and Marco shake hands mightily, then he turns to face me, holds out his arms, and says: "So?"

The newspaper falls from my lap to the floor. I clear my throat. "Well, it's no Jonathan Taylor Thomas . . . but still . . . you look . . ."

Marco bites back a laugh. "Great?"

"Yes," I manage. "You look great."

He turns to face the beveled-edge mirror hanging in the waiting area, pulling a hand down his neck, kneading at his skin. *Jesus.* "My neck's cold."

I pick up the newspaper, dragging my eyes away from him. "And your head feels lighter, right?"

"Yeah. It's fucking weird." He squints at his reflection while craning his neck left and right. I stand and cross the tiny waiting area to stand behind him. His hair is an otherworldly shade of black and without the extra weight, it falls into perfect S-shaped waves. "I think I miss my mullet."

I let out a sudden bark of laughter, tossing my head back. I think I startle Marco—I definitely startle myself. I haven't laughed that loud in months. "I *think* you'll adjust," I assure him.

His eyes are fixed on mine through our reflection, a smile on his lips. It's a very *Eyes Wide Shut* sort of intimacy, to meet someone's gaze through a mirror.

I'm wearing my bucket hat again, the brim curled upward, curls flattened to my forehead, coiling around my ears. I cringe internally at the sight of my body. I've always been a curvy girl but now my hips pull at the fabric of my short-sleeved green sundress more than they would have six months ago. Marco doesn't seem to mind, if the way his gaze is straying is any indication.

I yank nervously at the cardigan tied around my waist. "Come on, the boat leaves in forty minutes and I don't want to miss out on any of the freebies."

He pivots on his heels, turning to face me as he reaches for my hand, pulling it away from my waist, his fingers grazing the soft inside of my wrist. "You look really nice today."

I take a half step back, my voice trapped in my throat. "Oh—"

He laughs softly. "Am I making you nervous? It's just a compliment. That's what boyfriends are supposed to do, right?"

"Yeah." *Holy shit.* "I guess," I choke out.

"I was really in my head before, otherwise I would have said something sooner."

He's watching me, waiting for me to say something. I can't look at him, can't handle the weight of his eyes, which matches his words. A double dose of sincerity. *You don't mean that,* I want to say, defaulting to my factory setting: self-deprecating, evasive.

But I'm starting to get Marco. He means everything he says whether I like it or not. He's completely honest, and right now, that's a good thing. Maybe one day I'll wish he wasn't so forthcoming. Maybe one day he'll realize how good I am at hiding.

THE WHALE WATCHING ferry leaves from the private dock behind Barney's Sea Shack at 4:30 P.M. on the dot, no exceptions. Passengers are welcome to join Barney and his brother, Captain Bill, for an unlimited buffet of hot dogs, pizza, crab cakes, soft drinks, light beer, and ice cream inside the family-owned Irish pub before boarding Bill's watercraft and heading out into open waters.

One might wonder why Barney is giving away so much free food. One might even question the quality of such copious amounts of decadent treats. One might even begin to consider that perhaps Barney has a sick, nasty fetish for bodily fluids.

"I didn't eat meat for like, eight years," I say between bites of a perfectly charred hot dog. Marco and I are sitting on a bench on the dock, away from the indoor cacophony of our sea-mates getting lightly blitzed in anticipation of meeting Moby Dick.

Marco practically ran outside when he saw the volume of alcohol being handed out willy-nilly inside the pub, and, not to be outdone, I was hot on his heels, hot dog in tow.

"First time I ate a hot dog, I got a massive migraine."

Marco nods, expertly shoving half a crab cake sandwich into his mouth. "Had to go vegan for season five because they kept wanting me to take my shirt off for all these like, waterfall scenes." He rolls his eyes.

"Waterfall scenes? What did that have to do with the plot?"

"Bold of you to assume there was any plot at that point."

I'm laughing through bites of my dog. "So, what happened when you were a vegan?"

"Every time I cheated and ate cheese or ice cream, I'd have these crazy dreams. Like seriously fucked-up, prophetic shit. It scared the shit out of me."

"And your solution was to just start eating meat again?"

"I was desperate! It only happened to me when I was a *cheating* vegan, not when I was a regular carnivore. I had to set the universe right."

I pull back at how serious he sounds. The man is clearly traumatized. "*What the hell* did you dream?"

Marco considers telling me very carefully. He narrows his eyes at me and freezes, sandwich hanging limply midair, mouth open.

Then, he snaps his mouth shut and shakes his head. "Nah, another time. Too bleak."

Barney gets on his PA system and gives us a five-minute warning for departure and welcomes us to start boarding the *Miss Teak Skye*. I'm hell-bent on getting good seats right at the bow of the boat, so I force Marco to trash his final hot dog. We're in line, waiting to step off the dock and onto the ramp, when I hear a small voice behind me.

"Miss? Miss, excuse me?"

When I turn around, I realize I have to look down in order to make eye contact with the source of the nervous, thin voice: a five-foot-nothing, extremely pregnant woman clutching the hand of a little boy with messy chestnut hair. "I'm so sorry to interrupt your date, but I . . ." Her eyes wander over to *Miss Teak Skye*, terror bubbling up in her expression as the boat bobs willy-nilly in the reflection of her eyes. "I was supposed to take my son—Emmett, say hi—on the sunset cruise, but I just don't think I can do it. The doctor said I'm one speed bump away from going into labor and my husband is away for work and this thing is like . . . like, *fifty* speed bumps."

"Oh, wow, I—" I start to respond, but the little boy with the chocolate-rimmed mouth interrupts.

"Mommy." He grips her forearm, pressing his tiny, chocolate-lined lips against her skin. "Mommy, no. You *promised* we could go."

She gives him a taut, pained look before making the most intense eye contact I've ever experienced. "If I get on that boat, I will go into labor. Could you take him for me? Please? It would be such an enormous help a-and you look so kind and normal. I know it's a long ride—I can pay you! He's seven a-and *barely* uses the bathroom. He's a really good kid—"

"Mommy." Emmett's in a full-tilt panic now. He's seven, but he's not stupid. "I don't *know* her." Such a valid point.

"Of course," I say, hoping to temper the sudden swell of anxiety rolling off both of them. Marco's lingering at the edge of the ramp, hands in his pockets as he shuffles from foot to foot, eyes averted. Now that I know his triggers, I can feel his anxiety around being recognized. It has a palpable electricity to it. His entire body seemingly buzzes and a part of him sinks away, but I don't want this woman to be surprised to find out she isn't just handing her son over to a pleasant-looking woman in a bucket hat. She's handing her son over to a pleasant-looking woman in a bucket hat *and* a minor celebrity. "You don't have to pay us." I jab a thumb at Marco. "I'm with my friend. We've totally got this. Stay here and sit. Please."

"Oh." The woman's big brown eyes flutter shut in relief. She presses a hand to her enormous stomach. "Thank you *so* much."

"But Mommy." Emmett's on the verge of tears. "I don't wanna go alone!"

"Not alone, sweetie." She leans down as best she can to meet his eyes. "With a new friend."

"Hey, we're gonna have fun," I say, moving into a half squat to also meet Emmett's eyes. But he refuses to be so easily convinced—and rightfully so. He buries most of his face into his mother's long hair. I try again. "Do you know the names of all the original Poké-mon?"

Suddenly, Emmett gives me a deathly skeptical look, peeling his face away from his mother's side. "Kind of."

"Really? Maybe you can teach me. I always forget at least fifty."

His eyes dart back and forth between me and his mother. She gives him an encouraging pat on the head, and finally he detaches from her, like an octopus from the side of a ship.

"Maybe," he whispers from behind a hand, the majority of which is now lost in his nose.

"Cool." I reach for his unoccupied hand. "Come on, let's see if we can spot any Magikarp from the boat."

Emmett's mom and I exchange phone numbers, and I promise her repeatedly that she can call at any moment, for any reason, guilt-free. She doubts herself for one nanosecond, but I assure her I'm not a serial killer or a kidnapper by letting her scroll through my Instagram feed, which is functionally a promotional page for the produce stand. Lots of pictures of me in my work boots with cartons of peaches. It's humiliating, but it does the trick.

We board *Miss Teak Skye* and from the deck, we wave at Emmett's mom the entire time passengers load on. Marco makes a beeline for the bow of the boat, securing an area exactly where the helm comes to a point. When Emmett and I finally make our way over, as the ferry pulls away, Marco is watching me with an eyebrow cocked.

"I saw that kid absolutely destroying an ice cream sundae," he whispers, leaning close to me when I settle onto the bench beside him.

"Hush," I hiss, tossing my tote bag into his lap. "His name is Emmett, and he's a very good listener."

"Just saying. When we hit a rough patch, you're in the direct line of fire."

I glare at him. "Says the man who ate a crab cake, an ear of corn, and two hot dogs."

"One and a half hot dogs." He corrects me, looping one arm through the handles of my bag and bringing the other to rest behind Emmett and me on the railing. It's a small and paternal gesture that leaves me feeling weirdly protected—as if Marco's elbow could do anything to keep me from going overboard.

Miss Teak Skye gains speed as we pull away from the southernmost tip of New Jersey, heading out toward open water. Above us, the sky is a soft celestial blue, streaked with cotton candy clouds. It's five and the sun is still warm underneath the ocean breeze, but neither is strong enough to leave us uncomfortable. As we pull away, Emmett twists around to watch the shoreline grow thinner and thinner, his mouth falling open in awe.

"Pretty cool, huh?"

He nods. "My mom loves dolphins. She has my baby brother in her tummy."

I nod back. "Your mom's very cool. I'll make sure we take a lot of pictures of the dolphins. Right, Marco?"

Marco peeks around my shoulder. "Of course, pal." He holds up his camera. "I'll get the best picture I can."

ONCE WE MAKE it far enough from shore, Captain Bill begins his one-man show. I don't want to laugh, but he's pretty good at delivering a litany of dad jokes—lots of *I'm not the whale you're supposed to be watching* type of stuff. Marco's fully chuffed, basically slapping his knee. This delights Emmett endlessly and he switches spots to be between us, so he can get an instant replay from Marco without having to lean over me. He's entered that specific type of kid hysteria where words like *chum bucket* send him into a delirium of giggles. He's so gassed by the end of Bill's ten-minute set, we're basically holding him down to keep him from breakdancing on the deck.

"Alright, folks. We're coming up on our first big sighting of the evening. Usually around this time of day a pod of dolphins makes their way across the horizon. I ask that everyone stay seated as we are going to drop anchor and things can get *pretty* bumpy. Now, all I need is a little help from my crew—when I say *heave*, everybody shout *ho!* Ready? Heave!"

Everyone under the age of twelve is inebriated with joy, riding the free-sundae-bar sugar high, drunk on fresh ocean air. The first *ho!* is loud enough to split an eardrum and Emmett is nearly beside himself.

Marco, the world's greatest hype man, has Emmett by the armpits and with each *ho!* he tosses him into the air.

Heave . . . ho!

Emmett is hysterical, doubling over with laughter.

"Catch your breath, bud," I say, once Marco sets him down. "Maybe you can sit this next *ho!* out?"

Too slow. It's already happening again.

Heave . . . ho!

Emmett throws himself across Marco's lap, shrieking, "Again! Again!"

"I don't think that's a good idea," I warn Marco, but I'm not loud enough—or fast enough.

"Here we go!" Marco sings, grabbing Emmett around the waist and hoisting him upward.

Heave . . .

But now, Emmett is turning green.

"Marco," I warn him, urgency pushing my voice up an octave. "How about less swinging on the next one?"

"What?" Marco says through laughter. "He's fine! He's loving this."

"He looks *gray*."

"Heave!" Bill shouts, drunk with power.

But Emmett can't get out the next *ho!* He's standing statue-still, clutching a hand to his stomach, eyes tearing.

"I need . . . Mommy," he manages.

"Buddy?" I reach for his arm, and he stumbles forward toward me, his face waxen.

With the swiftness of an Olympic hurler, Marco scoops Emmett up under the armpits once again, but this time he aims him at the ocean.

"HEAVE-HO!" Bill crescendos with the rest of the passengers on *Miss Teak Skye*, and in that exact moment an arc of milky vomit bucks free from Emmett's mouth, cutting through the late-evening air. I've never seen anything like it. It's powerful. Majestic, even.

Everyone on the deck gasps.

I leap up, grabbing our jackets and my tote bag, and stand there, slack-jawed, at Marco's side. There's no way for me to help. There's *nothing* I can do.

Thankfully, the wind's on our side and Emmett's spew cuts cleanly through the air as we all watch on in horror. Marco cringes and recoils, evading the rare, rogue vom droplet that's flying backward.

While Emmett's blasting vanilla ice cream and hot dog chunks into the ocean, Bill's back to yukking it up over the intercom. *Jesus, read the room, William.* Isn't that the number one rule of comedy?

Marco pulls Emmett back into his chest, turning him around into an embrace while I rush over and wrap the boy tightly in my cardigan and Marco's flannel. My arms find their way around Marco's shoulders as I rub Emmett's back and promise him everything's okay, that he's okay, that we all just got *a little too excited.*

But the kid is traumatized. "I need my mommy," he blubbers over and over, throwing his head back to the sky as snot streams down either side of his mouth. "I need her! Mommy! My nose *burns.*"

"Call his mom," I order Marco, pulling my phone from my purse and shoving it into his chest while scooping Emmett out from his arms.

"Are you sure?" Marco has a faint sheen of sweat gathering on the fresh, clean edges of his new haircut. "What's your passcode?"

"One, two, three—"

Nerves gone. He rolls his eyes. "I think I got it."

BEFORE I HAVE time to panic about what the hell we may have gotten ourselves into, a flock of moms descends on us. Forget about the Green Berets, we need to think about militarizing moms. These ladies are on me in minutes with wet wipes, a teeny-tiny bottle of mouthwash, ice water, a cold compress, hand sanitizer, a ginger candy for Emmett to suck on once he's stopped full-body sobbing. As I hold him steady in my lap, wrapped in my gray cardigan with a hive of mothers around us, I find myself drifting out of the chaos and staring at Marco. He's on the other side of the deck, pacing back and forth, pulling anxiously at his bottom lip while he talks to Emmett's mom on the phone. I can hear him, faintly.

"They're all taking good care of him. No, I promise. I promise. Hey, Jen. Listen." *Jen*. I'm not sure how I hadn't gotten her name before. He's better at this stuff, isn't he?

"You poor thing," a blond woman with kind eyes and one million freckles says as she rubs my back gently, pulling my attention back. "Your little guy's all worked up. You probably thought you were just having a nice afternoon at the beach!"

"Oh, no—he's not—"

"Oh, Daddy's back," she announces suddenly, eyes doubling as they settle behind me. Who the fuck is *Daddy*?

"Hey, baby," Marco interjects. Oh, got it. Marco's Daddy and Emmett's our son. Everyone on this boat is insane. The cabal of women around me parts immediately as Marco sits down beside me. "You okay? How about you, champ?" Emmett's resting his head against my shoulder, no doubt with cartoonishly big tears in his doe eyes. Marco thumbs his button nose. *Champ. Baby.*

"My stomach hurt," Emmett murmurs.

"It sure did, buddy. All you have to do now is keep an eye on the horizon for dolphins, okay?"

Emmett nods, sucking noisily at his special ginger candy.

The woman looks back and forth between Marco and me. She begins to mouth, *Is he the guy from . . . ?*

I shrug playfully. "Maybe," I mouth back.

"Well." The blond woman sighs loudly, looking at us with the most ooey-gooey, honey-covered, sickly sweet smile I've *ever* seen. "Ain't that a good man? We'll leave you three to your family time."

Marco gets to his feet, as if she's a guest in our home that needs to be walked out. "Thanks so much . . ."

"Katie," she demurs. "I loved *Dude's Ranch*, by the way," she adds with a shyness I know Marco appreciates.

"Ah." He smiles sheepishly, extracting a hand from his pocket to rest gently on her back as he expertly guides her away from us. "You're too kind."

I pivot Emmett and myself toward the ocean, letting Marco and the woman have their private conversation about the healing properties of Vinny Baldacco learning to ride a horse.

"Hey," I whisper to Emmett. "Knock, knock."

"Who's there?" he asks, mimicking my soft tone.

"Heave."

"Heave who?" I wait a beat and then he lets out a stream of giggles. "That's not a *real* joke."

"You're right. I made it up just for you."

WE'VE DE-ANCHORED, AND we're on the move. Bill's promise to us is that we will see at least one dolphin, guaranteed. If not, we can come back tomorrow for another sunset cruise, on the house. We bob in place, in an uninterrupted stretch of blue identical to everywhere else we've been today, for a good forty minutes before Bill announces he has a foolproof spot. The subtext being: *no way in hell am I hauling you all out again tomorrow night.*

"Why the eff did you call me *baby*?" I demand as soon as Marco returns from the snack bar with two Diet Cokes and an apple juice.

He shrugs a shoulder, popping the tab on my drink before handing the can over. "You're my girlfriend."

My jaw tightens. "Why did I think I'd get a real answer out of you?"

He takes a noisy sip before crossing his foot over his knee, draping an arm over the boat ledge. "You're easy to rile up." I can't see his eyes behind the mirrored lenses of his sunglasses, but I know he's looking right at me. I can feel it, the way his eyes work over me. "I like it."

"Ugh." I roll my eyes. "Am not. You just wanted to call me *baby*."

He shrugs. "You're right. I wanted to call you *baby*. I want to call you *baby* again, right now, actually."

"Please don't. This is all too wholesome. I'm gonna hurl."

"Do it. Let's see if you're as cute as Emmett when you puke."

I laugh. "No way. This'll be some real *Exorcist* shit."

"Hey, look—" Marco leans over to point and his arm finds its way around me and Emmett. He points out at the open, calm water. "Dolphin."

"Oh my goodness. Emmett, look—" A pod of tails break through the surface, one after another, catching the late, low sun.

Emmett gasps and twists around in his seat to get a better view. He's suddenly feeling agile and awake. "Dolphin," he gasps. Pure joy.

I pull my phone out of my bag and begin snapping a thousand pictures of Emmett pointing and laughing and clapping, leaning backward to get the best angle. I'm leaning deeper and deeper into Marco's chest but he doesn't move. He keeps his arm idling around me, fingers resting on the metal rail. He's laughing softly, chest vibrating against my back while I yell, *"Smile!"* over and over.

"Keep your phone still," he chastises me, tone playful. "Can you take one that isn't blurry?"

"I'm going for something avant-garde. Abstract. Dadaist." I tilt the phone and snap a sideways picture of Emmett with the extra-long zoom on. Marco's hand is in the corner, barely visible, and I catch myself thinking about how nice his fingernails are.

"Let me do it," he says, engulfing me in his arms, hands coming over mine. His lips are right next to my ear now. His grip is firm without being forceful, and the smell of him—human and smoky, with a hint of something petal-soft—overwhelms me. I'm releasing my breaths slower, slipping microscopically into his embrace. "See," he nearly purrs, his voice low and gravelly in my ear. "Hold. Steady."

I wonder if the blond woman is watching us, and I wish I could see what she sees. I want to know how I look leaning backward into Marco's chest, his chin resting against my shoulder. I don't think I've ever really seen what I look like with someone's arms around me, let alone someone like Marco. Someone who calls me *baby* and pops my Diet Coke open before handing it over. There's a slickness in my stomach that drips down, snaking through my abdomen into my thighs. Something inside that's foreign, long dormant, waking up.

Emmett suddenly tries to stand on the bench, gripping the railing with both hands. "Easy, buddy," I say, lurching out of Marco's arms as he also immediately adjusts his hand to steady Emmett, chin grazing my exposed shoulder.

Now I'm aware of how close we've been. How any micro-movement would make it so obvious how close we are, hurtling us head-first into self-awareness and then an acknowledgment that maybe we want to be this close. Or that Marco wants to be this close and I don't have it in me to move away.

My skin goose-bumps and he must notice because I can hear him doing one of his little laughs. I ignore him, focusing all my attention on keeping Emmett from slipping between the railing and the ledge of the boat, soaking in the look on his face as he watches the pod before anyone else. Bill will get on his PA soon announcing the dolphins' arrival and everyone will rush over, shrieking. We'll be surrounded on all sides by bodies and noise.

But for right now, only we know about the dolphins.

AFTER THE RAUCOUS and highly successful dolphin sighting, Bill says we can finally head back to toward solid land. The sun is setting and the early-May warmth has evaporated, sending almost everyone inside the boat's main cabin, a large room outfitted with old, moss-colored carpet and muck-crusted windows. Marco asks if I want to go inside, but I can't imagine trading our perfect seats for anything, let alone a stuffy, noisy room.

Now the deck's all ours. Emmett lies down on the bench, resting his head in my lap, and falls asleep tucked under my cardigan.

I'm texting with Jen, sending her picture after picture of her son pointing at the dolphins. She's apologizing profusely, no matter how much I reassure her that Emmett is actually an angel—the type of kid that tricks you into thinking you want your own.

I have to ask, she pivots.

Yes, I write back immediately, he is the guy from dude's ranch

Omfg. I knew it!!!!! Vinny Baldacco!!!! Wait are you two dating???

I bite my lip to hide a treacherous little smile. It's a long story.

Marco's on the other side of the deck, staring out at the ocean. He's put himself on whale watch duty for me. After Bill threw it in reverse, I'd made a small comment about how I'd really hoped we'd see at least a sliver of whale.

Marco had shrugged. "It's not too late." And then he planted himself across from me, staring out at the horizon. The wind is ruffling his hair, blowing it backward and sideways away from his face. Every once in a while, he raises the camera from around his neck and snaps a picture.

For now, yes, I say to Jen. I tuck my phone into my tote bag and rest my head on the metal railing, letting my eyes fall partially shut. I don't want to miss a second of this calm, but I can feel the day catching up to me. Exhaustion seeping into my bones along with the happiness, making me feel heavy and drunk.

I blink my eyes open slowly and there's Marco—standing in front of me, camera held to his eye as he maintains his balance with tensed legs.

"Don't move," he instructs me.

I groan. "Why?"

"Because there's a whale right behind you."

"Behind me?" I lift my head and he lets out a stream of *eh, eh, eh*s like I'm a dog.

"Almost got it." The camera shutters once, twice. "Perfect. Quick, look now, before she's gone."

I turn just in time—just as a tail breaks through the water's surface, bringing with it a burst of water. Elegant and enormous, big enough to produce a rainbow, sun rays catching and exploding from marigold into prismatic Technicolor. The air smells like summer. I press my forehead to the railing and watch the whale as she grows smaller and smaller, as we speed farther and farther away.

Marco drops down next me, so close I can feel the warmth of his chest, the flapping fabric of his T-shirt. His arm slips around me.

"Why whales?" he asks.

"I don't know. I've just always felt connected to them. They're beautiful and powerful, but hunted—constantly in danger. You know how sometimes kids think all dogs are boys and all cats are girls? I think I've always felt like all whales are women."

"All whales are women," Marco repeats with a nod, pushing out his bottom lip, satisfied.

"Yeah," I say, my voice soft. Knowing he's there, I let my eyes fall shut, let myself sink deep into the moment. "All whales are women. Boats are also women. Stingrays are men."

He lets out a soft laugh. Memories from today flicker through my mind. Marco lifting Emmett to see the ocean, Marco managing and handling Jen over the phone, keeping her calm. Marco popping the tab on my soda. It's all too much to resist, isn't it? And it's nice to know sometimes you aren't facing a crisis alone. That if you're tired, you can lean on someone.

So, I lean back into his chest. Immediately, I feel Marco shift to welcome me, the rise and fall of his chest against my back. He doesn't touch me; he lets me fall into him.

"Tired?" His voice is warm, gentle against my ear.

I nod, only a sliver of the ocean visible now through my closing eyes.

As I lie perfectly still, I feel his arms snake around me. *I'll let myself pretend,* I think. Just for now. Just until we reach the shore.

Monday, May 8

On Mondays, Soph and I deliver produce to a few restaurants around the island. Our day starts at the ass crack of dawn with an hour drive inland to Soph's farm. There, we load the flatbed of their truck with hand-packed crates filled with lettuce, broccoli, peppers, potatoes, and lots of herbs. We work in silence, only pausing to take steaming-hot sips of coffee from our thermoses. When Soph agreed to let me work with them, we'd talked at length about my energy levels—how much physical labor could I handle and how frequently. I promised them over and over that I could do this, I could handle it. I wanted to be able to handle it.

I'd been a biker and a runner for years. I'd always dreamed of a more physical job, one where I got to use more than my brain and my wrists. The months I'd spent languishing in bed, doing nothing but staring longingly at the ledge off my fifteenth-floor apartment window, had ruined me almost as badly as the months leading up to getting fired.

I needed to move. I needed to feel useful.

As I'm rearranging the back of the truck, I can feel Soph watching me from underneath their furrowed sandy-brown brows. The sun has barely broken above the horizon. We've been moving through the inky, indigo dawn in almost complete silence, as we usually do on these Monday-morning shifts.

I pull off my gloves and turn toward them with my hands on my hips. "You're staring at me, babe."

They push up their glasses with the back of a ruddy hand. "Nuh-uh."

"Yuh-huh."

They shrug, averting their guilty, anxious gaze. "You look a little tired."

"It's five-fifty in the morning, Soph. You look a little tired, too."

"I don't want you to get hurt o-or, you know—"

"Sick?" I joke, but Soph doesn't laugh. They're very serious. A Capricorn. "Look." I hold up my hands and flex my fingers. "Dexterous."

"If you felt like shit, you wouldn't even say anything," they accuse before taking the world's fastest sip of coffee from their thermos. "You'd just let yourself get hurt."

I press my lips together. Soph is right; I can't even pretend to be offended. "Exactly, so why worry? No matter what, I'm going to just power through." I turn back toward the last stack of crates we need to load up before heading back to town.

"Because you were out late last night."

"I got home at nine-thirty."

"If you need to take a break, it's okay. Just let me know."

I stuff back a groan. *They're just looking out for you,* I tell myself. *Accept their kindness.* I take a moment to collect myself then nod. "Thanks. There's two more cases of chamomile in the greenhouse that I couldn't carry. Too heavy for me. Can you grab them?"

Soph looks satisfied with that. "Sure. Of course."

"Do you miss being a writer?" Soph asks.

The question throws me off for a second. We're stopped in late morning traffic on the Malaga Bay Bridge, a soft hazy sunlight falling over the road.

I'm still a writer. I write every day. Even on the days when I'm too tired to put pen to paper. On my phone before I fall asleep, I capture a few words. In my mind, I write poems and sketches and jokes. If I could play an instrument, I'd be writing songs. I don't love writing; it's just writing is the only way I know how to make sense of anything well enough to know how it's really made me feel. It's the only way I know how to let go.

If I hadn't been able to write down how the last few months have made me feel, I'd still be lying in bed in my apartment in Philly, staring at my shaking hands, paralyzed by the thick, inky pull of shame and self-loathing. But when I found out I had lupus, I documented all my symptoms. Then, what I did in a day and how it made me feel. Eventually, all the conversations I had with different doctors. The meals I ate, the dreams I had.

"I still write," I say simply.

"I mean writing commercials. Do you miss seeing your writing on TV?"

"Yeah." I kind of laugh. "Actually, I think I miss being able to tell people my writing's on TV."

They smirk. "You hotshot. Now what do you tell people?"

"That I'm a fucking farmer."

Soph laughs. And I laugh. We laugh all the way to Rucci's Pizzeria, where we deliver twenty-seven pounds of red onion.

"YOU GOT A package," Allie sings out to me as Soph and I bust through the front door, jackets heavy with morning dew and sweat.

I pull off my work boots. *"Moi?"*

"Yoi." Allie holds the package out to me. Weird. It's not in any sort of delivery service parcel; it's a brown-paper-wrapped box with a little white note card taped to the top. There, in ransom note handwriting, someone has written *NADIA*.

"Why aren't you at work?" I wash the grime off my hands before drying them on the hem of my sweaty T-shirt. "Did you see who dropped it off?"

Allie leans a hip into the kitchen island and takes an enormous bite of her apple. "It's state testing day. And no, they left it in the carport, and I almost ran over it."

"Awesome. How normal. Do we think this is a bomb or something only vaguely threatening, like a picture of me showering?" I rip open the note card. *Figured you need a new one.* No signature. "What the fuck."

"What's it say?"

I ignore Allie and start tearing away the paper, hungrily palpating the box, trying to get the lid to come away. When it finally does, tissue paper springs back and there, in the middle of the box, is a brand-new gray cardigan.

"No *fucking* way."

It's a lot nicer than the cardigan I wore last night and accidentally left behind, wrapped around Emmett as he slept like a little angel in the back seat of his mom's SUV. The fabric's softer—way softer—and the thread is too silky and finely stitched to pull or pill. It smells new and floral, like a department store.

"What is it?" Allie asks, ditching her apple to circle the kitchen island and snoop over my shoulder. "I don't get it."

I unravel the sweater from the box, revealing chic monochromatic buttons and drop sleeves. It even has two patch pockets, just like my old cardigan, but these aren't stretched from holding the weight of my phone and car keys.

"Wait, there's another note—" Allie pulls an envelope from the box, opens it before I can stop her, and begins reading out loud. "*Nadia, I'm sorry I can't keep my end of the* Sweet November *deal for the next few days. A work thing came up and I had to head back to New York*—Oh my God, this is Marco, isn't it?"

I've basically gnawed my thumbnail off. "Keep reading!"

"*I had to head back to New York for a work thing. But you're still my girlfriend*—Jesus Christ, Nadia!"

"Shut up and read, Allie, before I shit myself!"

"*But you're still my girlfriend for the month and I'd love to see you Wednesday at seven P.M.*—and then there's an address for a restaurant in Manhattan."

"He's insane. He's lost his mind." I snatch the note card out of her hand. "Don't touch the cardigan. I'm sending it back."

"Too late." Allie's pulling her arms through the sleeves and wrapping herself in the heather-gray fabric, pressing her nose to the collar. "Mmmmm. Smells like famous boyfriend."

"He's not my real-goddamn-boyfriend, Allie!" I jump up and immediately start pacing.

"Mmmmm famous. Mmmm musky."

"He wants me to meet him at Taigen Izakaya? *Spike Lee* eats there. *Kate Winslet* loves their nigiri." My voice is trembling, as if he's invited me to be his date to the Oscars.

"Awwww!" Allie yanks the card out of my hand and presses it to her chest. "You love Japanese food."

"I didn't tell him that. I didn't tell him my shirt size, either."

Allie rolls her eyes at me. "Because that's so hard to guess?"

"Then explain the Japanese food!"

"Dude." Allie takes me by the shoulders and forces me to look at her, directly into her icy-blue eyes. "He guessed."

I find myself shrinking underneath her touch until I'm leaning fully against one of her bony shoulders. "We went *whale watching* last night. He took a picture of me—with a *whale*."

"Okay." Allie laughs, running a soothing hand up and down my back. "What's the problem with that? You agreed to this whole November thing, didn't you? He seems like he just kind of likes being thoughtful."

I pull away from her, anxiety brimming in my voice. "No, he doesn't. He's a *vampire*. I'm being *sucked*."

"Poetic." She peels the cardigan off and flops it over my shoulders. "Make sure you say thank you."

"I told you, I'm not keeping it." I grab my phone off the kitchen island and scroll for what feels like eons, trying to find his number while keeping up my rant: "He's playing games—mind games, emotional games. I've been playing checkers, meanwhile *he's* playing 4D chess. This is a strategy, and I will get to the bottom of it." When I finally find the number and manage to call him, it immediately goes to voicemail. *"That little fucker."*

Allie watches me with an eyebrow cocked before returning to her apple, flipping lazily through her favorite piece of literature: the Vermont Country Store catalog. "Poor baby, you're just gonna have to keep the fancy cashmere and eat the fancy tuna."

I examine my new sweater with its elegant ribbing and soft tag that reads *Handmade in Peru*, before reluctantly holding it to my nose. It does smell like him—faintly. Like maybe he'd held it to his chest for a moment while browsing the rest of the cardigans, unsure if this was the one, or maybe he'd draped it over his arm as he walked to the cash register. Maybe Marco had flashed the cashier one of his full-throttle, lopsided smiles and said, *I can box it myself.*

When had he even had the chance to buy me a new sweater? Soph and I had pulled into the driveway a little after eleven; half the island was still drinking their morning coffee. Had he driven onto the mainland, to the mall? Or had he pulled it from an enormous pile of hashtag-gifted cashmere in the back of his closet? Marco, like most wealthy people, moves through his life in a way I can barely conceptualize, unburdened by *store hours* and the omnipresent concern of *coming on too strong*.

I drop the cardigan onto the island and grab my phone, crafting the beginnings of a text to Marco.

> **Nadia:** Why in the name of God

No, too dramatic.

> **Nadia:** Ok very smooth but

Backspace, backspace, backspace.

> **Nadia:** Listen here, idiot

Too mean. *Way* too mean.

I slam my phone down and address the sky. "*Why* is he being *so nice* to me?"

I'm pacing the width of Allie and Soph's kitchen, from the sink to the balcony doors, gnawing at my lip. I haven't left Evergreen in months—not since I moved here in January. I'd resigned myself to being a townie—the type of person who shows up to zoning committee meetings with a tub of caramel corn and a codified personal vendetta against anyone who has ever *parked in my spot*.

Allie's shoulders bounce with poorly suppressed laughter. She's trying to hide the fact that she finds me pathetic by taking an in-ordinate amount of time to throw out her apple core. "Because he's not some mid-level advertising executive with a Medusa tattoo and a face that screams, *I ate lunch at the peanut allergy table.*"

I knew Allie hated Kai, but—*damn*. Perhaps she's on to some-thing.

I stop pacing but keep chewing at my lip. "How do I get to New York?"

"You could drive into Philly—"

"No shot in hell."

Allie rolls her eyes. "You take a bus from Atlantic City?"

To think I'd been so content with the idea of never reentering polite society ever again that I'd *cut all of my hair off*. I figured: maybe I'll move back to Philly, maybe I'll get a job at Trader Joe's for the health insurance, maybe I'll join one of those acoustic gui-tar churches where I can contribute with enthusiasm to a monthly potluck.

Meanwhile, Marco's in New York working; that means acting or auditioning, being around other famous people at the very least. And I'm going to, what? Show up Wednesday with a raggedy Vera Bradley overnight bag, rattling with the different medications I need to take just to feel like I'm half alive? Not to mention Marco doesn't even know about my diagnosis. And I have *no plan* to tell him before the last day of May.

Right now, he sees me the way I want to be seen: healthy.

I come to a stop in front of Allie. "He doesn't know I have lupus."

Allie looks confused. "I mean, plenty of people have autoim-mune diseases, I'm sure he'd be really understanding."

"No, Allie. I don't *want* him to know. Right now, Marco doesn't really know anything about me and I . . . I like it. He just thinks I'm some quirky manic-pixie-dream slut that works at a fruit stand and occasionally lashes out about things."

Suddenly, her brows fall into a frown. "You were planning on going all of May without ever letting him into any part of your life?"

"I was gonna tell him *some* things."

"Like?"

"Like I'm . . . a sister. And a daughter."

"Wow, *intimate*."

I collapse into a chair at the end of their kitchen table, flopping forward onto the cool surface. I squeeze my eyes shut. "The first night we went out, he told me he's a *user*. He quite literally said: *do not trust me*. And now, all of this? I don't think he's being insincere, but . . . what happens next? What if he's like, mining me for content? I don't wanna end up as some anecdote in his memoir or a side character in a movie about his life."

"Honestly . . . that's extremely fair, Nads."

I blink an eye open. "Really?"

"Yeah, I mean . . . " She pauses to gesture at the discarded box—a wonderful gift, a potential red flag. "He's a nice guy, but I think your concerns are valid. He's probably used to getting what he wants, and you're a little bit of a challenge or a . . . a fun idea." She reaches across the table and lays her hand over mine. "I support you keeping some secrets."

Hearing my best friend say this should be a relief—but it isn't. I want her to tell me I'm being insane and ridiculous, that Marco is clearly and totally in love with me, how could he not be? We're perfect for each other, as everyone can see.

But that's just my ego talking.

I fold the sweater and place it back in the box, gathering up the note card. I take the wooden steps that run along the side of the house, leading from Soph and Allie's floor up to my apartment.

Inside, I finally shower off my long morning. It's one of those days when my legs are throbbing and the backs of my knees prickle with inflammation, but my mind is wide awake. I certainly haven't done my nervous systems any favors. I close the blinds, blocking out a wet, windy spring landscape, and crawl under my duvet.

A soft rain falls and each droplet against the window lulls me closer to sleep—or closer to delirium; I have less control over where my mind wanders. Back to the boat, last night. Back to the car ride home.

We should have been too tired to talk, maybe even should have run out of things to say to each other, but the ride home to Evergreen was filled with his laughter, my chatter.

He let me watch him, graciously, never meeting my eye. At the last light before we entered Evergreen, all he did was move a hand from the gearshift to my knee, where he gave me a brief squeeze. A microdose of intimacy that sent my stomach tumbling.

Back on the island, the stars and sky were blotted out with ocean haze and diffused light. Marco turned on our seat heaters and rolled down the windows.

"I love this smell," I admitted, my head lolled back against the headrest and my eyelids heavy. "I wish they would bottle it and sell it."

Marco made a small noise in the back of his throat, a hum of agreement. His eyes were narrowed and glassy, fixed straight ahead as he drove down Neptune Avenue, as if he was holding the gaze of someone he loved dearly.

"I've missed it here," he said eventually, pulling his eyes off the street to look at me. I took in the crow's-feet etched around his eyes, the permanent indents on either side of his mouth. *Smile lines.* The car slowed to a stop and I looked away.

"Today was really fun," I said. I hoped he didn't take it for granted—because it's a cliché to say something like that. But I don't really speak in clichés. I hoped he could tell that I really meant it. "Best date I've been on."

I think then he believed me, because he reached over and briefly, so briefly, brought a finger to my chin, running the pad of his thumb over the acute angle of my jaw. Like he wanted to hook his finger underneath and pull me to him.

Instead, he dropped his hand and leaned away. "Ever?" he asked, voice low and deliciously set in the back of his throat.

I couldn't hold back a small laugh. "Yes, Marco. Best date ever."

THIS IS WHERE my mind picks up as I lie in bed. Now, while I lie under the perfect weight of my covers, I imagine catching his wrist with my fingers, closing the gap between us. I imagine what Marco's mouth tastes like, without all the beer and tequila and cigarettes in the way. I wonder what it might be like to actually be with him; I think about it until my thighs ache.

I miss the sound of his voice, rough and unpretentious. I miss the smell of his skin. I miss his laugh and how frequently he does it.

I'm tempted, so tempted, to pull myself from oncoming slumber to send him a message that says exactly that, but even half asleep I know I can't.

I know there are only so many days in May.

Tuesday, May 9

To Liv's credit, she's excellent at making her presence known. The live updates of her drive to Evergreen begin promptly at 7 A.M.

> **Liv:** Loading up the car. Do you have a blowdryer?

> **Liv:** Getting gas

> **Liv:** Stopped to pee. Got coffee.

> **Liv:** *[Blurry picture of a rabbit nibbling a leaf outside the Farley Plaza rest stop]*

I'm already awake, unloading the dishwasher and trying to figure out what the hell to text Marco. I need to thank him, of course, but I also need to assert my dominance. Reclaim the upper hand in this little fantasy we're building together. My fortress has never been infallible, but the very least I can do is not swing open the doors, let down the drawbridge, and shout, *Come and get my ass! Hurt me so good, baby!*

I pour myself another cup of coffee and step out onto my deck.

I settle into a rocking chair and open our text thread. The last thing we'd said to each other had been when Marco was at the snack stand on the *Miss Teak Skye,* and I'd decided I also wanted a Diet Coke.

> **Nadia:** I changed my mind lol can I have a DC?

> **Marco:** Can you have a DC . . .

> **Nadia:** Pleaaaaaaaaaaaaase

> **Marco:** there we go

Another little rush of pressure and warmth through my belly as I reread our texts. The easy intimacy he's so good at is like toxic waste inching closer, threatening to gobble me up and turn me into someone unrecognizable.

Suddenly, Liv texts me. Omg boardwalk is crowded????

Shit. That means she's on the island. She'll be here any minute.

Time's up. Without thinking, I open my phone's front-facing camera and take a picture of myself in the loose cardigan, fabric pooling around my wrists, coffee mug in hand. I cut out most of my face except for my tongue, which is poking out between my lips.

She's beautiful, I caption the photo. Thank you . . . and I'll see you tomorrow.

Marco replies, immediately, with a heart.

"RAPUNZEL, RAPUNZEL! LET down your long hair!" Liv shouts up at the balcony from the carport. I'm still reeling in the bathroom over this damn heart emoji, rubbing skin tint into my face with one hand and gripping my phone with the other, when I hear Liv. She really missed her calling as an opera singer or foghorn.

Also . . . *hair.*

I look up at my reflection.

"I should have warned her," I say out loud to my reflection. We stare at each other, terror in our eyes, pixie-length curls and coils smoothed neatly into place. It's a great look; I'm a huge fan. But I know Liv will take this dramatic physical change *very* personally.

Whatever. Rip the Band-Aid off. How many Liv meltdowns have I dealt with in my life? *You'll survive,* I tell myself. A real rouser of a pump-up speech.

I give myself one last stern, meaningful look before exiting the bathroom and heading toward my fate.

Instead of running out onto the balcony, I jimmy the living room window open and pop my head out. Then I shout, with all the charm of a prison guard: *"Ta-daaaaaaa!"*

LIV THROWS HER purse onto the couch, kicks off her shoes, opens and slams shut every cabinet, grimaces and scoffs at all my belongings, then asks me a series of questions, including, "Have you seen my hair straightener from middle school? Did you steal it?"

Apparently, the haircut has stunned Liv so profoundly, I actually overrode her freak-out feature.

I lean against the archway to the hall, watching her spin around the kitchen and living room in an endless huffing frenzy. She yanks open all the blinds, pulls back all the curtains, and tosses open the deck doors.

As much as I hate to admit it, it does feel markedly less dreary in here.

"Aren't you going to say something?" I demand when she pauses to hunt for a snack—nuts, specifically. Salted, mixed nuts.

"About what?"

"About my *hair*."

Liv pulls her head out of the fridge and appraises me for a moment. "I don't know, it looks good. Can you make me a coffee?"

"That's it? It looks *good*?"

Liv pares me with a look of total exhaustion. "Jesus, what do you want me to say? Fine. It looks *awesome*. Happy?"

Awesome is my least favorite word ever, and Liv knows this. She's being a bitch—but a different type of bitch than usual.

After brewing a fresh pot of coffee, we fill our mugs and head down to the stretch of quiet beach on the far side of the houses. There, we kick off our shoes and begin walking along the chilly, damp sand.

"So." Liv eyes me over her mug. "Tell me all about this episode you're having."

"An *episode*? You sound like Mom."

"Everyone always said I was the dramatic one, but you're really making up for lost time."

"You're not wrong." I take a sip of my coffee, pressing my toes deeper into the sand. All those frail Englishmen were onto something about the healing properties of ocean air. I'm feeling better almost instantly once we get walking on the solid, sturdy shoreline sand, the muscles in my neck and back relaxing under the soft sun. "I'm sorry I didn't tell you about my hair."

Liv shrugs. "I would have found out from Mom eventually."

"That's not true! You always get the news first."

"Since when? You never told me you got fired or about your nose ring or about that weird mole on your stomach that kept bleeding. Mom had to break the news on all three. You've never told me about a single boyfriend—"

"Because I've never had a serious boyfriend." I rush to defend myself and then immediately feel a pang of embarrassment. *Ha, gotcha! I'm incapable of emotional intimacy!*

"What about that fireman guy from Edison—Dante?"

I roll my eyes. "Unknowingly being someone's mistress does not count."

"Oh, yeah." She giggles into her mug. "He was like, the fourth married fireman that year."

"Two thousand eighteen was a year of learning and growing," I confess into my cup of coffee. We've organically reached boyfriend talk, and I know what I have to do. My haircut may have been forgiven, but withholding Marco would land me in the Hague. "Speaking of boyfriends . . ."

Without missing a beat, Liv shoots me *the eyes*. It's a look that transforms her face into a carbon copy of our father's. It's terrifying. Nicky calls this act of eyeball contortion her *gobstoppers* because no matter what you're about to say, the eyes stop you in your tracks and make you think twice. A mix of shock and forewarning floods her gaze, then she tilts her head down and arches her eyebrows. "Don't tell me you're in love with an Evergreen townie."

"No," I say with a nervous laugh, "and I don't really even have a boyfriend. It's more like . . . like an arrangement."

"Oh God." She comes to a complete stop. "Not another married guy, Nadia."

"Shockingly, no—"

"You're a sugar baby?"

"What? No, let me tell my story—"

She gasps. "Oh my God, you're a sugar *mommy*."

"Jesus, Olivia." I give her a shove strong enough to send her stumbling toward the water. "Let me talk!"

"You know, when most people go fancy-dress shopping, they don't usually stop for Auntie Anne's and Nathan's Hot Dogs first."

"That's because most people are fucking boring," Liv replies, handing me my cinnamon-sugar pretzel and my coveted frozen lemonade. Around us, the Surf City Mall glistens and glitters with midmorning energy as we settle onto a bench by the fountain, mismatched snacks in hand.

Big to-dos go against everything we believe in, but Liv has a particular affinity for keeping things utilitarian and pragmatic. It's why she's worn OPI Bubble Bath on her nails for the last ten years, and also why one day, she will run a small totalitarian ethno-state. She hates bridal parties, vanilla cake, overpaying for mediocre food, and saying hi to family members who can't recall her birthday off the top of their head. Needless to say, this puts us all in a very tricky position when it comes to anything matrimonial.

So far, she's handled all of the planning in the most Liv way I can imagine: I was unceremoniously dubbed maid of honor via text message; a bridal shower was declared ILLEGAL at Sunday dinner; then we were all asked, via email, to *keep Halloween free*.

And now, we're dress shopping at a living shrine to the late nineties.

"Should I take a picture of you deep-throating that dog and send it to your soon-to-be husband?"

Liv gives me the finger. "Should I take a picture of you in your Crocs and send it to Marco fucking Antoniou?"

"Ugh," I scoff, dusting my sticky fingers off on my bike shorts. "He'd probably write back something like: *wow smiley-face emoji nice feet heart-eyes emoji.*"

After wiping some relish off her maw, Liv cocks a brow. "He's that into you?

I let out a small, noncommittal grunt. "I don't think he's *actually* into me. I think he's into *the idea* of me or maybe just women in general."

"I have no sympathy, Nads. You have a rich, famous hottie in your DMs and your pants for a month." We start meandering with our food and drinks.

"He's not really in my pants," I murmur, trying to suppress the sudden memory of my overalls on his bathroom floor.

"But he could be—or would be—if you stopped being such a tight-ass about everything."

"Oh, hi, kettle. You look *great* in black."

"Oh, come on. I'm less of a tight-ass than you."

"*You* have the tightest ass out of everyone in our family. You could crack a fucking coconut with your ass, that's how tight it is."

I don't realize how loud we're being until a group of women in matching Lycra outfits across the fountain silence their chatter to glare at us.

"I don't know why you're hesitating so much. Don't you love flings?" Liv says, pulling me by my wrist in the direction of the boutique where we have an eleven o'clock appointment.

I did, or I used to *prefer* flings. My reservations about Marco are almost entirely wrapped up in the simple truth that there is a chasm in my life—a before and an after. I know how fragile I am now. I know how easily I can break, how delicately my body and mind are connected. I'd just gone through that, and I'd only just barely glued myself back together.

Liv has always known exactly what to say (and how to say it) to make me feel like I'm being exceedingly childish and thoughtlessly overdramatic, even when I know I'm heeding to my own deep-rooted instincts. Whatever Marco's intentions—even if they are just to have a real and true no-strings-attached month of fun—I would hold on tight to my right to be scrupulous, and I would hold my diagnosis as close to my chest as I possibly could.

But before I can think of a succinct way to shut my sister down, she's yanking me through the doorway of a brightly lit storefront sandwiched between a toy store and the restrooms. The shop window showcases a veritable explosion of tulle and sequins, mermaid dresses and mermaid-y colors.

"This is where they buried Liz Claiborne's final Horcrux."

"*Shhhhhh*, shut up," Liv stage-whispers, death-glaring me into submission. "Mike's mom knows the shop owner. Do *not* misbehave."

"*Me?*" I hiss back. "You're the one who looks like a bug just flew into your mouth."

"So?" Liv retorts while glowering at an enormous peach-pink organza mess strapped to a mannequin. "At least I'm not being a smart-ass."

I respond by miming that I'm locking my mouth up and throwing away the key.

Eventually, after thumbing through an entire wall of hot-pink prom dresses, we're approached by a woman with a very geometric haircut, corralled into a dressing room, and interrogated to the point of perspiration and dehydration.

"You have to know at least one thing you want in a bridesmaid's dress," she chastises Liv, dressing her down in a way that brings me *so* much joy.

"Uh, black? Satin, maybe?"

Miss Geometry is appalled, and we are instead given an armful of eggplant and mauve war crimes.

I try on a litany of dresses—some tragic, some kind of nice but nothing interesting enough to move Liv out of her current position: head in her hand, nose scrunched. She gives me a little "Nah" or "Meh." Only one dress is bad enough to merit a loud and swift "Ugh!"

"Okay, we're done." I throw my arms up in defeat. I'm trapped in a trumpet-cut dark blue nightmare. It's long-sleeved, but there are cutouts on my hips. I look both slutty and sad about it. "Why won't you just tell me how you feel about my hair?"

Liv is already standing up, grabbing her sunglasses and purse. "I told you it looks great. What else do you want me to say?"

I try to shuffle after her, but my shins are imprisoned. "You don't think it looks great. You never think *anything* looks great."

"That is *not* true," she says, pushing her sunglasses up into her dark waves. "I think lots of things are great. Like—"

I don't even give her a chance to pretend like she can recall the last time she liked something. I lean over and yank a purple organza-tiered disaster off the designated *No!* rack and hold it back up against my chest. "You told that woman that you'd rather swallow a screw than look at any more dresses like this."

"Okay, so, you know I'm being honest! Clearly, I don't hold back."

I take a shaky step down off the platform, wobbling on my borrowed heels as I clomp back toward the chair where I left my clothes. "I can't deal with you anymore."

"Nadia, wait." To my surprise, Liv grabs my arm, nearly pulling us both off-center. I catch her eyes in the mirror as I trip over my own feet. She's chewing at the inside of her cheek. "I really do think you look nice."

"But?"

"*But* I don't think you cut your hair off because you wanted a nice, new haircut. I think you did it because you want everyone around you to fuck off and leave you alone, and you figured if you cut off all your hair, I might get so mad at you, I would fuck off and leave you alone and let you rot."

My breath comes out quick and tight. The lights overhead are buzzing and this dress, with all its buttons and itchy tags, makes me feel trapped and strangled. My skin prickles and itches, and I may start screaming.

"I'm not going to let you push me away anymore. It's stupid. You're being stupid. And I know things are hard right now, but it's me—"

"It's in my kidneys," I blurt out. "Lupus. In my kidneys. I found blood in my urine, and they ran some extra tests and now, I'm scared—terrified, actually. It's not uncommon, but—but it means I'm getting worse even with all the medicine I'm on. I'm *still* getting worse. I feel like shit, Liv. I feel sick and exhausted and—what if it gets so bad that I can't do it anymore? I just started to feel normal again, and I know you think I'm being dramatic, but there's so much I don't know right now—"

"Who else have you told?" She cuts me off.

"No one," I say quietly. "Just you, for now."

Without any hesitation, she pulls me to her chest.

WE GET HOME and change into sweatpants before driving down to the boardwalk to pick up a pizza, which we eat on the balcony, in our rocking chairs, facing the ocean. I wrap myself up in my new cardigan, delighting in how it clashes ridiculously with my mustard-yellow St. Cecilia's High School of Philadelphia sweatpants. We eat in silence, Taylor Swift playing from my phone. If Liv was cooler, I'd ask her to split the joint chilling in the ashtray between us. Unfortunately, my beloved sister is a narc.

"If you need a kidney, I'll give you one," she says, wiping grease from her chin.

I reach over and swipe at the single, thick droplet of orange she missed. "No way." I shake my head. "You have a semi-husband. He has first dibs—legally."

"Oh, yeah," she mumbles around another mouthful. "I guess he does. Maybe Marco can give you a kidney."

I let out a tut of laughter. "As much as I'd love to see that headline, I don't think I'll be making Vinny Baldacco aware of my internal organ situation."

"So," Liv says, dragging out her vowels. "Do we get to meet this guy?"

I furrow my brow at the horizon. For some reason, I like the idea of Liv meeting Marco. I think he'd actually really get a kick out of her. Liv is endlessly entertaining—she's so extremely normal, she's actually circled back around and become a freak again. Anyway, it doesn't matter. There's no way that could be arranged in the next twenty-some days. "Hell no," I conclude.

"Boooooring," she sings.

"It is what it is." I punctuate this piece of wisdom with an eye roll. "We're not actually anything. Twenty-odd days and it'll all be a memory." When I look up, she's giving me the gobstopper, but with a twist—she's grinning like she has a wild hare up her ass, like she's auditioning to play the Joker. "What?" I demand.

"Nothing." Liv's eyes twinkle. "You just sound sad, that's all."

Wednesday, May 10

My phone rings in the middle of the night, and it actually wakes me up—something a tornado siren couldn't even do. I answer with a grunting "Hello?" and a familiar voice fills the line, deep and rich.

"I can't believe I missed another whole day with you."

My eyes fly open. "Marco?"

"Don't tell me you're dating someone else for only thirty days," he drawls, voice sarcastic and sleepy.

I shift up onto my elbows, dizzy and confused and happy. "It's like, three A.M."

A throaty laugh ripples across the line. "It's midnight, babe." *Babe?* I roll over to check the analog clock on my nightstand. It *is* midnight, and barely at that.

"Don't you *babe* me."

"Why? Afraid you might like it?"

"Yeah, terrified." I yawn. "Where are you?"

"New York." He sighs these words. A door clicks behind him and suddenly his voice is farther away, flatter, without any echo. I can almost feel the hot city air. "I spent the whole day with a bunch of people I don't like thinking about how much I'd rather be on a boat with you."

I settle back against my pillow and decide to tell the truth. "I had a similar thought today. Which is weird."

"Weird?" I can hear the smirk in his voice; maybe something else too. Smoke catching on his teeth. "Not nice or good?"

"No." I dig the heel of my hand into my eyes. "It's weird. I've known you for five days. Are you smoking?"

"You're a slow burn, huh? A little stand-offish? Full of secrets?"

"*No.*" I sound very defensive. "I'm just not anxiously attached or a recovering addict. Now, answer the question."

"Damn. Right through the heart with that one." He sounds excited. He likes this, this me-being-mean thing. I like it, too. "And yes. Just one cigarette. I had a bad day."

"Poor baby."

He lets out a little growl and now I can definitely hear it, the sizzle of the paper as he inhales. "Exactly. More people need to feel bad for me."

"What's for dinner?"

"This cigarette."

"It's time for your favorite meal and all you're having is some toxic air vapors?"

Marco makes a tut of agreement. "I'd kill for a Pier Point BLT."

"With sweet potato fries or regular?"

"Regular. Who the fuck gets sweet potato fries?"

"Heart-healthy Americans," I reply, defensive.

Marco huffs. "If you *actually* swap regular fries for sweet potato, we might need to end this little experiment."

"Well." I bite back a smile. "Looks like you're single again, buster." And that makes him laugh very hard.

Liv and I both wake up around eight and take our coffees down to the beach for one last walk. For some reason, I feel like she's holding something back and this sensation only intensifies when I notice she's barely sipped her coffee. I'll never stop being acutely aware of Liv's body language, every micro-change in her mood. I'm getting ready to ask just as we reach the top of the steps that lead from the sand to the asphalt, but she beats me to it.

"I'll miss you," she says quietly, threading her arm through mine.

"I'm always here," I remind her.

"I know." She pulls back, then runs a hand over my hair, smoothing the frizzing little bundles away from my face. An uncharacteristically gentle gesture. "I just prefer when you're in the same house as me."

"We haven't lived together in a decade."

She gives my arm a squeeze. "We can change that." I'm not sure if I should roll my eyes or cry.

Her car's packed and ready to go. There's nothing left for her to do but leave. We dust the sand from our feet and she puts on her shoes.

We hug one last time, and when I let her go, pushing her toward her car, I yell after her, "Go on. Get out of here. Go home to your loving fiancé, the poor sucker."

Liv smiles at that, rolling down her window and shouting back at me, "Luckiest man on Earth!" while she drives away.

I DON'T HAVE too much time to pine after my sister. I have bigger, bolder matters on my mind, such as: What does a person even wear on a date to eat sushi with their K-list celebrity fake boyfriend? If I knew, I probably wouldn't be standing in front of my closet, completely naked, heart racing, thirty-five minutes before I have to be at the bus station. All I know is that I definitely cannot wear my bucket hat, lest he begin to think that I've had it surgically attached to my head.

I grab a slinky black dress and some gold jewelry, which I carefully pack into a bag alongside an unnecessarily cute pajama set, skin-care necessities, my medicine, a toothbrush, and a paperback historical romance titled *Her First Duking*. Because if I'm not having sex, someone should be.

Just to be safe, I booked myself a last-minute hotel room. And also, to be safe, I've shaved my entire body.

I'm still unsure of how deep the waters of our relationship cosplay are. How much Marco has decided to *go method* with his role. Is he actually excited to see me? Has he missed me over the last couple of days? Or does this fantasy only work if he plays out every part of it—romance included? Because if Marco just wanted to have sex with a woman for thirty days and then fuck off out of her life forever, he could have easily done that—with a more easy-going accomplice, might I add.

He'd said it himself: I'm stand-offish. And when I want to be, I can be as frigid and inhospitable as the arctic. Maybe that was part of the appeal—*my* appeal—to him. Traversing a hostile environment, struggling to reach the summit, and then, ultimately—uh—planting his flag in frozen earth. Of course that would appeal to a certain thrill-seeking type, wouldn't it?

With five minutes to spare, I pull into the Atlantic City bus station and book it to my terminal, where an ungodly long line has formed. Perfect, I'll be seated somewhere close to the toilets in the back, sandwiched between a teenage runaway and a man in khakis with pamphlets. Despite the temperate, sunny weather, I'm a sweaty, sticky mess.

Finally, I settle into a seat—not as close to the toilets as I thought I'd be—and attempt to stuff my overnight bag down between my legs. A young woman slides into the seat next to me and immediately pops in her AirPods. *Thank God.* It's one thing to be a chatty passenger on a cushy Amtrak ride, but on a charter bus? There simply is not enough oxygen for that type of behavior.

As the bus lurches out of the parking lot, I open my conversation with Marco and shoot him a text: Made it onto the bus with 37 seconds to spare. If you wanted to ghost me, you're too late.

> **Marco:** Just got out of my last meeting of the day, thank fucking God.

> **Nadia:** Do I get to hear about this top-secret job that's kept you so busy?

> **Marco:** Maybe. Do I get to hear about your week?

> **Nadia:** I've got two hours and a king-size Snickers bar. AMA.

Then, suddenly, my phone's buzzing in my hand.

His name appears on my screen: Marco Antoniou. What kind of person has the confidence to cold-call people multiple times? *Sociopath.*

Stunned, I pick up. "Hello?"

"Why are you eating a king-size Snickers bar when you're two and a half hours away from the best meal of your life?" His voice is light and airy, like a perfectly whipped Italian meringue, a stark contrast to the immediate punch of city noise it's set against. It sounds like somewhere very close to Marco, someone has fallen asleep with their forehead against their car horn.

"Don't you snack-shame me. That's twice in twenty-four hours."

"Someone has to," he says. "If you leave me hanging tonight because you ate too much caramel and peanut—"

"It was a joke, I swear. The only thing I've had today is a thimble of water and a single arugula leaf."

"Man," he laughs, "I wonder what it would be like to know one, actual thing about you."

The ribbing about me being a dark horse is nearing dangerous frequency. Is it that obvious I'm holding something back? We've agreed to spend a month together, approximately one-third the lifespan of your average American egg. What do I really owe the guy? But I can offer one, small truth. I gnaw at my lip. "I'm wearing the cardigan you gave me. There ya go."

"Yeah, right. You're probably wearing a T-shirt that says *I hate Marco Antoniou*."

"I swear! I'm wearing your cardigan, jean shorts, and no bucket hat."

"Damn, baby," he jokes, but I still feel a twinge deep in my stomach. "What else you have on?"

"Chaps, lasso, big red honky nose."

"Wow. Please, stop, I am about to cum."

I bite back a laugh. "Tell me about the very important business that stole you away from me."

"Ahhhh," he coos. "You'd like that, wouldn't you?"

"Well." I guffaw in response. "Never mind, then."

"I'm working on a potential project—a nonacting thing that is very cool."

"A nonacting thing, huh?"

"Yes, but I don't want to jinx it so . . . that's the only intel you're getting."

"Fair enough. Must be pretty great if you're willing to sacrifice two perfectly good days of our *Sweet November*."

"I hope." He laughs softly and the noise of the city dims behind his voice. "I've missed you," he adds after a beat.

I compress my mouth to keep from smiling, as if he's right beside me. "Yeah, right."

He laughs again, louder. "I wish I could have put money on you saying that."

"I should go—I think talking on your phone on a Megabus is the last felony they flog people for."

"Fine." He sighs. "I'll see you soon, Nadia."

"See you very soon, Marco."

"Text me a picture of you in the cardigan."

"You really think I'm lying?"

"I just wanna see your face," he says, a smile on his voice. "But yeah, kinda."

I can't hide the smile in my voice anymore, either. I lean my head back against the fabric seat and let my eyes fall shut. "Goodbye, Marco."

An hour later, we pull to a screeching halt in Port Authority and I begin my official descent into a manic fugue state. I drop my things in my hotel room and quickly change into my carefully packed outfit before ordering a rideshare. I'm rushing, but I still manage to take my meds before heading out—all the usuals, plus my first love: Prozac. I'm like a walking advertisement for the shortcomings of the modern generation.

With a swipe of lip gloss and one last scan of my final look, I head out into a perfect May Manhattan night.

THE RESTAURANT IS packed—elegant in its soft, dim light and abundance of noise. The lobby's choked with bodies, clouds of Coco Mademoiselle and Baccarat Rouge rolling in from every direction as I try to navigate my way through martini-clutched hands and sport jacket backs to the hostess stand, flashing apologetic smiles left and right.

It's amazing that I haven't forgotten, after months, how to move through a space like this—solipsistic glamour glides, and when you know the rhythm, you can join like a fish to its school. My heart thrums in my chest, my pulse in my neck, and I remember suddenly what was so appealing about the way I lived before. Every night began the same: feeling like it might be *the night*, so epic as to change the rest of the nights that would follow, for the rest of my life.

There's more than just designer scents in the air in a place like this; there's hope.

Marco's at the bar. Everyone around him is beautiful, finely dressed. But Marco, somehow, glows. He's sitting with a leg casually extended to rest on the bottom of the stool next to him. His profile in the bar light makes him look like Apollo or Ares, powerful and warm. Full lips curling backward in a winking laughter, eyes crinkling at the corners, biceps strangled by the soft knit fabric of his shirt. His thick, dark hair flows in neat waves away from his face and behind his ears. There's something so sexy about the muscular curve of where his neck meets his ears that I'm once again overwhelmed with the urge to bite him.

"Hi, welcome. How many in your party?" the hostess asks, pulling my cannibalistic sex-fantasy tangent to a halt.

"Oh, uh, I'm with—" I point at Marco. But then I realize that I'm just some lady pointing vaguely, so I add: "My boyfriend. He made a reservation, I think." It feels so indulgent to call him that. *My boyfriend.*

She doesn't give a shit. Her eyes are already back on the screen built into her kiosk as she pokes away. She dismisses me with a chilly, "Enjoy your dinner."

I cut through the crowd, and Marco's still engrossed in conversation with the bartender. But something is happening in my body and now all I care about is ripping him away from everyone else and burying my face in his neck, kissing every tendon that stretches and tightens as he calls me baby. I want to feel his hands in my hair; I want his lips on my throat.

"Jesus Christ," I mutter to myself, smoothing a hand over my stomach. I'm so horny I might die. That's also part of being alive, I guess. *Desire.* It's a hunger that feels like I'd never possibly be able to satiate. *I* feel like a vampire, dreaming about his neck and skin and eyes.

How am I even going to say hello? Do I tap him on the shoulder? Do I just slide onto the stool and wait for him to notice? Should I go for a coy *hey, you*? A jaunty *oh, hi*? I cannot for the life of me remember how I usually greet people. Is it possible I've never said hi to anyone, not even once?

The bartender catches my eye as I'm creeping up behind Marco, and the ignoramus foils my plan by giving me the famous White People Smile (no lips, no teeth, lots of eyebrow) and saying something to Marco that sounds like "I think she's here."

He turns in slow motion. No, not slow motion—regular motion. But I swear to God, everything goes flat except for Marco. Have I ever really looked at him before? Maybe not. Maybe I'd always kept my eyes downcast for this exact reason.

He leans back, pulling himself up to his full height. "Nadia." He says my name like he's exhaling a heavy breath.

His fingertips find my waist and then we're hugging. Briefly. His palms slide to the flat of my back and around the smallest part of my waist, sending an ache through my hips and crashing into my knees. If that's what a palm to my spine can do, I'm worried what will happen if he ever actually touches me.

We separate before I pass out.

"I made it," I say, situating myself on the stool, carefully navigating the high chair in my even higher heels.

"You . . ." He gestures toward the stool swiveling underneath me. "You need help?"

"I got it." I laugh. "This place looks incredible."

"You look . . ." He pauses briefly to furrow his brow at me, but the bartender is back with a heavy-bottomed tumbler filled with a dark liquid.

I look between Marco and the glass. "Is that alcohol?"

"No. God. I promise." Marco's fingertips are still resting on my waist, a gentle throb of heat at my side, but when the bartender says, "Cheers," he pulls away. "Dan, this is Nadia. Nadia, this is my very good friend Dan."

Dan flashes me a sweet smile as he garnishes Marco's glass with sprig of rosemary. "This is an Old Classic—my spin on an Old Fashioned. Homemade bitters with a sassafras-infused, nonalcoholic Italian aperitif, topped with caramelized herbs." He finishes his explanation by lifting a mini torch from his apron pocket and setting the rosemary briefly ablaze.

"Well, Dan. What an introduction." I deeply regret calling him an ignoramus. He has a kind baby face and sweet blue eyes.

Dan gestures at Marco's glass. "Give it a taste."

Marco lifts the tumbler to my lips and I sip back the mocktail. "Wow. I don't know how to tell you this . . ." They're both watching me, rapt. "This tastes exactly like Dr Pepper."

Marco lets out a huge laugh as Dan drops his head, shoulders slumping. "Goddamnit. It *keeps* happening."

"What? That's a compliment!" I assure him.

"Not when you're soft-launching your mocktail business," Marco leans in and says to me, not-so-sotto voce.

"Ah." I pat my lips with a cocktail napkin. "Then I take it back. This sophisticated, groundbreaking beverage tastes *nothing* like Dr Pepper."

Dan gives me a wry look before turning to Marco and quipping, "Your girlfriend's a liar." There's something about the way he says it—smooth, unflinching—that sets my insides on fire. Tonight there are no parameters; we just are. Then, Dan gets pulled away to make more drinks and Marco turns his *everything* on me.

"No one kidnapped you," he remarks, swiveling on his barstool to face me, drinking in my entire body with a slow, smooth look.

"Was that a possibility?" I ask, cheeks heating under his focus.

He shrugs, lifting his glass to his lips. "Cute woman on a regional bus route."

"Cute?" I raise an eyebrow. "That's it?"

Marco pauses, drink suspended at his lips. "If I tell you you're sexy, will you make fun of me?"

"Of course." I smirk. "But I thought you liked that."

AFTER A ROUND of nonalcoholic drinks, the hostess comes back and taps Marco gently on the shoulder. "Sir, your table's ready."

"Oh?" I remark, as soon as she's out of earshot. "Very impressive. Celeb treatment."

Marco shrugs me off and for the first time, I wonder if he's actually gone ahead and pulled some strings. We say goodbye to Dan and make our way back to the hostess stand, where the previously disinterested woman perks up significantly, leading us to a set of steps beneath an enormous, glistening chandelier.

"Hey." Marco slides his hand into mine and gently pulls me back, until his lips are a hair away from my ear. "You look unbelievable," he whispers.

I have to keep moving or my knees may turn completely gelatinous and send me tumbling to the ground. I give his fingers a squeeze, then guide his hand to my waist as we move through the crowd. His other hand meets my other hip, and my mind goes blank except for one single thought—what if he pulled me back against him? How would it feel to have his hips against me, his hands pressing into the soft flesh of my hips? A shiver runs through me; I hope he doesn't notice.

We're guided to a quiet corner of the second floor, where the music turns to low, groovy Muzak. Up here, the only light comes from votive candles in the center of each table, illuminating couples bent low toward each other, sharing plates of steaming gyoza and tonkatsu.

We drop into our chairs and the hostess leaves us alone.

"It's no Ernie's, but it'll do," I quip. It's hard to read Marco's face in such dim lighting. His expression is usually so clear, painted over his features in broad strokes. The man is mostly incapable of keeping a secret, immediately betrayed by the overactive muscles around his mouth.

Marco laughs, carefully unfolding his napkin. "You can take the girl out of Evergreen . . ."

"Should I order a Twisted Tea?"

"Absolutely. Assert your dominance."

"Should I ask for a fork, too?"

He winces. "Eh, there's such a thing as being *too* down to earth. Let's start slow with the Twisted Tea."

I'm failing terribly at keeping my cool. "Since when are you funny?"

Marco throws me a wink. "I'm just trying to keep up with you."

I meet his eyes full-on for the first time since I walked in. There's a fire behind his gaze. I think I may be making us both more nervous than we need to be, so I pivot. "Jen sent me a picture of a drawing Emmett did at school today—it's us on the boat with *his* dolphin."

"Really?" His eyes light up and he leans toward me. "Let me see."

I slide my phone across the table to show him the picture Jen sent me, completely forgetting that the entire exchange culminated in me telling her about tonight, to which she replied: will you tell me if you bang??? pls nadia

"Damn, Jennifer."

Heat rushes to my ears. Of course he's snooping. "Can you not read my messages, please and thank you?"

"It was right there! Underneath the picture her kid drew."

"No excuses." I take my phone back and make a show of sliding it into my purse.

"Jen, Jen, Jen," Marco tuts, flipping open his menu. "What are we going to do with you?"

We order potentially way too much food. Pork buns and pick-led vegetables to start, chicken katsu with curry sauce, nigiri and sashimi. I ask Marco a million questions about his life, rapid-fire, between bites. He's gracious with his personal deets, and in the absence of alcohol, carbohydrates relax us back into the slick, cool material of our chairs.

"Siblings?" I ask, biting into my fifth or fiftieth piece of yellow-tail tuna sushi.

"An older half sister and a younger half brother," he replies. We're both middle children. Very interesting.

"Favorite Evergreen pizza?"

"Genie's. Duh." We agree that this is the only respectable an-swer.

"Biggest fear?" I pause and point my chopsticks at him. "But fun stuff only."

He laughs, wiping his mouth with the edge of his cloth napkin. "Sure. Tropical bugs. How's that for fun?"

"Worst sex of your life?" Then, I quickly add: "And I don't count."

Now Marco pauses, eyebrows tenting as his gaze drifts to the chandelier hanging over the center of the room. His fingers slide back and forth over the angle of his chin, and I try to not imag-ine what it would feel like if they carved that exact path over my waist. "Worst sex . . . ever? I guess when I got roped into a weird love triangle with an Instagram fitness model." Then, for context, he adds: "She was like, twenty-five, which in retrospect was maybe too young for me."

This one cuts weirdly close to the bone. I *hate* imagining his tan forearms flexing around some faceless woman. "Too nubile for you?" I tease. *I hope you like stretch marks,* I think. I can't even imagine my nude body on display for a man who has almost exclusively dated models and actresses without nearly barfing up my gyoza.

He catches the edge in my voice and looks suddenly quite proud of himself. "Way too nubile. And too blond, yuck."

"You know." I set down my chopsticks and lean forward, narrowing my eyes at him. "I used to spend a lot of money on being a blond woman. Hours of my life were wasted in salon chairs scorching my scalp so I could have some of that fun."

"You? Blond?" Marco feigned deep reverence. "Tell me more. I know you used to love to run—and you used to be blond. What about now?"

Now.

What do I like now? Who am I now? With our knees almost touching under the table, I can't get out of answering this question. Not in this dress, not in high heels.

"Well," I say slowly, searching my mind for even the most basic facts about myself. "I love a really strong cup of coffee. More than anything. If I had to pick between a last meal or a last cup of coffee, I'm going coffee, all the way. And I like to paint—I make all the signs for Soph's stand. And cook. I don't cook as much as I should but I think . . . I think I really love to cook."

Without realizing it, I've delivered my mini monologue to the votive candle between us. When I lift my eyes to Marco, he's watching me with widened eyes. "Underneath all that attitude . . ." He lifts his fingers and swipes them gently over my cheek, a movement so smooth and quick I wouldn't have known it happened if I hadn't been totally pulled in by his gravity. "You're just a sweet little grandma."

I throw my head back and laugh. "Oh, fuck you."

OUTSIDE, AFTER DINNER, the night air feels like a cool rag over my flushed neck.

"We should have followed your rule," I groan, pressing a hand to my stomach. "No page twos."

"I don't know." Marco stretches like he's just taken the best nap of his life, rubbing his stomach with both hands. "Page two was where we did some of our best work."

"Mmmm," I groan, leaning back against the building, actively fighting off the food coma. "I'm deeply regretting saying no to the green tea."

"Come on." He laughs, reaching for my hand. His fingers lace with mine. "Let's walk it off. You can wait for a cab at my place."

A cab at my place. What a gentleman.

It takes everything in me to not ask—*is this a line?* But realistically, if Marco had wanted to sleep with me, he might have tried before suggesting we split an aquarium's worth of fish.

The night is aglow with streetlights trapped in fog. We turn a corner and somehow, we've slipped out of Chinatown and the crowds of twentysomethings and tourists fall away. We're the only ones walking on a cobblestoned street under zigzagging fire escapes and electrical lines.

I let him lead the way, let his fingertips dance down my wrist until his fingers lace with mine. In heels, I'm almost as tall as Marco.

"I can't believe you live in a neighborhood this glamorous," I comment with widened eyes.

He shrugs a shoulder. "It's no Evergreen."

I let out a small laugh. "You read my mind."

I try to keep a straight face as his fingers travel back up my wrist then migrate suddenly to the small of my back. I'm beginning to suspect Marco may be an ass man, given how frequently tonight I've felt his heavy gaze settling on that curve of my body. His fingers pulse for a moment on my hips and I feel a tidal wave of warmth strong enough to buckle my knees break loose from my stomach.

"Cross here," he says. He's just guiding me—devilishly. Marco's building is a grand stone-facade high-rise. He greets the doorman with a quick dab. I want to analyze his face for micro-expressions— does Marco do this often? Did he do this yesterday? How many times has he brought home a woman in a skintight black dress after a fancy dinner?

But Marco's walking too fast, the doorman's totally unfazed. I can only wonder.

We step into the elevator and all around us are mirrors, reflecting the tiny space into infinity. My crisp profile, my short hair. The fabric of my dress, clinging to every curve and dimple of my body. His laconic, crooked smile and his heavy black waves that fall around his gaze. Marco shoves his hands into his pockets, but his eyes beckon me. *Come here.* No words, no fingertips. All it takes is a look.

The elevator glides upward without a sound, picking up speed with every floor we pass. His eyes travel downward, dripping over every inch of me, leaving a volcanic heat in their wake. My skin goose-bumps; my nipples harden.

"Come here," he whispers, pulling a hand from his pocket and hooking a finger on the strap of my purse. With the gentlest tug, I fall forward toward him. I'm liquid.

We're inches apart. He reaches for me, taking my hand in his. His lips graze my knuckles, the inside of my wrist. His mouth moves over my skin so gently I have to remind myself to keep my eyes open. Desire blossoms in my belly and I feel like an orange, peeled open, soft flesh pulled aside.

"This okay?" he asks, his voice a warm breath against my wrist.

I nod, taking another microscopic step closer to him.

Up close, Marco's still boyish, even at thirty-three—even with the fine dusting of gray through his stubble. His brown eyes glow yellow under the light and his heavy brow softens. His other hand finds my waist and all the space is collapsing between us. His full lips part, like he's going to say something.

The elevator dings.

Eleventh floor.

Too late.

"Wow." I MOVE slowly through Marco's living room, dragging a hand over the long, suede back of his couch. "You *own* this place?"

"I bought it when I was twenty-two, immediately after season one." Marco says this like it's some sort of discredit to the fact that he owns property in Lower Manhattan. I can tell he's vaguely self-conscious of his celebrity, but to be honest, I'd completely forgotten. Somewhere along the way he'd just turned into Marco, the filmy mug shot and the overly photoshopped promo photos of him in a cowboy hat gone from my memory.

He's in the kitchen, divided from the living room by an enormous glossy island, making us both an espresso. The distance is sobering, and I'm desperately grabbing at conversation topics.

How could I let myself turn to goop at his feet in the elevator? I need to keep my wits about me. *I need to stay vigilant.*

Marco's watching me, tongue running over his bottom lip, arms flexing as he leans back against the kitchen counter. He picks up a piece of mail and idly fiddles with it.

"But I thought you filmed in Los Angeles?"

"Yeah." He snorts. "Idiotic. But I was positive we'd get canceled, and I missed the East Coast."

"Did you want to get canceled?"

Marco ruffles slightly, like retrieving whatever memory that just dawned on him has caused a cellular-level cringe. "Not right away, but a season and a half in? It just seemed inevitable. The writing was bad, no one got along, the idea was stupid."

"Did you like anything about the show?" I ask.

Marco smirks. "Misha Landon." Of course. Misha played some sort of bombshell neighbor with a trite, mid-aughts take on gender roles. Girl Mechanic. Sexy Miss Monster Truck. Hot Plumberina.

"Of *course* you did."

I've wandered over to a wall covered in black-and-white photographs, grainy and filled with a familiar warmth. An old man sleeping in a plastic chair somewhere in the Mediterranean next to an old man sleeping in a plastic chair somewhere on an American beach. A woman asleep on the subway, tepid sunshine casting her face in a milky, godly light.

"You asked," Marco says, pulling my attention back to him. Another smirk as he presses another espresso shot into his fancy machine. "Don't be jealous. She was the biggest asshole out of all of us."

"I am *not* jealous. I was just hoping you'd say something like *the experience* or *getting paid to make art*."

"Art? It was a show built entirely on a pun." Marco rounds the island with our coffees in hand, socked feet padding softly on the parquet floors. He flicks his head in the direction of the couch—

enormous and pure white, covered in a million pristine pillows. I'm both terrified I'll spill coffee on it *and* dying to belly flop down. "If I asked you your favorite part of working with vegetables—"

"That's not my career," I interrupt quickly, defensive. "It's just what I do."

He raises an apologetic brow. "What's your career, then?"

Caught. I walked right into that. And Marco knows it. He's practically vibrating as he settles into a corner of the couch. I can see it in his eyes—*finally got something out of her.*

I kick off my heels and follow behind him. The dress I picked for tonight has become unbearably uncomfortable and the arches of my feet are killing me. I sink down into the couch like it's a warm bath, letting out a groan of delight. "What a meal, am I right?"

Marco narrows his eyes at me. "Don't think you can change the subject on me."

"I worked in advertising, at an advertising agency, for years." I tuck my feet underneath me and lean forward to take my espresso from him, but never quite manage to pick my cup up. Instead, I say mournfully, "I started off as a copywriter, like the lowest of the low, but over time, I worked my way up to being an assistant art director. I had a team of copywriters and . . . yeah, that's all."

"Damn. Really?" He sounds incredibly impressed. "That's cool as hell."

"It was. It was a lot of things. Fun, toxic, stupid. But—" I shrug. "I don't know. Life's different now."

Marco drains his cup and sets it back down on the large glass coffee table in front of us. He's working his lips between his teeth, gaze fixed on me again. "Was your favorite part making art?"

I tilt back my head and laugh. "Good one. *Nothing* about what I did was art. We had briefs and budgets and legal copy and timelines. And if you tried anything different, you'd piss off some girlboss and never hear the end of it." I purposefully leave out that, frequently, that girlboss was me. I untuck my feet and extend my legs, flexing and stretching my toes. "This is a *really* nice couch."

Marco slides toward me and then, as if he's done it a thousand times, he pulls my feet into his lap. He possesses an otherworldly ability to move my body, to move my mind, to coax me out of myself. I don't fight him at all, not even when he takes my foot in his hands. His touch turns my legs to jelly, warmth spreading upward from his fingers and down through my abdomen and thighs. We left something unfinished in the elevator. My coffee stays put on the coffee table, growing cold.

"Jesus, you're tense." His hands work up over my ankles, over my calves.

I suppress a shiver, sliding down lower, moving deeper into his touch. "Blame the patriarchy."

Marco makes a small noise in the back of his throat. "You didn't have to wear heels for me."

I narrow my eyes at him. "Of course I did. We went to a fancy restaurant. That's what you do. What if someone had taken a picture of us?"

He lifts his eyes to mine, shining and playful, and gravely announces: "Never again."

"Never again," I agree.

We fall quiet while Marco's hands steadily work at the tensed muscles of my calves. I want to ask him more questions—a million more questions—but I can't think of anything right now. I don't notice that my head has fallen backward or that I'm making a soft humming noise until his hands have made their way up behind my knees, my lower body entirely draped over his lap. His fingers still, and I lift my head back up, blinking my eyes open.

Marco's watching me, cheeks flushed.

"What?" I ask, my voice little more than a whisper.

Then, as if we're performing a practiced, choreographed dance, Marco leans in as I lift myself up. His fingers find my jaw and for a moment we linger, nose to nose.

"I'm going to kiss you," he says, so quietly I may have only tasted his words. "Again."

I can't remember if I say *yes* or *okay* or if I slip my fingers into his hair and find his lips myself.

Then, every inch between us disappears, along with all my anxieties about time and place and who I am versus who he is. All of it falls away until the only thing I can focus on is the feeling of his mouth against mine, soft and persistent, the pressure of his body as we move against each other. Marco takes a firm hold on my lower back, coaxing me into his lap, his hands traveling the length of my spine in a feather-soft touch that has me melting. Electric desire moves between us, an infinite loop of half-rendered thoughts and feelings. I *knew* I wanted this—I just didn't know how bad.

I shift to straddle Marco's lap, his hands sliding back down to squeeze at the thickest, softest part of me, a growl lodging in his throat as I roll my hips against his, against the eager strain of him against his zipper. Then, with almost no effort, he shifts us, gently placing me onto my back so he's over me, hands sliding up over my hips, my waist, my breasts.

Marco settles between my legs, easing me down further onto the couch, teeth nipping at my jawline, at the hollow base of my throat. I can't keep track of where his hands have fallen, until they tease so very close to the tender edge of my inner thigh. As a moan slips from my mouth, his teeth snag my bottom lip. Blind desire eclipses everything, and I press into his denim-clad thighs rough against mine, bare and soft, as he brings his hips to meet mine again.

"*Nadia,*" he breathes, lips on my jaw.

We're a cart careening down a hill; no brakes, no steering wheel, only momentum. I drag my hands down his chest, pulling the fabric of his shirt loose as I wrap my legs around his waist. Marco lets out another noise of encouragement against my neck, his erection pressing into the thin fabric of my underwear. My back arches instinctively as his breath hitches.

I press myself upward, trying to catch my breath. I'm losing my mind, unable to pull back and regain my usual control. I push my hands into his hair as his lips meet the exposed triangle of flesh between my breasts.

"How do I get this dress off you?" He pants against my skin, fingers skating along the elastic edge of my underwear.

"Like this." I yank the material up over my thigh, then my hips, and finally over my head. I fall back down onto the couch, my breasts spilling sideways. Marco sits up and back on his heels, eyes dark with desire. He slides his hands from my knees up over my thighs, taking his time to feel the soft, downy flesh.

I hook my fingers into my underwear and push them down, kicking myself free.

A muscle in his jaw jumps. "*Fuck.*"

Like this—me naked and Marco fully clothed—there's a power imbalance. Finally, he's in *my* light.

He wants me. So badly. It's written all over his face. And I want him, more than I would ever, ever admit. For months I've been dormant, asleep to myself. Maybe I've been asleep longer than I realized, because now, I feel like I've reentered my body and with every fresh connection of his mouth with my skin, I forget why I ever, ever wanted to be gone.

Wake me up, I think.

Suddenly, his lips are on the base of my throat. With a groan and a murmured encouragement, his tongue, tentative and slow, travels with restraint over my nipples, heavy-lidded eyes pinning me to the couch. He slides a hand up between my thighs, until I let out the tiniest gasp, head falling back.

"You're quiet," he whispers, tone wry.

"What do you want me to do?" I pant. "Sing?"

He chuckles, eyelashes fluttering as his mouth descends, hands working, until they meet somewhere in the middle.

Just when I think I can't take any more, Marco pulls away, sitting back on his thighs—chest rising and falling, dark hair mussed and falling forward. He smooths it away from his face, biceps flexing, strangled, underneath his shirt. He's hard, the outline of his dick visible through the material of his pants.

"What . . . " He pauses to catch his breath, tongue catching on the corner of his mouth as his chest rises and falls. "What are the ground rules for this?"

I pop up onto my elbows. "What?"

"This—for this. What are the rules?" He blinks, eyes heavy-lidded with desire. "You can't ghost me."

"I wouldn't do that."

"Sure." He brings his mouth to mine, snagging my bottom lip with his teeth. "You're a fucking heartbreaker. I don't trust you."

"Are you kidding me? *Vampire.* Gone in thirty days."

I regret those words as soon as they leave my lips. Marco cocks an eyebrow, mouth pulling upward into a smile. "Why? Do you want me longer?"

The question grates. *Enough.* I sit up and reach for his belt buckle, narrowing my eyes at him. "You'd like to believe that, wouldn't you?"

Marco rests his hand over mine, pressing my palm into his length. "Promise me you won't sneak out in the middle of the night and delete my number."

I bite back a groan at the feeling of him. "Promise me you aren't just using me to fill some freaky void in your big, beautiful, empty life."

"Specific," he growls, unzipping his pants. *Holy shit.*

I sit up, pushing Marco back as he pulls his shirt over his head, unveiling the muscular planes of his chest. He's built but soft, and I love the sight of his articulated, lived-in body immediately. His arms are thick and toned, his pecs muscular and broad. He looks like he could change a tire or smack an ass with authority. I want him to do both.

Without another thought, my mouth is on his, then his neck and his chest. His breathing is heavy and ragged as I push him back to the couch and straddle him. We break apart so he can work his boxers down over his thighs.

Then, he's pressed against me, our bodies shaking with anticipation. Marco's fingers dance down my stomach, his mouth quirking, eyes flashing with desire.

He pushes into me as I lower myself to meet him, as slowly as I can manage, a gasp snagging from me with every inch. He grips me tight, fingers digging into me harder and harder as he gives in and lets me take full control. We're both a bundle of nerves, tightened and tightened again, so close to snapping.

Marco takes a palmful of my ass in each hand, head falling back against the couch, Adam's apple bobbing in his throat.

"Give me a second," he whispers against my damp skin, pressing his mouth into the base of my throat. I grip the couch behind him, thighs quivering. I need one, too.

WE MOVE FROM the couch to his bedroom upstairs, in an open loft over the kitchen, never breaking apart. His mouth and hands and eyes stay on me.

Marco's bed is enormous. More pristine white, more luxe fabric. Eventually, we run out of condoms and move to the shower, where the steam cloaks us, obscuring our bodies. His chest is solid and warm, and I decide that pushing my fingers through the dark curly hair on his chest is my favorite sensation in the world. He holds me tight against him, then maneuvers us so my back is pressed against the freezing-cold tiles. He pins me there with his hungry, eager mouth.

Out of the shower, we collapse side by side on the bed. Marco's hair ink black against the pillow, his lips swollen and red from the near-constant friction.

"You never answered my question," he says, still trying to regain control of his breathing.

"Which one?"

"About your career—was your favorite part making art?"

I'm limp, exhausted, profoundly satisfied. My guard is down and for the first time in months, I feel like I'm one with my body. Is it possible Marco has melded me back together, cured me, penilely? Because right now, I'd tell him anything. I'd tell him about my diagnosis, my failing kidneys, my completely stalled out and empty life, my relationship with my sister that is alternately full of love and total shit. My cowardice in the face of my own mortality.

I'd like to start over, I could tell him. I could go completely insane and blurt out: *I want to start over with you.*

Instead, I let out another satisfied sigh, like a cat in the sun. I'm melting in the mattress, sleep coming for me quickly. Marco moves around me, tucking an arm under my head. I can feel the stubble of his beard against my shoulder and the soft dance of his fingers over my arm.

"Yeah," I say softly. "It was."

Thursday, May 11

When I wake up, I have to peel myself off Marco's broad, sweaty back. We've kicked off the duvet and top sheet, both of us sprawled toward each other. It's a miracle that we spent the entire night intertwined like this, my face buried in Marco's neck, his arm slung over my chest. In the middle of the night I could feel him pulling me closer, kissing my shoulder blades, fingertips grazing my stomach.

Marco looks peaceful while he sleeps, olive skin flushed and bright against the ivory sheets around him. My hands and feet are swollen, and I quickly sneak out of bed and into the bathroom. Under the steaming-hot water, my thigh muscles ache with an unfamiliar strain. Like I climbed a fucking mountain.

When I come out of the bathroom, Marco's in the kitchen, hair mussed in every direction, throwing together a pot of coffee.

"Hey, sunshine." His back muscles flex and relax as he moves, scratch lines from my fingernails still fresh and pink down his shoulder blades.

I pause, towel wrapped around me. "I helped myself to some of your hot water."

He laughs. "Take as much as you need. If you're not in any rush to get back to Evergreen, I wanted to take you to breakfast."

I swallow roughly. "I'm not in a rush to do anything." This is my attempt to make good on my promise last night that I wouldn't disappear. "I don't have to work until Friday. I just have to check out of my hotel by eleven."

He turns away from the percolating pot and crosses his arms over his chest. "There's an exhibit in Brooklyn I really wanted to see."

I can feel the edges of my comfort zone quickly approaching, an invisible wall looming somewhere in the distance. And I can also see the challenge in his eyes, the same flicker I saw in them that first night we went out.

We're standing there, staring at each other, thinking the exact same thing: *How far can I push this?*

Marco waits for me outside while I run up to my hotel room to change into a pair of floaty pants and a cropped top. My hair is a total mess—frizzing and coiling away from my scalp in little jovial bundles.

I dig through my bag for a hat after checking the UV index. Today is weirdly going to be a scorcher. I take my morning meds then slather myself in SPF, taking special care to not get any on my shirt or necklace or eyebrows, before hastily packing my overnight bag and booking it downstairs. Knowing Marco is there, waiting, has me moving at double speed.

Outside he's chatting on the phone, a hand lost in his hair. With his arm extended like that, I can make out a hickey on his bicep, a hickey I'd strategically placed to be diagonal to the one on the inside of his thigh. My belly tightens at the memory of him propped up on his elbows, gaze heavy on me. The raspy way he'd growled *fuck*.

I'll never be able to look at him the same—not without a sensory flashback. The weight of his chest against mine; his stubble against the inside of my thighs; his fingers tightening, tightening, tightening on the soft flesh of my hips.

The film camera hanging around his neck pulls at his shirt. Just the sight of him, spied through a window, fills me with an electricity. I push out into the humid morning, and he drops the phone from his ear, lips twisting into a half smile.

"Hey, pretty—"

I cut him off, grabbing a handful of his shirt and pressing my mouth to his. He meets my eagerness with a gentleness that has me melting against his chest. He tastes like himself, sweet and exciting, like the bitter coffee we drank this morning, and like my sunscreen. His fingers find my jaw just as we break apart. Marco's mouth comes away glistening, just like his eyes.

"What was that for?"

I shrug, running my thumb over his bottom lip, taking with it some of the moisture I'd left behind. "I wanted to kiss you."

Marco blinks slowly, clearing away the desire in his eyes, then presses the back of his hand to my forehead. "You feeling okay?"

"Shut up." I laugh, swatting him away. But he doesn't let me get far. His hand falls from my forehead to my shoulder, finger tracing down the inside of my arm. "Let's get breakfast. I want something sweet."

He's watching me with a mixture of incredulity and joy.

I'm sick of wasting time, I realize. I can't believe how much of it I've already wasted, the way I've been tossing days away like used paper towels.

I let him stare at me like that while I link my fingers with his and pull him with me. It's May 11, and we only have three weeks left together.

"TRUTH OR DARE," I ask, mouth full of French toast. We stumbled onto a diner in SoHo with no line and agreed we'd eat concrete if it meant avoiding a huge wait.

Marco ordered an improbable amount of protein as part of a breakfast I've dubbed Man Meal. It's about thirteen scrambled eggs, eleven slices of bacon, and enough toasted rye bread to feed every duck in New York State.

The waiter took the order without flinching or looking us in the eye. If he recognized Marco, he did a damn good job of acting like he didn't.

Marco considers his options carefully, mouth twisting sideways. Finally: "Dare."

Shit. I don't have a dare lined up. My plan was to use the sexy and adult allure of truth to coax information out of him about his current career-slash-life situation. In all the hours we've spent together, Marco hasn't yet dropped a single hint about this new career *thing* he has going on, and I'm desperate to know, in spite of myself.

"I dare you to tell me what you want to do in the next six months." Ham-fisted as hell, but I think it works.

Marco's eyebrows immediately fall into a frown and finally, he takes a bite of toast.

"Hmm, six months?" His gaze travels from mine out to the busy street behind me. "I guess in six months I'll have six months sober, which is good. It's a nice, solid number. I'll be back in LA." He winces at that but keeps going. "I'll be thirty-four."

"That's all you're gonna give me?"

"You really want to go there?" He pops an eyebrow, lifting a forkful of eggs to his mouth. "Truth or dare, Nadia."

I bite the inside of my cheek. "Truth."

"Why are you in Evergreen?" he demands, without missing a beat.

The French toast turns solid in my stomach, like I've swallowed a brick whole. At a loss for my own words, I borrow Liv's. "I ran away. I lost my job, and I was humiliated and embarrassed, and I just wanted to be somewhere no one would find me. I'm hiding like a coward." This is all true, if only partially.

Marco's gone completely still. "Same."

"I thought you were house-sitting for your uncle."

He scoffs. "That house has more security cameras than a Manhattan vape shop. Why would he need me?" Marco shakes his head. "No. Am I staying at my uncle's house? Sure, but it all started when I didn't get that part in *Brokeback*—the one I *really* wanted." He lets out a terse laugh at himself. "I've never wanted an acting job this badly before. I was always on autopilot, doing what I had to do because I had no other skills or because my mom really needed money or because my friends needed me. But this one . . ."

He pauses, reorganizing his features to push back the hurt bubbling right up to the surface. "I don't know, this one was for me. I took years off, went to college. I studied acting and filmmaking. When I didn't get it—when my agent called me—I knew right away I was going to relapse. I was like, cool. Hung up and something in me *decided* I was going to relapse. I knew I had to get out of town . . ." Marco clears his throat. "And then I did it anyway, kind of. So, here I am—what? Seven days sober? I'm thirty-three, and I'm starting over."

I search for his foot under the table, circling his ankle with my feet. "Me too." *Tell him,* a voice whispers. *Tell him everything.*

I shove the voice away, stuffing it deep inside myself. This moment isn't about me. I want to be there for Marco—maybe in a way I wish someone had been there for me. "Look, just because you wanted to relapse and just because you drank—that doesn't mean it isn't amazing that you've stayed sober all those years. It doesn't make it any less impressive how far you've come. I mean this in the absolute best way possible—you are *so* normal."

Marco's expression pulls and for a moment I'm terrified I've said too much, somehow accidentally dropped all my cards on the table. He pushes his eggs around before taking another bite. Then, his eyes flicker.

"It's so unfair." This comment is directed at his coffee mug. "You've just existed all these years, and I only get to have you now."

My heart skips and stalls, and I have to keep from actually pressing my hand to my chest. Marco's suave. He's charismatic; he knows what to say, when to say it. I can feel it when he's turned on that light inside himself—the one that got him Vinny Baldacco at eighteen with no prior acting experience. Now, in his thirties, Marco is as rehearsed as he is raw. I can tell vulnerability like this isn't in his playbook.

No, this comment comes from deep inside him and as soon as the words pass through his lips, he looks like he's torn between grinning and taking them back.

I tighten the grip I have on his ankle under the table, knocking my knees against his. "Truth or dare."

Marco gives me a flat look as if he's saying, *More?* "Truth."

I run my tongue over my lip. "Why one month? This . . . this doesn't seem like something you usually do."

He laughs softly, a chuckle in the back of his throat. "Well, for one, I think you're fucking beautiful. And I guess I knew there was no way I'd get you to agree to go out with me again after that first disaster night. So, I had to trap you." He lifts a piece of bacon from his plate, flailing it at me. "Even when you really want something, you have to prove to yourself that you *actually* really want it."

I narrow my eyes at him. "And you think I really want you?"

My barbing perks him up again. Marco straightens in his chair and swivels his hat around to face forward, dragging his teeth over his bottom lip. He lifts his chin at me. "Truth."

I nod, accepting his demand. "Hit me."

Marco folds his arms on the table and he leans forward, eyes creasing at the corners. "Tell me the last time you had sex like last night."

A heat ignites in my hips and spreads over me instantly, starting deep and low and working upward over my chest and neck, until I know my ears are pink. He waits patiently for me to answer while I squirm in my chair, but under the table I can feel his knee knocking against mine.

Finally, I relent, meet his gaze full-on. "Never."

THE SUBWAY TO Brooklyn is so packed, we have to force our way into a car. Then, we claim the last open spot in the dead center of the train, between a man in a winter coat and a woman with a suspiciously large backpack. Marco squares his hat and pulls the brim low, placing one hand on the small of my back and holding on overhead with the other. The car's so hot, I immediately feel the fabric between us dampen. Everyone's this close—the woman behind me bumps her backpack against my shoulders over and over, while another woman, seated, presses the spine of a hardcover book directly into my hip—but no one's facing each other, inches apart.

No one is looking at each other like Marco's looking at me.

Or like how I'm looking back.

His eyes dance with amusement as he takes each lurch and bump of the subway as an opportunity to graze his lips, just barely, over my cheekbones. Underneath the loose cotton of his T-shirt, I can feel his heart beating as fast as mine.

"Claiming your territory?" I quip in a whisper when the subway makes a sharp turn and his fingers flex and tighten around the curve of my ass.

He makes a hum in the back of his throat, bobbing his lips down to my ear. "I don't care if people know you're mine. I know you're mine."

An electric throb passes through my chest. "Confident," I whisper back.

His hand slips higher, his thumb brushing up and over a sliver of exposed skin at my waist before dipping momentarily under the hem of my shirt. "You like it."

"Stop." I press my fingers into the taut planes of his stomach, feeling for where the waistband of his boxers hugs his skin just above his belt. "Or we're going to get ourselves banned from the MTA."

He shrugs a shoulder. "I can control myself."

"Barely."

"Hey." He untangles his hand from my waist and brings his thumb to my bottom lip, a finger hooked under my chin. "We were both there last night."

Jesus Christ. I need to physically separate from this man. My eyes are practically rolling back in my head from just a graze of his fingers over my chin, memories of last night coming rushing back to me, sweeping through my body. His firm yet gentle hold on me, the unbearable weight of his eyes watching me, the scent of his skin.

I curl my fingers around his wrist. His lips part, half a word formed as I bring my mouth to the soft, hollow skin underneath his ear.

Then, absolutely sick of our shit, the subway doors fly open and everyone shoves their way through us.

"IT'S HUGE," I gasp. We're standing underneath the glass ceiling in an old, converted warehouse deep in Brooklyn. Around us, shipping containers have been stacked and converted into cellular gallery spaces for various artists. But the exhibit Marco really wanted to see hangs over our heads.

He has his film camera held up to his face, pointed right at me. My neck is tilted all the way back. Above us hang hundreds of shards of sea glass—each one ranging from the size of a penny to a hubcap—intertwined and connected like a wind chime. They split the light, splattering geometric rainbow explosions all over the floor and walls and me. Underneath them, I feel like an ant standing in the center of a spring snowfall. The last frost before everything blooms. The light warms me from the inside out, like everything has over the last few days.

"Now, there's something I've never heard you say before." Marco laughs, his camera shuttering in his hands. "Look to your left."

I follow his instruction while letting out another over-the-top gasp. "This one's even bigger!" A stalagmite of sea glass dangles precariously close to my head—maybe six or seven feet above me. One snapped wire and I'm done for. How *thrilling*.

Marco takes a few more pictures, directing me to look this way and that, to extend my arms and relax my hands, even though I complain almost continuously that I hate pictures of myself.

"These aren't supposed to be thirst traps. You look beautiful," Marco assures me.

I'm tempted to make a joke about how he better send them to me for my Tinder profile when this is all said and done. Just to see how he reacts.

Afterward we wander from gallery space to gallery space. I'm particularly taken with a glass artist from Emilia-Romagna who creates anal beads from recycled Murano chandeliers.

"Come *on*," I beg Marco, clutching his biceps. "If we split the cost, we can both use it! It's an investment piece."

"No shot, Fabiola. I'm not paying two hundred dollars for something that goes in my ass when we have four perfectly good hands."

"But it's artisanal." Then, I gasp. "Artis-*anal*."

"I'm walking away," he deadpans, dislodging his arm from me. "I'll see you on the second floor," he calls over his shoulder, tossing a two-finger salute at me.

Eventually, Marco says he wants to show me something and pulls me toward the very last gallery on the second floor, which overlooks the Hudson.

While the other makeshift exhibit spaces have logos affixed to their front window, business cards set out on little silver trays, or even have champagne flutes filled with sparkling water, this cell has only a simple black-and-white sign on an easel that reads *ADAM WEST PHOTOGRAPHY*.

Adam West has turned the small space into a sort of canvas. The lights have been dimmed and the walls are covered in enormous black-and-white prints, larger than most gallery-displayed photographs. Somewhere, distantly, I swear I hear ocean sounds—waves crashing and gulls. All of the galleries are freezing cold, but only in Adam's does my skin goose-pimple.

"I recognize this one." I point to a print that takes up the majority of the back wall. Here, the contrast and texture of the photos paired with their size make the figures within them look alive. Like they could stand up and step out of their poses. "From your apartment; it's the same artist."

It's my favorite photo of all the ones Marco had on display: the two men, sleeping in their beach chairs, side by side and a world apart. The man on the left holds his lolling head up with a thick, deeply tanned fist. The man on the right is reclined, fingers intertwined over his pecs, mouth slightly agape. A placard underneath displays the title: *Rest*.

"Yeah." Marco nods. He's gone unusually quiet, camera tucked under his arm and hands deep in his pockets. "I collect his work. Do you like it?"

"Really? I *love* it. It's vibey, evocative." All of the prints in Marco's apartment by this artist were of people sleeping; in this exhibit, West has expanded on the theme by including shots of people laughing with their eyes closed, squinting against the sun, meditating by various bodies of water. Everyone has their eyes closed. It's powerful, strangely sexy. There's one photo in particular I can't stop staring at. A woman with a million freckles splattered across her face and shoulders shot from an upward angle. Her eyes are scrunched close and her unfathomably thin body twists against a cloudless sky. Her mouth is open, her jaw jutting to the side, black hair flying against a pale gray sky. She might be singing or yelling, dancing or thrashing. I reach out to her and almost run my fingers over her face.

"Did Adam inspire you to take up photography?"

Marco nods. "In a way. I discovered his work while I was in film school. I liked being behind a camera, but I didn't like dealing with all the people."

"Nice." I laugh. "Doesn't sound like you."

Marco shrugs, threading an arm around my shoulder and redirecting me toward the exit. "I'm an introverted extrovert. I like doing things on my own terms."

"Wait." I dig my heels in, craning to get one last look at the woman. *Is she singing? Is she yelling?* Five more minutes and I think I could figure it out. "I wanna buy a print."

Marco hesitates before trailing a hand down my arm. "How about I give you one of mine? We gotta have our picnic before the sun sets."

WE SPEND HALF an hour running around the Whole Foods in Dumbo, filling a basket with an array of cheeses, crackers, and olives. Turns out Marco is very particular about his snack foods, with an undeniable allegiance to his heritage. Our relationship almost implodes over a very heated asiago versus feta decision.

We won't make it to Central Park before the sun sets, so Marco picks a grassy knoll in Brooklyn Bridge Park and we spread out with our spoils. It's even more magical than Central Park, honestly. Better than any picnic I'd imagined for myself. Marco takes over snack arrangement, leaving me to sip my sparkling kombucha and watch the sun halfway behind the Brooklyn Bridge. My contribution is yelling out fake names for all the dogs that go trotting by on the path below.

I pull the cardigan Marco gave me out from my bag and slip it on while he prepares us a makeshift charcuterie on the paper plates we splurged on. When he catches me wrapping myself in the material, his eyes flash with a smile.

Suddenly, my phone pings. I tap the screen to life and find two notifications that nearly send me into cardiac arrest: 1) a calendar alert that my bus home leaves in *twenty minutes* and 2) a text from Soph asking if I'll be home in time for my shift tomorrow. A jarring reminder of my reality; that this is *not* my reality.

"Ah, shit," I mutter, stumbling to my feet. "Shit, shit, *shit*."

"You okay?"

"No, I'm a total idiot." I dust my hands off on my thighs and begin throwing together a message to Soph. It's 50 percent apology, 50 percent incoherent ramble. My hands are shaking and I can't stop misspelling words. "My bus leaves in twenty minutes and I'm supposed to work tomorrow morning." I stare back longingly at the garlic-stuffed olives Marco has arranged lovingly on my plate. "Shit."

"At the farmers market?"

I nod. "Yeah. Soph's gonna kill me. I'm already the world's most lackluster fruit vendor."

"Hey, no sweat." Marco lifts his chin toward the plate he's put together, now balancing on the palm of his hand. "I'll make sure you get home in time."

I frown at him. "What?"

"Stay the night with me and I'll make sure you're home in time. We'll leave tomorrow morning. Bright and early. Four A.M. No way you'll be late."

I return to my spot next to him, taking the plate off his hand. "You're okay with that?"

Marco leans back against the hill, popping an olive into his mouth. "I was never going to let you take the bus home."

"Oh." I fiddle with my phone, then revise my text to Soph to a way simpler yes boss! With the saluting emoji. "Thanks."

He shrugs a shoulder, lifting the bill of his hat to run his fingers through his hair. "Just what a good boyfriend does."

"I guess it is." An evening breeze ruffles the trees above our heads and I bring my knees closer to my chest. "I wouldn't really know."

Marco watches me for a moment, nervousness pulling at his mouth. "You've never dated anyone before?"

I point a finger gun at him. "You said *good* boyfriend."

He makes a noise in his throat I can't decipher then falls completely quiet, which, I'm starting to pick up, is pretty rare for Marco. He's always making some kind of noise—talking, laughing, humming. I've realized in just one day that this nonchalance doesn't really sit in his face. If anything, his features are worn and wise, in direct contrast to his bouncing walk and quick, dangerous smile. Now, Marco lies on his side, head propped up on his hand, pulling at strands of grass, his food untouched.

"Hey." I toss a kalamata olive at his head, purposefully aiming over his shoulder. "Did I say something wrong?"

"Not at all." He reaches for my ankle, giving me a quick squeeze. His fingers linger. "I'm thinking about how nice this is."

It is *so* nice. Pure decadence, and I don't want to stay to watch it spoil. I nod in the direction of Manhattan. "Let's go home."

"Home?" He smirks, pushing himself back up to sit. "Do I need to clear a drawer for you?"

I roll my eyes. "You know what I mean, nerd."

We clean up and leave the grassy knoll in pristine condition. There's not even an ass print left in the soft ground. It's like Marco and I were never even there, and with a last look back at the spot where we were lying, it dawns on me that this is what my life will be like, too.

There will be a before and an after with no evidence left behind.

I SPEND THE subway ride trying to leave something behind. If I tangle myself with him tight enough, when I pull away there'll have to be a mark.

There's a stillness about the empty car and a timelessness to the smell of grass on Marco's collar, and I'm intoxicated by the way he hums and sighs when my lips trace the soft, smooth skin beneath his ear. It's like I've never kissed anyone else before. I wouldn't have been able to stop myself even if I wanted to.

Maybe it's his breath, warm and ragged on my neck as he slides his hands down over the curve of my hips until he's pressing into me, lifting my hips to meet his. Marco whispers in my ear that *this* is what he's wanted all day. His voice vibrates through me, and I let go of the last shred of *whatever* has kept me imprisoned for months.

Friday, May 12

As promised, Marco wakes me up at 4 A.M. He rolls on top of me, covering my throat with kisses, even as I moan and whine in protest, muffled under his mouth on my chin and neck, his hair falling into my face. I can feel the weight and heat of his naked body through the thin sheet and only that stirs me.

"You know," I begin, running my nails over and around his shoulders as he plants lazy kisses on the soft planes of my stomach. "Two weeks ago I didn't even know who you were. Now you're pressing your dong into my thigh to wake me up."

"That's love, baby," he mumbles into my skin, and I try to ignore the ache in the center of my chest.

We cross the bridge into Evergreen and every part of me relaxes. *This is home.*

I quickly change and drop off my stuff before running down the steps. I actually can't wait to get back to my place behind the till, the crisp, sappy smell of fresh-picked peppers and green beans and onions all around me. Soph left extra early to haggle for a better spot, away from the food trucks, and suddenly, this feels deeply exciting. I imagine our little stand accruing more customers.

Allie's waiting for me on the last step of the porch with a thermos of fresh coffee. "I need to know everything. *Everything.*"

"We fucked," I say, taking my thermos and pressing my lips to her cheek. "Gotta go."

She gasps—a wild, uncharacteristically loud sound for such a country mouse. "Oh my God. You're obsessed with him."

I screw my mouth up into a grimace as I buckle my bike helmet under my chin. "I am. I'm so obsessed with him. It's a real problem."

"*Wow.*"

"An absolute pickle."

Allie wraps her arms around herself, a barefoot bundle of hoodie and sweatpants in the morning breeze. "What if he's your soulmate?" she shouts after me.

I laugh as I swing my leg over my bike. "That would suck, wouldn't it?"

"You cannot leave me like this." She's hauling ass after me down the driveway as I'm pedaling away. "I need details, specifics, timelines! Give me content, Nadia!"

"I promise," I call back, picking up speed. "You'll get details, but if I'm late again Soph's going to kill me and then you'll never, ever know."

I zoom down Neptune until it meets Brambleberry, then I make a left and pedal past The Billiards and the record shop and Cecily's Hot Donuts and the bench where I lay down after my first night out with Marco. The sun is heavy and orange, dripping like honey down the vinyl-clad roofs. My phone is playing music from my bike basket, and I'm feeling sensations I haven't felt in weeks. A tingling in my hands, in my wrists. A quickness in my pulse.

I want to write something. A script, a story. Something complete, more complete than scribbles on the notepad I keep next to my bed. I want to sit down and try to capture this feeling—this type of aliveness. It's like I've glimpsed a butterfly resting on a purple dahlia, and I know I have to take a picture because this is rare. So rare that in twenty years it might no longer exist.

Happiness has that feeling for me now. A depleting resource.

I start to piece together some words—barely fragments. I like the butterfly metaphor. I'll keep it. I'm not ready to start a big project, but a few lines about last night I could do, and that feels incredible. Maybe I could blow the dust off my laptop and even open a Word document.

I'm pulled away from my music and my thoughts when my phone starts buzzing in the basket of my bike.

I wouldn't stop this song for anyone else.

"Hello," I call out to Marco. "You're on speaker."

Marco chuckles, his voice deep and sleepy. The man laughs at everything I say. Preemptive joy. "Okay, I'll keep it PG. Listen, I just got some really good news. Remember that work thing I said I didn't want to jinx? Well, it's happening—soon, too. This week, and I want you to come with me."

"Come with you?" My pedal strokes grow languid. I thought he'd retired from acting, given up the whole shebang forever. "On location or something? Is this a movie?"

"No, it's something totally different. You'll just have to trust me. It's in Rome."

I come to a sudden, total stop. "Rome? *Italy?*"

"That's the one. What do you say, Fabs? Wanna come on a Roman holiday with me?"

"I'd . . . love to. I just . . . I'm not sure . . ." I'm stuttering, a thousand thoughts coming together and dissipating. *I can't travel.* Travel requires togetherness—constant togetherness. No sneaking away to take medicine, to recover, to cry in the shower or nurse a migraine.

If we travel, he'll absolutely figure out I'm sick.

Maybe he won't. Maybe it doesn't matter.

Maybe I'm not even really sick. Maybe if I just keep—

"You have a passport, right?"

I frown down at my phone. "Yeah. I do."

"Perfect. I'll take care of the rest, I swear. Hotel, plane ticket. I really want you there, Nadia."

Fuck. He sounds so excited. "Can I let you know by tonight?"

"Of course." His voice lilts with a tinge of disappointment. "Take your time. But . . . not too much time. I have to leave tonight, so your ticket would be for tomorrow."

"Tomorrow?" I repeat, barely containing my shock. He really meant it when he said *it's happening soon.* "Marco, I can't just abandon Soph and my job and—I know it doesn't seem like much, but . . ."

The line falls completely silent. For the first time ever, I've stunned Marco.

"Yeah," he says finally. "Yeah, that's totally fair. I don't know what I was thinking."

"It's okay," I say softly. But it's not. I know what I have to do. I know that the only way I can have Marco is if we stay here in Evergreen.

Soph is grinning at me across the church lawn as I secure my bike and make my way over. "There she is!"

In all the months I've known Soph, I've never heard them sound *this* excited.

I duck my head, because I know my face is red. "You and your lover look like fucking Cheshire cats."

"I didn't think you'd ever come back." Soph pulls me into an awkward sideways hug as I slip my apron over my head. We never really touch, so I take this as a sign that they really missed me, and that alone is enough prompting for me to pull Soph into a real hug, to show them that I did, too.

"*Duh*, I came back. New York's nice and all, but I missed this."

"Is Marco back, too? Is he gonna stop by?"

"No idea." I turn so Soph can help tie the strings of my apron while I pull on my gloves. Knots can be a bitch when my hands feel swollen and achy. "I'm trying not to make him my life. Therein lies disaster." I busy myself rearranging the display of chamomile and rosemary, which we have an absolute deluge of. I should probably update the chalkboard sign to include directions for drying the flowers to make tea.

"Or." Soph shrugs a shoulder, fiddling with the quart-size green cartons of shishitos and jalapeños. "You two could really date? Like, you know, just make it a thing."

I press my lips together and shake my head. "Not an option. He's made it extremely clear he won't be in Evergreen after the end of this month—and he definitely won't be moving to Philly, which is where I would end up. And also . . . I read an article."

Soph looks at me like I'm insane. "Like a newspaper article?"

"Well, it's not 1960 so the article was on the internet—but yes." I suck down a breath as I prepare to make my confession. *Forgive me, Father, for I have googled.* I tell Soph about Sage Liu's article— Marco's cageyness about romance that read like a very-well-media-trained way of saying *I don't do relationships.* For extra evidence, I throw in the casual comment he made about having sex with a twenty-five-year-old.

"So, he's a commitment-phobe that has basically locked you into a temporary sex contract?"

I swallow roughly. "When you say it like that, it sounds way worse."

"I mean, but that's what you guys are doing. It's just a no-strings sex thing."

No, no, no, I want to say. *We're like the same person; we completely get each other. He loves being sad and watching old movies and picnics! We're friends.*

Are we friends? If I don't go to Rome, I'll probably never see him again. *Sweet November,* over.

THE MORNING PASSES at a steady clip as the usual suspects wander from stand to stand. I'm not sure if it's the afterglow of the last few days or the Evergreen gossip mill working at its usual lightning pace, but I keep getting looks.

"All smiles today, aren't we, dear?" Jeanine remarks while thoroughly thumbing a basil plant.

Nancy Birch, my former favorite waitress from the diner, is holding court by the last remaining ashtray at the base of the church steps. She's surrounded by a cabal of similarly horny community elders. "They're saying he has a *girlfriend.*" Then a woman with very blunt bangs shushes her loudly while making direct, unbroken eye contact with me.

"Boomers are so fucking weird," I whisper to Soph.

"Don't even get me started." They roll their eyes. "Oh my God, Annetta Silva's headed for them. She's about to mess their shit up."

Annie, endlessly chic with her crisp gray bob and repertoire of caftans, is hauling ass over to the group, pulling along a gorgeous brown-eyed toddler I've never seen before. Annie opens her mouth and in a booming voice calls out: "For the love of hummus, Nancy, are you *really* smoking outside the house of *God*?"

Don Bilovich drops by with some hefty bulbs of garlic from

his garden and a sob story, looking for a deal on Soph's award-winning rainbow chard. While they haggle it out, I step away from the stand and pick up my phone, which has started buzzing in the front pocket of my apron.

"Hello?"

"Amazing news," Liv blurts out. "You're *never* gonna believe this."

"Ooooh, exciting." I transfer my phone from one ear to the other, waving at the book club ladies who are collectively gawking at me from their usual spot under the awning of the coffee truck. Nancy is among them, and I've most definitely pinpointed that epicenter of all juicy Evergreen goss. I add an uncharacteristically big smile to my wave—something that says, *Hello ladies! I fucking see you!* "Hit me," I say to Liv.

"Do you remember Celeste Taldi's older sister? Long hair, weird nose?"

"Dionna Taldi?"

"Right! Okay! She came into the shop and told me she's looking for someone to help the dental office with social media—"

I groan. "Oh jeez . . ."

"*Hush.* She's going on about how she needs help getting followers on social media. They want more patients—younger people. And she's not the only one. Turns out tons of people are looking for someone to help with social media. TikTok and all that. I mentioned you and she lit up. She was like, *Nadia's always been cool.* Isn't that crazy? You could totally start your own business doing this. I told her you'd probably love to—"

"Thank you, Liv, seriously. But I'm just not interested—"

"Why not? It's basically *free* money. These businesses run themselves, you'll just have to post a few times a day or whatever. You can move back to Philly!"

I pinch the bridge of my nose, stuffing back my growing frustration. "It sounds amazing—really. But I'm just not in the headspace to do marketing stuff again. I'm happy in Evergreen—"

"You're *happy* in Evergreen? Doing what, growing mold? Hanging out with Marco?" That stings. It stings badly. Of course Liv would choose this moment to make fun of me, a time when I'm already feeling slightly battered and bruised, preemptively sad over how Marco will react when I tell him I can't come to Rome. Proactively sad about another piece of life I'll miss out on.

And of course Liv would make fun of me about the one man I've chosen to open up to her about—if the one passing conversation we'd had on the balcony could even be considered "opening up."

Now I'm pissed and ready to pounce, but I'm not fast enough. I'm never fast enough to get Liv before she gets me. "Rotting away in Evergreen and fucking some guy who doesn't even care about you enough to give you a real shot isn't going to make you less sick, and it isn't going to take your life off pause. You're spinning your wheels and when Mom and Dad—"

A sudden, ancient rage sparks to life in my stomach. Is that what she thinks of me? Of sex? "*Fucking* some *guy*? Real classy, Liv. Really nice. You know what they say about South Philly girls—"

"What, because you're not from here, too? I'd rather be trash than be a fucking depressive shuffling around in my bathrobe all day."

Oh. We're both out for blood.

"Real clever. Calling me a snob, once again. It's the only insult you have."

"Yeah, snob. You're a snob. Snobby, lazy, and *boring.*"

"Oh, I'm boring? At least I'm not marrying the first guy to message me on Myspace."

The situation is deteriorating faster than either of us can pull the emergency brake. If she was here in person, we'd be pulling each other's hair and clawing at each other's necks. We're too old for this. I know we are. But I don't care.

Every argument I've ever had with Liv has started for the exact same reason—everything has to be on her terms, and if I can't match her enthusiasm, then I deserve the worst of her ire.

"You'd die to have a guy like Mike, you cantankerous old cun—"

No. We cannot cross the *cunt* Rubicon.

"Olivia," I shout into the phone. Loud enough to get her to shut up and loud enough to turn a few heads from the stands around me. I turn away from the growing crowd of post-brunch retirees and grit my teeth. "I can*not* do this right now. This conversation is over. I am at work, at my job. I cannot take extended breaks in order to scream at you. So, please, shut the fuck up."

"Work." She huffs. "You're playing farmer with your friends. Great use of that college degree."

It takes everything in me to not bash my head against the stone side of the church. "Look, I'm sorry it is so personally offensive to you that I don't want to go from being an art director at one of the most well-respected ad agencies on the East Coast to making memes for some fucking pill mill."

"There it is. The truth comes out. You think this is below you."

"It's not below me! It's just—look, it's not what I want right now, okay? *God*. I'm sorry if that hurts your *feelings*."

"What do you want, then?" she demands. "If you don't want to come back to Philly, then what do you want?"

"I have no fucking idea, Olivia! But you know what's not going to help me figure it out? You calling me in the middle of the day to berate me."

"I'm not calling you to berate you. I was calling to do you a huge favor."

"I don't need favors! I'm fine!"

"Fine!" she shouts back. "Be an asshole! Goodbye!"

My whole body shakes with rage. My entire skull aches from how hard I've been clenching my teeth together. I look down at my phone, trembling in my hand. My fingertips are pink from how hard I'm gripping the device while my heart hammers against my rib cage. I still have more fight in me. *Why?* I want to text her. *Why are you acting like this?*

But I don't. Instead, without a third of another thought, I'm calling Marco.

He answers on the first ring. "Nadia?"

"Hey," I say, but I have to clear my throat to hide the way it cracks, still raw with emotion. "I'm in for tomorrow. You can buy me a plane ticket."

"Really?" He's ecstatic, the thrum of his voice matching the city noise around him. He's a shooting star of energy, a punch of alkyl nitrites right up the nose. For the first time in my life, I have someone to call when everything is going wrong. Someone who can immediately and totally make my pain go away.

"Fuck yeah," I exhale, slumping back against the church.

"*Fuck* yeah," he repeats. "You'll be ready to fly out tomorrow night?"

"One thousand percent."

Saturday, May 13

M arco lands in Rome at 3 A.M. Evergreen time, and I wake up to fifteen texts about our hotel room, including a video of Marco struggling then succeeding to set his phone up while he posed with an espresso cup, completely nude save for one of those souvenir aprons with David's stone torso and tiny, flaccid penis. Marco looked *very* satisfied with himself. Just when I thought it couldn't get any better, he turned around—all firm ass and defined back muscles. For the first time ever, I notice a little tattoo above his right knee and another on the inside of his left arm. I must have missed them, the last time I saw him naked. We'd been *very* preoccupied.

Disgusting, I reply, sinking my teeth into my bottom lip, nervous jitters keeping me on the verge of a very-out-of-character giggle. Blocked and reported.

But then I keep replying to every picture.

Holy shit.

Holy shit.

Omg.

Omg.

Marco takes a little while to reply, but when he does, it's all heart emojis and the Italian flag.

Bring at least two fancy outfits, he tells me.

What does *fancy* mean to Marco? Before I can even reflect on the clothes I have in my closet, I'm in a full panic. Is this a red-carpet event? Am I going to be photographed, heaven forbid?

What kind of fancy? I ask in earnest, my terror undoubtedly palpable to Marco. Unwisely, I follow up with: My Cracker Barrel best or Olive Garden chic?

Making a joke was a huge mistake, because the only thing Marco says back is: You scare me.

"YOU'RE WADING INTO the danger zone," Allie tuts, holding up one of my lacier pairs of underwear before folding it and tucking it into my carry-on.

Soph is draped over my bed as Allie and I carefully pack my suitcase. After some back-and-forth, Marco helped me pick out two outfits for the mystery job–related things we'll be doing: a white linen pantsuit with wide legs and a flattering high waist and a muted orange dress that still fits perfectly over my curves. It's a miracle that somehow these items ended up here in Evergreen with me. Otherwise, I'd be showing up in my dad's fishing boots and Nicky's altar server robes.

"What danger zone?" I ask, doing my best impression of an absolute moron. I'm so far up my own ass, I'm surprised I don't emerge from my mouth every time I speak. "We're going to do the same exact thing that we were doing here, just in Italy."

Soph rolls over onto their back and lets out a labored sigh. "I hate to say it, but I'm with Allie on this one. You're heading into a love pressure cooker. An accelerated timeline. If we were in a movie about the multiverse, the version of you and Marco in Italy gets married and sails off into the sunset in a gondola."

"*What?* Why? Because Rome is *so* sexy?" I'm sputtering like an old garden hose, fists pressed into my hips. "They have a *very* horrible graffiti problem."

"Are you sure this maybe isn't some sort of . . . overcorrection?" Allie offers. "With everything that you've had going on?"

I throw a pair of sandals into my suitcase a little harder than necessary, fighting off flashbacks from my phone call with Liv. "What's *that* supposed to mean?"

"We just want you to find a middle ground, sweets. To do what makes you happy—"

"I am happy," I pout, crossing my arms over my chest. You know, like happy people do. "*This* makes me happy. Marco makes—we're happy right now."

Allie tilts her head to the side and looks at me for a moment like I'm kind of tragic. "But it's temporary, babe."

My mouth almost falls open. What an unbelievable argument. "So what? Does that mean I don't get to have fun? Do you cry while you eat ice cream because you know it won't last forever?"

Allie shrinks slightly, a flush of pink dotting her fair cheeks, and I can tell I just made a really good point. "We just don't want you to end up like after Kai—"

"My breakup with Kai had *nothing* to do with Kai—plus, who is this *we?*" I cut Allie off viciously, turning my angry gaze on Soph. "Do *you* think that's what's going to happen?"

Soph sits up, pushing their glasses up and off their nose as they rub at their eyes. "I'm not getting involved. But just think before you say or do anything, okay? We don't want to spend a month scraping you off the bathroom floor."

Allie nods, pride beaming off her at Soph's dad-like delivery of that final line. Then, she points at me. "Yeah. Don't write a check your ass can't cash."

That's a Nadia-ism, used right against me.

Sunday, May 14

On my flight from Philly to Rome I was seated next to an older woman on the way to Basilicata to visit her family. Her English wasn't great and it seemed like maybe her Italian wasn't either, after years of living abroad. I fell in love with her watery eyes and soft, thin black hair immediately. She didn't look anything like my nonna had—a heavy-set, sturdy woman with warm brown eyes and solid forearms—but she seemed cosmically connected to all nonnas, and therefore I had to protect her.

When turbulence hit, we held hands and looked at each other, giggling, embarrassed by our fear.

"It's okay!" I whispered. "We're okay!"

"Mamma mia," she said softly, gripping my hand.

Now I levitate through passport control and baggage claim, basically running to the arrivals hall. I only make one pit stop—into the restroom to pop a handful of pills that will hopefully ease the horrible throb in my back, brush my teeth, and scrub away the old mascara underneath my eyes. I smell a little funky, but Marco's a big boy. He'll survive.

I step through the automatic doors and search the crowded, chaotic hall for his face and I find him immediately. While Marco should blend in with his olive skin and dark, wavy hair, there's something so American about his face. He looks like a gum-chewing, sunflower-seed-spitting baseball player with his square jaw and thick arms crossed over his chest, waiting for me on the other side of the railing that separates arrivals from arrival recipients. I pick up speed toward him, a grin on my face, and I'm still running when he wraps his arms around my waist and hefts me to him.

His teeth are bright and white and his skin is glowing and he looks like the safest place on Earth.

"*Buon giornoooooooo,*" he trills, spinning us in a circle, almost knocking us into a group of discombobulated teenagers. It's so ridiculous, so over-the-top. Any other person and I would be mortified.

"Put me down, I'm flashing the entire airport!" I shout, trying to keep the shapeless linen sack I traveled in from flying up over my waist.

He obliges, but we don't stop moving. "This hotel is crazy. I can't wait for you to see. It's right in the middle of everything—right in Piazza Trilussa. Oh, and there's this restaurant we have to try—"

"Jesus, slow down. Can we stop for coffee?"

He comes to a complete stop and turns back toward me so fast I almost flat-tire his perfectly white sneakers. Marco takes my face in his hands, improbably gentle and firm all at once, bringing his mouth to mine. When he pulls away, we stay close, foreheads pressed together. It's disgusting, how sweet it all is. He watches me through heavy lids, mouth curving. I've abandoned my luggage and wrapped myself around him. "*Certo, amore.*"

I squeeze his bicep. "You've got worms in your brain."

He laughs, but doesn't let go of me. "*Si, amore.*"

Marco drives us back toward the center of Rome with every window of his rental car rolled down and the radio blasting. He keeps taking his eyes off the road, over and over, to look at me and just *smile*.

"Stop it." I laugh, shouting over the wind. "We're going to crash."

"You actually came. You're here."

"Did you think I wouldn't?" I raise my eyebrows at him. "Even with a ticket?"

He shakes his head, pressing his lips together. "I never know what's going to happen with you."

I look out at the ancient skyline, breaking through the umbrella pines under a wildly clear azure sky. "I'm not an asshole, Marco."

I sound like Liv. Our argument flashes back like a cold blade over my skin, and I actually shiver—even though it must be eighty-plus degrees. I hate how we left things, but I can't think about Liv and her obsession with trying to scale me down to a more recognizable shape. I turn back toward Marco. "I'd never go out of my way to hurt you. You know that, right? You know I care about you? Even if this . . . this relationship is fake or temporary or whatever, I'm not pretending I care about you."

"Hey, of course." He looks so serious suddenly and I realize it's because *I* look serious. "Of course. I was just kidding."

Rome is like a Renoir. A Matisse.

The air smells like jasmine flowers and honeysuckle, heavy with heat and diesel fumes and melting garbage. Everything's ancient and rotten and beautiful, lush green life bursting through broken concrete and abandoned buildings alive with wild vines. We park near the Tiber River and step out into the morning rush, immediately absorbed into the pace and rhythm of the city.

There's so much to look at, I'm not where to start and I think Marco can tell.

He pulls me through the crowds of tourists that clog the narrow, cobblestoned streets of Trastevere, my bag slung over his shoulder.

He's glowing like I've never seen before under the late-morning sun. The sky is preternaturally blue, and suddenly I remember that Italians have about eight different words for light blue. All different shades, all different combinations of soft consonants and decadent vowels.

"Coffee!" I remind him, tripping over my feet in an effort to keep up as Marco leads me by the hand down a winding *vico*, so filled with sunshine it looks like it's been dipped in saffron.

We stop at a coffee shop en route to our hotel. The building is a faded shade of amber, crowded on either side by nearly identical palazzi, ivy and graffiti mixing together to disguise where one building starts and the other ends. The entrance is bookended by two tables of old men sitting with their newspapers and morning cigarettes. If Marco had a tail, it would have been wagging at the sight of a delicious 8 A.M. smoke. I have to practically pull him away by his collar.

"God, I wish I could just have one vice without taking it too far," he remarks, running a hand through his hair, *jonesing*.

"Woof, how personally should I take that?"

Marco rolls his eyes. "Sex isn't a vice."

"Oh, no?" I pop a brow. "You're a *very* bad Catholic."

He smirks and says with great pride, "Greek Orthodox, actually. I'm a bad Orthodox Christian."

We order frozen espresso, shaken out of a liter Coke bottle into shot glasses, and sip them while standing at the bar, no one else around us. The radio crackles over our heads and Marco keeps a hand lazily glued to my lower hip, something I would have never allowed in Evergreen, but the magnetism of his happiness draws me closer and closer. Suddenly, I'm compelled by the spirit of a corporate-girlboss demon to sputter out the sentence, "What . . . are your goals for this trip?"

Marco's arms find their way around me, his fingers tracing the length of my spine over my linen dress. "What are my *goals*?"

"Like, what do you want to accomplish?"

"Did you hit your head on the flight?"

"I just . . ." I attempt to shrug out of his arms, but he tightens his grip on me. "This is really romantic."

"Okay." He laughs, lifting a hand to smooth my hair away from my face. "And?"

"What about our feelings?" But before he can answer, I course-correct. "Soph and Allie told me I need to be careful with this. They're worried I'm going to . . ." I lose my nerve, just like the waitress from that very first night at Ernie's. I roll my lips over my teeth. "You know."

"Ah, of course," Marco says gravely, pressing his lips to my forehead. "You're going to fall head over heels in love with me, by accident."

"Right." I laugh, all the anxiety falling away from my voice. *Am I being ridiculous?*

"Do you think that's possible?" he asks earnestly. "To fall in love with someone against your will?"

I grimace. "I don't know, I spent a lot of years really horny for Conan O'Brien."

He pulls back, admiring me for a moment. "Conan? Really?"

"One hundred percent. He's *so* funny. And charming. And I guess I love a redhead."

Marco smirks. "You know, I could probably get you his number."

"Oh, *honey.*" I wrap my arms around his waist. "Don't make me *beg.*"

MARCO PUSHES OPEN the door to our home for the next four days, and I let out an audible gasp, pressing both my hands to my chest.

Without an ounce of irony, I announce: "I want to live here *forever*."

Marco's grinning, the proudest I've ever seen the man. "I did a good job, huh?"

"This is the nicest place I've *ever* been."

Gray terrazzo floors, stone archways through which each room flows into the next, leading to a balcony that overlooks the piazza below, angles of sunlight falling across the bed from behind doors that nearly reach the ceiling.

The bathroom is bigger than the whole suite with a deep, white stone soaking tub that curves lusciously like a gravy boat. I kick off my shoes and climb in, Marco watching me bemused from the doorway. He's leaning against the frame, arms crossed over his chest, sunglasses pushed up on his head, as I point my toes at the ceiling.

"Holy *crap*. We could both fit in here!"

"You think?"

"Yes, absolutely. Get in."

Marco carefully removes his sneakers before climbing into the tub. Our legs interlock and we stare at each other, almost doubled over with the type of silent laughter you assume becomes impossible with age.

"We . . . look . . . like . . . babies . . ." I manage through enormous gulps of air and wheezing laughter.

"Babies?" Marco repeats, beside himself.

When I finally get ahold of myself, I crawl across the space to him, his arms wrapping around me, and my head settles onto his chest. I can hear his heart beating, his breath moving in and out of his lungs as his thumb traces the curve of my shoulder. A window is open and sunshine and church bells and distant voices pour in. My eyes flutter shut and an extreme sense of peace blankets me.

"I love this," I say, the words falling from my mouth before I can catch them. It's how I feel, down to my core. And it just comes from me, before my ego can step in the way. I do. I love this.

Embarrassment pinpricks in me immediately. I shouldn't have said that. "Being here," I add without lifting my head or opening my eyes.

A soft noise of agreement moves in Marco's chest. "Me too," he whispers. "I love being here with you."

I INSIST ON seeing as much of Rome as possible, even though the city seems to still—haphazardly—observe the holy day. Through the bathroom's slated balcony doors, I hear the hushed excited chatter of two little girls, followed by the slapping of their sandaled feet on the Sampietrini. I can sort of understand what they're saying—something about a little gray cat. It takes everything in me to not throw back the shower curtain, pull on a sundress, and run downstairs after them. Their voices carry on the sweet late-morning air, curling and twisting with the steam from my shower while I towel off my hair, shaking myself dry like a puppy. Instead I wrap myself in a towel and follow the smell of moka pot coffee into the kitchen.

"It feels like a waste to not spend every *single* moment—thank you," I say to Marco, pausing to take a boiling-hot espresso cup from him before taking a series of sips. When I look up, he's smirking—leaning back against the little kitchen stove, sunshine painting his face in a honey light. "What?"

"Nothing." Marco shrugs, arms crossed over his stomach. With a look of great satisfaction, he sips his own coffee. "I just don't think I've ever seen you this excited before."

"I-I . . ." I stutter. "What about the whale?"

"Eh." He tilts his head from side to side. "The whale made you smile—but the whale was also your idea."

I grin, batting my eyes. "It *was.* I'm a genius."

With a soft chuckle, he sets down his demitasse cup and shifts toward me, nearly closing the space in a single step. Before I can finish any of my thoughts—about whales, about Rome, about how incredibly smart and perfect I am—Marco's in front of me looking so unbelievably handsome, my breath actually stalls. Then, he's taking my face in his hands; a frustrated growl half forms on his lips before he tilts my face to his and kisses me—slow and hungry. I curl my fingers around his wrists, falling into him—soft and malleable against his chest.

He pulls away, keeping a firm hold on my face between his hands, and looks down his nose at me.

"What was that for?"

His gaze meets mine, eyes shining. "Good. You're still grinning." He swipes a thumb over my lips. "I was getting really jealous of that damn whale—and this city."

THE FATIGUE OF travel and jet lag are coming for me, ready to make me their bitch, crush me into a fine powder and blow me into the wind. But for now I'm delirious and slap-happy.

Out in the heat and haze of a Roman afternoon, Marco seems completely, totally in his element. This is a version of him far more confident than I'd seen in Evergreen and New York, a man I'd surrender to wholly. I'd let him manage my finances and my sleep schedule.

He knows the best ways to the best places; we zigzag around crowds and slip through streets so narrow they must be hidden passages. He tells me about different personal landmarks like: Piazza di Santa Maria in Trastevere is his favorite of all the piazzas, the communist bar around the corner with cheap beers is the best in the entire city, and the *supplì* shop two streets over has the best potato croquettes and roasted chicken. Does he like *pizza alla pala*? Yes, but only the kind with fresh mozzarella from the shop across from the park, on the other side of the piazza. He speaks Italian well enough to make me instantly jealous. When a woman speaks to me in an aggressive, rapid string of Romance-language perfection, I smile like a Midwesterner and gesture his way.

"So, what's the deal with you and Rome?" I ask Marco over the *margherita* we're splitting for lunch.

"We're just having casual sex."

"Oh, yeah?" I quirk a brow. "Just for the month of May or . . . ?"

"Very funny." He rolls his eyes at me, reaching across the table to dust a bit of semolina flour from my chin. "I don't know—I came here with the cast years ago and just . . . fell in love. It's a city with everything, you know? Literally everything. It's like the entire universe contained between seven hills."

"What about Greece?" I ask, shimmying two slices of pizza apart. I push one in his direction.

"Greece is beautiful, but—it can be a lot, being so surrounded by family and tradition."

I make a noise of deep, guttural recognition, so he keeps talking. "Rome feels like my place. My memories, my traditions. Every way I feel here is something *I* discovered."

"No one's telling you how to feel. No boardwalk clown music."

Marco nods. "No boardwalk clown music."

WE JUMP ON the tram and ride it to the end of the line. He takes me to a bookstore with four stories and endless shelves of glossy paperback editions. I see so many authors and volumes I lust for, I have no choice but to feel crushed with the knowledge that I'll *never* possibly read them all. I stand at the table of Elena Ferrante novels with their Italian covers, as God intended, tears bubbling in my eyes.

Marco laughs and takes my picture.

In the center of it all, I feel an ancestral ache. Am I home here, too? Am I as home here as I am in Evergreen? Two places connected by an ancient pathway, carved out and worn smooth by millions of people. I see Liv in dark-haired women that zoom by on mopeds, brows set in determined concentration. I see my mother's soft, lined smile in the faces of different shopkeepers, with their arthritic hands and reading glasses hanging around their necks.

We walk for miles until we reach Piazza Navona, and I stand awestruck at Neptune's feet.

"Can we stay forever?" I ask Marco, arms outstretched. The sun sets in an ultraviolet explosion of indigo and fuchsia.

He makes the little *eh, eh, eh* noise and then snaps my picture from a crouching position. When he pulls his camera away, he's watching me with a smile in his eyes. "It definitely suits you."

The way he looks at me makes my skin goose-pimple, my stomach lurch into my chest.

It does, I think. *I think I'm healed here. I think I'm all better now.*

The thought comes in an instant—and then it's gone.

Monday, May 15

Marco pulls me from a deep, dead, jet-lagged sleep with his mouth on my bare shoulder and a gentle hand coaxing my knees open underneath the crisp sheets. The sounds of traffic drift up toward us, rising off the Lungotevere, as we'd fallen asleep with the balcony doors open. I don't do anything to resist or protest. Instead, I blossom to his touch, purring like a content cat.

When Marco pulls the sheet down over my hips, I don't stop him. When his mouth skims my stomach and his hands slip underneath me, I don't suggest we close the doors.

I SLIP INTO the bathroom and unzip the pouch that contains all my medicine—a series of loose, chalky pills floating around in a bag. I shake out what I need, my hand trembling slightly as the pills slide out one by one. They seem to grow every time I dole them out.

Fuck, I need water.

I shoot a furtive glance at the door, which I've left ajar. Marco's on the balcony taking a phone call, his voice waxing and waning as he paces from one end to the other.

I spin around toward the sink, and just as I'm about to turn on the tap, his voice fades completely. I stay perfectly still, even holding my breath, listening for the sound of his sneakers on the stone floors.

But there's nothing.

Stillness.

I tighten my grip on the pills, turning more and more powdery in my sweaty palm.

Then, Marco laughs—a big, booming noise that makes my stomach and shoulders lurch. Suddenly, a burst of air whips through the room, tossing the balcony doors open, throwing around the hand towel. I cringe as everything clatters and bangs around me, sun streaming out from behind a cloud and falling over me and my mess, throwing us into harsh relief—even the spinning, shining particles of dust in the air look, suddenly, like jagged bits of glass. I tighten my fingers around my medicine.

"Nadia?" Marco calls out to me. "You okay?"

I must have made a sound.

My chest tightens, my breath catches. I throw the handful of pills into the toilet and flush.

Then, I spin around.

But Marco's not behind me.

It was just a gust of wind. That's it. *A gust of wind.*

I press a hand into my chest, willing my heart to still.

The toilet drains with an immense amount of noise. My pills swirl away, and my eyes turn dry as I stare on in horror.

Anxious heat prickles down my neck, every exposed inch of my skin coming alive with dread. How much of my medicine had I been holding? Not all of it. No way. I wouldn't have—couldn't possibly have—

"Nadia?" He raps at the bathroom door with his knuckles. "Everything okay?"

I press my lips together until they stop trembling. *I'm okay,* I tell myself. *I will be okay.*

"Yep," I call out finally. "All good."

Tuesday, May 16

I haven't checked my phone in two days, and even though I know my sister well enough to not anticipate any sort of open, vulnerable communication, I still crave it. While I shower, I let my mind wander to a daydream, a fantastical near-future where my sister picks us up from the airport. She meets Marco; she comes back to Evergreen; she pulls me aside and tells me, *You two are soulmates. It's so obvious.*

No way, I'd say back.

I feel pathetic for yearning so completely for her *acceptance,* yuck. But shouldn't it be enough for her—to see me deliriously happy, even if it's just for a little while? It's been so long since I've been *this* happy.

After drying my hair, applying makeup, and stealing a sip of the coffee Marco's just brewed, I connect to the apartment Wi-Fi and wait for my phone to ding.

Marco still hasn't revealed to me the *work* reason for this trip, but not for my lack of trying. With little to no information about our upcoming evening, I put the decision about my outfit completely in his hands. He chooses the white linen pants and matching blazer with nothing but my golden skin and black bralette underneath.

I'm securing the strap of my sandal around my ankle when Marco appears in the doorway, leaning against the frame, floating on a cloud of cologne and shower steam. His outfit is simple, elegant, and all black. Next to each other, we'll be in perfect harmony.

He lets out a slow whistle when I look up to catch his eyes. *"Damn."* He looks rugged with a few days' worth of stubble on his chin, his heavy bottom lip pulled back between his teeth. Our eyes meet and he moves toward me like my eyes contain a magnetic quality.

"You like it?"

"I . . . I love it." He takes my hand in his and pulls me to my feet, then to his chest, closer and closer until our lips meet.

"Can you tell me anything about where we're going?"

"Wait just a little longer. The surprise is worth it, I swear."

"Better than this?" I ask

"Hm, no." His eyes dance over my face. "Definitely not better than this. Nothing is."

Very suddenly I miss Evergreen so much it hurts my chest. I miss the smell of bay and salt air and the way Marco had looked at me the very first time I saw him. I long for that moment, want to crack it open like a walnut, see what lives inside. I miss his nervous eyes and his mullet; I miss the first time I felt like I wanted him, on the dance floor at Ernie's and maybe even before that, on the boardwalk.

It's not that days have passed and I know our time will be up; it's that this is the best thing that has ever happened to me and I want it all over again, from the beginning.

Whether this entire saga ends with us looking at each other on the edge of this bed or if everything ends in ten days or ten years, I would want to replay it all. I'd rewind over and over again, memorizing every moment, charting the course from where we started to where we are right now, so if ever I were to lose my way as profoundly as I lost myself back in November, I'd have a map back to this. *Joy*. A feeling intense and perilous and so deep and clear, I could drink it and never feel thirsty again.

Marco brings me joy.

"You're a flirt, Marco Antoniou," I say into his neck. We're swaying now, back and forth, to invisible music.

His hand tightens on the small of my back, sending an electric throb through my hips. "Not a flirt. Just personally invested in making you feel amazing."

I'm not sure how it happens—how it's possible to have never experienced something before, but to know deep in my stomach, in my soul, that I'm falling in love.

A BUMPY, JITTERY taxi ride where my heart skips with every cobblestone we hit lands us in a piazza somewhere north of Castel Sant'Angelo, which Marco points out to me, sliding across the back seat, a hand lazily draping over my thigh. I'm so fucking nervous, I don't even care about the enormous, gorgeous stone structure smearing by in a blur of orange streetlights and inky-blue sky. I just want to turn in to his chest and close my eyes.

"Can you give me a hint? Or at least let me know if there's going to be five thousand cameras or if I'm going to have to give a speech?"

"Nadia." He laughs, shaking his head as he pays the taxi driver. "This is supposed to be fun, not an acute form of torture. I promise it'll be worth it, okay?"

THE PIAZZA IS filled with a post-dinner crowd, couples lounging in chairs that face a brilliant, glittering fountain while the marble terraced steps that lead to the water display fill up with teenagers, tourists, panhandlers, and drug dealers. Marco leads the way to the far end of the square toward a building with enormous carved doors and a boisterous crowd spilling out into the night. I can hear a fluid mix of Italian and English, as I crane my neck to try and parse out the details of what we're headed into. No red carpet, thank God. No groups of autograph seekers. No cameramen, no microphones, just a single photographer and a security guard standing stone-faced at the top of the marble steps by the door.

As we draw close to the building, I can make out a large fabric sign hanging over the doors. In enormous white letters, it reads:

ADAM WEST
"REST"
MOSTRA IN ANTEPRIMA
16 MAGGIO–1 LUGLIO

We slow to stop, and Marco drops my hand. "Well?"

"Your favorite photographer? We're here to see his exhibit?" That can't be right. I guess again. "You modeled for Adam?" That feels wrong, too.

What else could it be? I recognized the photographs from his apartment at the exhibit we went to in Brooklyn. The grainy black-and-white portraits of people sleeping—or looking at least like they wanted to sleep—made sense for an exhibit called "Rest." All of the photos I've seen taken by Adam are candid shots. Maybe it's a small film premiere?

"No," I jump in before Marco can correct me. "You're not a model."

"Uh, *ouch*." He laces his fingers with mine and pulls me along with him.

"You had a mullet when I met you," I remind him. "Did you model the mullet?"

His eyes glisten as he says, "Let's think about it—what have I brought on each of our dates?"

"A winsome smile. A huge boner."

"Besides that."

"I don't know . . ." I feel like an absolute idiot. I stop walking and stare at him in horror. "A gun?"

"Nadia." He takes my face in his hands, laughing. He plants a kiss on my top lip. "I always bring my camera."

"Wait." I pull back from him with a gasp. "You're not Adam West, are you?" Marco responds by pressing his lips together until they disappear. "*Holy shit*, Marco. *You're* Adam West? This is *your* premiere." I rip myself out of his hold altogether. "Holy *shit*!" Then, I throw myself forward, arms circling his neck, laughter exploding out of me. "Adam *fucking* West."

"You're not mad, are you?" he asks through a laugh, stumbling backward at the sudden weight of me against him, his hands coming to gently rest against my hips.

"*What*? Why would I ever be mad? This is. . . . this is *amazing*."

"But I didn't tell you about any of this—about this part of things."

I pull away from him and take his face in my hands. I'm not crying, but I should be. "Baby, you don't owe me anything."

He lays his hands over mine. "Did you just call me *baby*?"

"You deserve it," I say. "You look stressed."

"Yeah." Marco throws a look over his shoulder toward the building. "A lot of people I want to work with are here tonight. From fashion brands and bigger galleries around Europe. Plus, some people I really need to make things right with. Old coworkers from different projects over the years. The whole team worked really hard to help me get my foot in the door. I haven't been this nervous since I was a kid. I've never done something like this before—like, stood on my own as an artist. They've invested time, energy, love."

"Your work is incredible, Marco. *You're* incredible. You've got this."

He takes a deep, steadying breath, squaring his shoulders. "Well, either way." He reaches for my hand. "I've got you here."

WE STEP THROUGH the grand doors, squeezing past the guard, who greets Marco with a handshake, and into a high-ceilinged front room. Marco's arrival—and mine, too, I guess—sends a ripple through the crowd and everyone explodes with movement. Turning heads and double kisses, one on each cheek. The space around us is choked with bodies and noise, and while everyone grabs for Marco, he holds on to my hand the entire time. Everyone's smiling at me, and they're warm and fragrant like the Roman night.

They're looking at me like they know me. The walls are high and stark white around us, with gallery lighting but no art. Through another pair of double doors I spy what has to be the exhibit. I can hear the same soundtrack—the one that played over the speakers in Brooklyn—of waves crashing, gulls crying. Sounds, I realize, from Evergreen.

The crowd moves us through the room, like a multitentacled beast, depositing us into various groups of gorgeous, important people. I meet those who have job titles I dreamed of, even job titles I once had, but somehow they seem *more* valid. Art directing for fashion houses and beauty brands and mononymous individuals. Not for failing media conglomerates or ointment manufacturing companies.

Someone presses a flute of prosecco into my hand, and I take it, suddenly overwhelmed with gratitude. I really do need a drink. Tonight is outside of everything usual and typical. I can't even think about medicine and dosages; none of that exists here—in a place so close to perfection. Dosages, triggers, aches and pains—those can be tomorrow's problem.

I lean close to Marco while he chats with a very large Dutchman, trying my best to not interrupt what sounds like a bone-dry discussion of public art policy. "Would it bother you if I have some champagne tonight? Just a sip, to celebrate."

"Whatever you want," he assures me, pressing a hand into my lower back.

The first sip of alcohol I've had since our first date. It fizzes on my tongue, dry and electric. My stomach immediately comes alive with fire and my nerves mellow. For a moment, my mind flickers back to other moments I drank to soothe myself—a quick snap of terror and dread in my chest. But just as quickly as it arrives, the memory is gone.

I'm okay, I tell myself. *Tonight, I'm okay.*

Once again, the crowd bucks and moves us forward, like high tide at our back pushing us to shore. Finally, we arrive at the second set of doors. The exhibit.

I tighten my grip on Marco's hand and he squeezes back.

Here, the crowd parts for us as we step into a different world. This room is cooler, less cramped. All the noise of conversation and glassware clinking and lo-fi music is gone. Like in a movie, everything dims.

My feet fail me and my hand falls from Marco's, cool and moist. His photographs are enormous splashes of black-and-white, fantastic explosions of life stretched across canvas. There's only one or two on each wall, except for the farthest wall at the other end of the room. There I see only one photo, lit from above.

My breath snags, and my feet carry me forward. As I cross the room, heads turn. They smile, they look twice. They see me, in double.

Because there I am.

In black-and-white, six feet off the ground. Lit from above.

The moon hangs heavy in the sky, bold beside the soon-to-fade afternoon sun that drips like milk-white honey over the surface of the ocean. Sunlight unravels like a bolt of ribbon down from the sky, over the ocean, then to the handrail slipping over the edge of the boat and, finally, over my face. Over my close-cropped hair, my full, curly lashes and closed eyelids, the angle of my nose and the pout of my sleeping mouth, over my fingernails glinting at the tips of my limp hand, tucked under my chin.

And just behind me is the arch, smooth and long, of the whale jumping.

I can almost hear this photo. The powerful, quiet sway of the ocean. The gulls overhead. Marco telling me to stay still.

For a moment, the room falls away and I'm back in Evergreen, the place that has kept me, made me feel safe, while I rested.

My eyes have fallen shut, and when I blink them open, he's next to me.

Without pulling my eyes away, I say: "It's me."

"It's you," he says softly. "I hope you don't mind. It's my favorite photo from the set." He runs his tongue over his bottom lip before adding, "I can't tell if that's because it's my best photo or my best subject."

"I . . . I love it, Marco," I manage. "I can't believe that . . . that's *me*. I look so peaceful."

His mouth tugs to the side. "That's definitely you." He lifts his chin toward the sunset. "You and your whale. Two beautiful women."

THE WALLS OF the exhibit are filled with photos of people from Marco's life—his mother and his aunts sunbathing all in a row like roasting ducks; his little brother face down on a tattoo bed, vibrating needle pressed into his spine; a man with pierced ears and a face etched with heavy lines appears over and over, and it dawns on me that Marco definitely has a best friend—other than me, *of course*. There are other women on display. I don't know who they are—how long they were in Marco's life and how deeply he felt for them. There's the woman who dances, her hair fanning around her in a sunbeam of joy. There's another woman asleep in an armchair, a book draped over her thigh and a dog at her feet.

It's a patchwork quilt of small moments, a story of how easy it is for Marco to slip into people's lives and warm them. On the other end of his lens, we all look at peace.

Am I special to Marco? I don't know anymore. I don't know how I fit into the landscape of his life—am I as big to him as I am in this gallery? The thought hounds me as I move from photo to photo, turning over each piece of his work like ancient artifacts. I hunt for meaning, for clues. Has he done this before—tricked a regular woman with a silly, little life into falling head over heels into his world?

I don't mean to, but I drink my whole glass of prosecco.

EVENTUALLY THERE'S A dimming of lights and lots of shushing and a thin woman with a loose, low bun steps into the center of the room with a microphone.

I don't really understand Italian, but I gather that she's introducing Marco, whom she gestures at continuously. He ducks his head as all the eyes in the room turn to him, and suddenly I am extremely grateful for my glass of prosecco. I've been to enough weddings to know what's coming—one of us is going to have to make a speech. And like *hell* will it be me.

For the first time all night, Marco leaves my side and the crowd erupts into boisterous applause that ricochets off the walls and comes back twice as cacophonous.

"Good evening, everyone. *Buona sera a tutti.*" I find myself thinking, *When did Marco learn Italian?* But it's a dumb thought because Marco could have known Italian his whole life. I've only known him for less than two weeks. What else don't I know? So much. A pang of anxiety strikes me in the back of my throat and travels down to my stomach. I'm on the edge of a spiral when he clears his throat and begins:

"Thank you all so much being here. I've dreamed of tonight for many months—ironically, I've lost countless nights of sleep, terrified and exhilarated at the idea of finally sharing all these images in one place as 'Rest.'" He pauses politely, pulling a tan hand down over the angle of his chin, while laughter ripples through the crowd. When he looks up again, there's a new emotion in his eyes. "All the photos on display tonight are candids, moments I was lucky enough to actually witness. When I was deep in my battle with addiction, I never slept. Sleep terrified me. Sleep was, in my mind, a tiny stream with many precarious mouths that all opened up to a violent river that could sweep me away. I thought about death constantly. I thought about my value, my legacy—who would remember me, *why* would they remember me? I couldn't sleep because if I did die, I would die a loser. A failure. That shame controlled my life." Marco's gaze is pure fire, yet perfectly still. No fear, no nervous energy. I know that gaze. I'd seen it in myself, weeks ago, when I'd lifted the shears and held them to my hair and made the first cut. *Pure purpose.*

"When I found sobriety, I finally found the beauty in rest. In closing my eyes and handing a part of myself over. Once I found that beauty, once I recognized it, I saw it everywhere. All the small moments we hand ourselves over—the quiet moments when we let ourselves become vulnerable. I recently had a small setback, and all I could think about was how I never want to live in a world where I can't see that beauty. That was scarier to me than death. Bigger to me than shame. The people in these photos changed my life. They taught me this lesson. So, please—" Marco pantomimed lifting a glass. "Join me in thanking them."

I'M INTRODUCED TO dozens of people and each time Marco tells me one thing about them he appreciates.   •

"This is Paola, she's a genius winemaker—she's always giving me great ideas.

"This is Pierdavide. He runs a small press, I owe so much to him.

"This is Tia—the best curator in the world.

And then, he introduces me in Italian. *This is Nadia, from the photo.*

It hurts how badly I want to be more.

I SLIP OUT of bed, the cold terrazzo stinging the bottoms of my feet as I creep into the bathroom. Just the sound of my thighs brushing together and toes cracking. I shut the door behind me and start the bath, water bubbling and tumbling noisily with no respect for the sanctity of night. My head is pounding from what feels like a toxic mixture of prosecco, medicine on an empty stomach, and Marco's speech.

When the deep, white basin is full I slip into the water, barely suppressing a moan of relief as the water melts me inch by inch.

Months ago, this sort of midnight madness took everything out of me. I was still learning the rhythms of a sick body—how I could physically be so exhausted while my mind was so awake from the pain. It was tedious and boring, especially when it already felt like life was being wasted on me. What about all those fathers taken from sons too soon? All the mothers who went out for groceries and never came back?

Now I understand the pain, anticipate it, even wait for it. These moments are deeply lucid, and I feel incredibly awake.

I sink down deep into the bath until my hair is wet, warmth seeping into me through the back of my skull. Then, I wet a washcloth and place it over my eyes, throbbing in their sockets with every jolt of blood routed through my veins. Sickness has a way of making you aware of every dimension of yourself; I swear I can feel the difference between tissue and bone. I've never felt more 3D than when I hurt.

Fragments of the night move through my mind intermixed with sunbursts of color, a private little light show from my brain. Marco's eyes on me. Marco talking about shame, shame controlling his life.

Me too.

Shame has an iron grip on me. There are many reasons why I can't tell Marco about my life, but none of them as compelling as the shame I feel. Maybe I'm not afraid to fall asleep, but—worse yet—for all those months, I'd been afraid of being awake.

And even still, I thought we could find a way to make this

work. Without any form of confrontation with my reality. How idiotic.

Now, I see exactly how far away Marco is from me, how finite our time together is, how easy intimacy is to cultivate when you're beautiful and charming and find someone as *starved* as I am for something I'll probably never really have.

Liv was right. She's always right.

"You okay?" a hoarse, sleepy voice says from the doorway. Moonlight slips over his broad shoulders. I make out the soft swish of skin as he crosses his arms.

"Can't sleep," I say to Marco.

"Jet lag?"

"Headache." I pull the rag off my face completely. Blue moonlight falls in from the balcony, cutting a harsh pattern across the stone floor. The entire room has an otherworldly glow. A hard knot seizes in my chest. I don't want Liv to be right. "Get in."

Marco listens; he slides out of his boxers and into the tub opposite me. The water surges and overflows then settles around our shoulders as he weaves his legs between mine.

He looks tired, eyes heavy and soft. He reaches beneath the surface and takes one of my feet in his hands and I sink lower, until the soap bubbles lap at my chin.

We don't speak at first. Not until I say: "I keep thinking about your speech."

He lets out a hum. "Was it okay?"

I nod. "I think I get it now . . . why you wanted to do this."

"Tell me."

"Nothing in life has ever been effortless for me . . . ever. I thought I did everything right. And it didn't get me anywhere. Actually—" I laugh. "It almost killed me. And I think . . . I think you're like that, too." He nods, so I keep talking. "It feels like there are some people—me and you—that no matter what, we're always gonna be on the outside. Even if we do everything right, we're always going to *feel* wrong. And it becomes this self-fulfilling prophecy. We feel so lonely and then we make ourselves unreachable. We realize we'll never be enough. We'll never be everything for everyone. Or we'll never be the right person for our right person. So . . . so, you just said fuck it. And I guess I did, too."

"That's . . . that's exactly it," Marco says, his voice soft and urgent. "When we met, all I could think was, what if? What if it wasn't so fucking hard to make something good or even something mediocre? What if I just chose to be okay? What if I just chose a person and went with it?" I lift my eyes from the glistening surface and look at him. His eyes are tearing into me, dark tunnels that press me against the porcelain. "I know that's not romantic."

"I think it's . . ." I swallow roughly. "Very romantic. Or maybe there's something better than romance and we're the only people who've ever found it."

"I'd like that. To have something that's all our own."

I sit up and reach for Marco. He drops my foot and lets me into his arms, sending a tidal wave of water lapping at the edge of the bathtub. He pulls my mouth to his, gentle yet hungry. *Famished.* He kisses me like he wants to sink through me, and I kiss him like I want to give him every ounce of me. Every secret I've ever held inside me. I kiss him like shame doesn't control me.

"Tell me something true," he whispers against my skin, his voice wavering under the weight of restraint or emotion or maybe both.

My body is shaking; it's like I've just had my mind read, every piece of myself pulled out and laid bare. What else is there left to say? Isn't it all obvious? *I'm in love with you. I'm not okay, and maybe I never will be, but I love you.* More than anything I want to ask him why I can't feel the way I looked in his photo.

I close my eyes and press my forehead to his temple. "I feel . . . like I'm in love with you. But I don't know if that's just because I'm finally remembering how much I love being alive."

He tightens his grip on my waist. "We could find out," he whispers back.

"Marco," I say softly, pressing my face into his hair. "If you broke my heart, I would never recover. If you left me, if you hurt me . . . Worse, if I hurt you. I don't know how I'd—"

"Hey." He pulls back, tilting his head so he can look at me. The moon glints off his eyes, heavy-lidded with desire, carving a hard edge over his features—the long slope of his nose, the hollows of his cheeks, the square pout of his mouth. He runs his thumb over my chin. "Me too, okay? Me too."

Then, his thumb keeps moving, slipping over the slick skin at the base of my throat, over my collarbones, and down between my breasts. Underneath the water, I feel him hardening against me, pushing into me. Around us the water cools, and I shiver. His touch is so light, yet persistent and firm. A groan, a raw bid of desire, builds in his chest as he touches me. Under my breasts, around my waist, his fingers travel, his mouth following. Marco takes his time, teasing every inch of my skin until I'm vibrating with desire, every hair follicle on my body raised. His tongue finds the soft, sensitive spot on the side of my neck and his fingers slip between my thighs. A sound catches in my throat, and I arch my back.

"You're sexy when you moan," he breathes into my ear. "Why do you try to keep quiet?"

"I'm trying . . ." My voice comes out in a pant. "I'm trying to let go."

"Stop biting your lip, then," he commands. His voice is rough, deep in the back of his throat.

"I have to hold back. I have to . . ." But I'm not holding back, not anymore.

"That's it," he whispers into my skin, smoothing my hair away from my face. "Much better."

Wednesday, May 17

We sleep late, tangled together in a towel on top of the sheets. When I blink my eyes open Marco's still dozing, sun-kissed cheek flat against his pillow and the soft sound of his breathing. That's when I realize that I'm staring at someone I love.

He blinks his eyes open, as if he can feel the realization settling in my stomach.

I love you, I mouth.

His lips twitch. *I love you, too,* he mouths back.

While Marco sleeps, I sit on the balcony with my bare feet pressed against the wrought iron bars, letting the sun soak into my skin. I don't know why but after months of ignoring almost every part of my "old" life, I open my email. It's an absolute moratorium for a world I no longer recognize.

One email stands out to me. The subject line is just "Hey" and I see it's from K. W. McClain. The sight of his initials sends an immediate, reptilian jolt through me, like a betta fish seeing its own reflection. If I were a cat, I'd be hissing.

Kai.

Hey, not super proud of how we left things. Not gonna lie, I miss ur energy. If it were up to me, I would have pushed for a per-

sonal improvement plan and some vacation time. Srsly, ur talent
is missed greatly.

Btw, New York office is hiring a Creative Director. Ud be perfect.

No hard feelings?

-K

I stare at the email until my eyes go dry.

No hard feelings. A long-lost rage needles at my stomach. Is this
who I used to subject myself to? Grown men who can't be fucked
to type out an entire three-letter word or attempt an apostrophe?
He didn't even have the decency to send such an anemic, vacuous
email from his iPhone. No, he *opened his laptop* and chose to type
like a seventh-grade boy who'd recently discovered negging.

I miss ur energy?

Such a load-bearing sentence. So few words with such little
substance and yet he'd been relying on them to do *so* much. In
Kai's mind, I was probably still sitting dead-eyed and exhausted
with tearstained cheeks, gripping my last advertising award for
Best Thirty-Second Short, praying he'd call. I was never capable
of moving on from the emotional potency of our situationship. It
was just too good, wasn't it? Watching him talk, uninterrupted,
about A24's latest juggernaut after five minutes of vigorous, silent
humping.

Forget about me moving to a new city, getting a new job, and
finding someone so wholly, so *globally* better than him.

What an embarrassing little fuckface.

Oh, Kai, I want to type. *You sweet idiot. There's no going backward for me now. And you are so very, very backward. I've met a man who takes my picture. Who gets jealous of whales for being my favorite animal. Who brings me to Italy and makes love to me in a way that makes me want to use the phrase "make love."*

But I won't do that. The door to that part of my life is closed, locked.

There is no going backward.

My fingers quiver with energy, with excitement, as I delete his email.

"PAOLA INVITED US to her family home in Fregene tonight. It's about twenty minutes away, right on the sea. She said we can stay the night."

"Wow." I look up from the creased paperback I'd been trying and failing to read. Marco's sitting across from me at the breakfast table situated in the corner of our bedroom, eating an apple in front of his laptop. It's kind of funny, and I think back to Allie's wonderment and delight. *Celebs—they're everywhere.* Eating apples. Typing on their laptops. Going to the beach. Making people fall in love with them. "That sounds amazing."

"Good." He stands and stretches, idly running a hand over the soft, curly hair that runs down the center of his chest. Then he comes around, looping an arm around my neck and bringing his sticky, sweet lips to my temple. "Bring your bathing suit."

"Oh, no *way* am I letting any of them see me in a bathing suit."

"What the fuck?" Marco jerks back, away from me. He sounds genuinely pissed. "I love your body."

"Sorry to yuck your yum. I'd just feel *weird* in a bikini around people like that. They're all bony in that generationally wealthy sort of way." I shrug, shutting my book and tossing it onto the table. "I'm not their type of person."

Marco brings his hands to rest on my shoulders, fingers crossing over my throat. "You're exactly their type of people, Nadia."

I'm flattered he thinks I could somehow be a person in his world, but certainly not delusional enough to believe him. I tilt my head back against his stomach. "Are any of them writers?"

"Not like you." He gently chucks me under the chin. There's a hum of pleasure through me. *Not like you.* "I think Giorgio runs an online Marxist zine." We both roll our eyes. "Paola directs plays for the English theater, but I don't think she writes anything."

I guess I am a real writer, even if I've sold my soul for pennies on the pound. "Won't they call me a sellout?"

Marco's mouth twists into a wicked grin. "From behind their designer glasses? Maybe." He presses his lips to my hairline. "Everyone loves you already, I promise."

He pulls away and heads for the bathroom, but before he disappears behind a closed door, I call out to him. "Wait! I hate to ask this, but . . . will you be the most famous person there?"

He throws his head back and laughs.

WE DRIVE OUT to Fregene for a classically late Italian dinner, taking the beltway through a neighborhood that looks, theoretically, rough, but still, I find myself wondering desperately what it would be like to live in one of never-ending rows of brutalist, concrete apartment buildings with pollution-stained balcony railings. To line dry all my clothes. To sit out by a single-pump gas station and smoke a cigarette, watching the sunset over the umbrella pines, knowing that once upon a time, Hannibal and Julius had done this, too. Through thin lace drapes, I spy TVs turned to the news, soccer matches, and game shows; kitchen tables set with colorful cloth; overflowing ashtrays; and I see my parents.

This is where they fell in love. Young and beautiful and full of hope, under this sun.

Here, I kind of see Evergreen. The last few days have been an insulated bubble of privilege, completely submerged in Marco's world. A wonderful, warm escape. But I miss home, I realize. Not Philly, not the ultra-cool studio I used to rent near the El.

I miss Evergreen, the little beach apartment with the leaking skylight. Sitting on the balcony with my sister, smoking a joint with Soph and Allie on the beach. *I miss the produce stand,* I think when we drive past an Ape truck selling peaches out of its minuscule bed. *I miss my peaches.*

Marco squeezes my thigh when we're stopped at a red light, and I startle out of my daydream just as the road opens up and we turn toward the sea.

PAOLA'S FAMILY HOME is a low-slung vermilion villa on a gravel-coated country road that juts right up to the beach. When we pull up to the gate, it unlocks with a horrifying electric buzzing sound and then slowly, noisily rolls open. Paola's on the other side—all limbs and angles in a pair of linen overalls and a bandanna tied around her head. She's tanned deeply, even though it's only May, her black hair pulled over a shoulder.

"Buona sera!" she calls, waving us over to a parking spot under the shade of an olive tree. As soon as we step out of the car, she begins a double-speed monologue in near-perfect English, includ-

ing a posh British accent, while taking my hand in hers. To my surprise, it's warm and soft.

"Welcome to the countryside! We're so glad you two could make it. Giorgio's always sort of sad around his birthday, but I convinced him a dinner with our American friends isn't even *about* him." She throws a wink at me, leading us down a stone-lined path, past a pond and a row of squat palm trees, toward a pergola. Cicadas write their music all around us, and everything smells like honeysuckle. "Tia will bring a cake—of course, not for Giorgio. Who has dinner with no cake? And Martina, his sister—hold on, *Martina*!" Beneath the pergola is a long wooden table, already set for dinner. A woman with honey-colored hair, still wet from the sea, jumps up at the sound of what must be her name. "Martina brought a *parmigiana*, and Giorgio will grill lamb. Do you eat lamb?" This question is aimed at me.

"I-I'll eat anything," I stutter. In a house like this, I really would eat *anything*. Suckling calf. A human heart. The last Atlas lion. "Everything. Whatever you have."

She grins, revealing an adorable chip in one of her front teeth. "Good girl."

The meal unfolds like an orchestral symphony.

The best part is, for the first time all week, I don't feel like I need Marco. Of course I love having him next to me, squeezing my thigh under the table, his fingertips grazing idly over my upper arms as I answer Giorgio's questions about the upcoming American election and the newest litfic starlet. I love knowing he could drive us back to our hotel if I suddenly became too anxious, that if I said I needed a Band-Aid or wanted to eat half a dozen cream puffs, he'd be the first person to hunt down either.

Conversation flows easy, like the plum-colored wine Paola re-
trieves from inside the house. Giorgio sloshes out generous por-
tions from the wicker-covered cask (to everyone except Marco and
me), and about halfway through the bottle, the Overton window
shifts when Martina tells us titty-fucking is called "Spanish sex"
in Italian.

"That's *so* beautiful," I say. "We just call it titty-fucking. That's
the only name it's got."

"Tit-*tee* fucking?" Martina repeats, her mouth pulled down into
an exaggerated blowfish frown, a cigarette burning down to the
quick between her manicured fingers.

"Uh huh," Marco says dryly, leaning back in his chair. He has
one arm draped around my shoulders, his thumb burning a lovely
path as it grazes up and down my skin. "It's like *trash can* or *cross-
walk*. We just call things what they are."

I let out a deep hum of agreement and take my final bite of lamb
chop. "Exactly. Well said."

Marco's eyes slide sideways to me. He's smirking, eyes flickering
like the last embers in a bonfire. "Thanks, baby."

"How *vulgar*." Martina guffaws. Then, she holds up her glass for
a refill. "How horrible this *tit-tee fuck* sounds."

After cake and sorbet, Giorgio and Marco wander off toward
the property line to stare out at the last boats coming back in from
sunset cruises or a day of fishing. In lieu of singing "Happy Birthday," Tia demands that I make some sort of writerly statement. It's
such a crazy demand and all I can do is flap my jaw like Slappy.
They all egg me on and eventually I pull a quote out of my ass—
something I'd read in a book by Ferrante, underlining it until my
ballpoint pen ripped through the paper.

Eventually, I'd written it down on a Post-it note and put it on my vanity mirror, next to the note from Audrey.

It was a line about fucked-up people from a fucked-up place trying desperately to make sense of their own violence, against each other and themselves, each choice another turn down a dark hallway. That was how I'd felt, always.

Each time I made a decision that drew me farther away from my family, I turned another corner. Each time I tried to double back, I found the last place I'd been was now consumed by darkness. So, I wandered, room to room, darkened corner to darkened corner. All I wanted to be was a new whole version of myself—instead, I kept breaking apart.

Now, months later, I realize maybe that's the point. Maybe that's what being alive is. You don't get to resurface, new. You break away; you start again; you molt old skin, altogether too tight and wrong, and while scars fade, they never disappear. At least not right away.

I lift my glass filled with water and say, *"In what disorder we lived, how many fragments of ourselves were scattered, as if to live were to explode into splinters."*

Giorgio, with his big, wet eyes and kind smile, tilts his head. "Ferrante. Impressive."

I nod and lift my glass in his direction. "Cheers to another year of splintering."

TIA BRINGS OUT a platter overflowing with fresh fruit alongside tiny glasses filled with grappa. We watch the men trolling around the parameter with their fists pressed into their hips, giggling at how much they remind us of our fathers' friends.

"You're Italian, right, Nadia?" she asks, setting another scoop of lemon sorbet into the crystal plate.

I nod. "My parents are from the south, Calabria, but I guess I'm not really—"

"But you know a lot about Italy?" Paola jumps in, pushing a perfectly ripe fig in my direction. I'd already eaten one—the sweetest, creamiest fruit that had ever passed between my lips. Was I really allowed to have another?

"Of course she does," Martina says, with a series of shoulder shrugs. "She can quote Ferrante."

"That's because I want to *be* Ferrante," I gush suddenly. "I'm hoping to absorb some of her talent through osmosis. If I could just write one single grocery list as beautiful as her prose, I'd die happy."

"Of course you can," Martina says, throwing around her favorite phrase. To Martina, everything is *of course*. She slips another cigarette from her half-empty pack and pushes it between her lips. "You're Italian."

Her logic is so simple, it makes instant sense. I want to bottle up Martina's confidence and carry it around with me forever.

"I don't know," I say, nervous laughter dotting my speech. "I guess I haven't tried."

Paola bumps her shoulder against mine. "If you ever do, let me read it first."

"You will." Marco reappears, plopping back down into the chair next to me. "When you're ready to, you will."

"Well, excuse me," I say, turning in his direction. "How long have you been holding on to that astute little observation?"

He smirks, skimming his fingers over his hair, pushing it away from his eyes. "It took me a minute, but I got a read on you now."

Before I can come back at him with a clever retort, Martina grabs ahold of my arm and squeezes. "You should write one of those books where the narrator is a liar!"

"I love those," Paola gasps. I want Martina's confidence and Paola's ability to experience the world so orgasmically. "A saucy heroine with a deadly secret!"

Martina and Tia shriek and cackle. *"Daje!"*

A memoir, I want to say. Instead, I shove another fig in my mouth and let them cook up the perfect story.

WITH THE LAST sip of grappa drained from Giorgio's glass, we all kiss and hug goodbye. Marco and Paola take a moment to embrace, and I can hear him thanking her, over and over, for everything.

"Take her to the beach, Marco," she urges him, under her breath. "You *must.*"

Thankfully, he listens to her. We drive down to the end of the gravel road, where the pebbles turn to sand.

"That was quite the quote you pulled out," Marco says, grasping my hand and helping me up the steep incline that leads to the beach. "I've never seen Giorgio impressed before."

"I love your friends. They're brilliant." I couldn't possibly be drunk, but the softness of the evening has seeped into me. With one hand holding on to my shoes and the other wagging in the air to keep my balance, we make our way down toward the nearly silent tide. "Tonight was incredible. Fun and . . . and, I don't know, *electric.* I miss being around other artists, I guess." The shoreline is deep and the sand has retained its warmth from the day, grittier and sturdier than Evergreen's beach. I can imagine the sea as it looked when we drove by earlier—a lazy swirl of cobalt and aquamarine—but right now it's a glassy stretch of indigo calm.

The wind keeps us from moving quickly toward the tide, blowing back the fabric of my dress and melding Marco's T-shirt to the curvature of his frame. We find a spot where the sand turns moist and solid, then we sit.

Marco leans backward onto his elbows, looking up at me with an expression that must mirror my own: a hazy, heavy look of deep satisfaction. "I told you. You're meant for a world like theirs, for big things. You fit in perfectly."

For some reason, this hurts more than an actual insult from Marco might. I almost can't stand that he thinks my life is the way it is because I'm in a stage of transition. I almost can't stand how well I've tricked him into thinking I am still someone who takes great risks and lives an interesting life.

I can't stand that he thinks he's just a pit stop on a very long road unfurling ahead of me, filled with just the right amount of twists and turns. To Marco, it's certainly not a road that ends abruptly, when I'm still young. It's not a road checkered with gaping potholes or endless loops backward.

No, I want to say, *falling in love with you is the greatest thing I will ever do. Being here with you, under all of these stars. This is me peaking.*

He takes my silence in stride. Marco is, after all, very good at listening. He takes the quiet the way he takes my words.

I bring my knees into my chest, hugging myself. Finally, I say: "I like living a small life. I like living by the beach and working for Soph. Maybe that sounds sad or pathetic, but when I keep things small . . ."

When I keep things small, I can manage. I can manage my depression. I can manage being sick.

I squeeze my eyes shut and try to find different words. "Getting to where I did in my career before took *everything* out of me. That job was my life, and I can't even believe what I missed out on because of it. I wouldn't see the sun for days sometimes. I'd get to work before the sun rose and leave when it was dark out. I'd fall asleep at my desk. I kept an emergency toothbrush and change of clothes in case I had to stay all night. And doing what?" I shake my head. "Writing commercials? Designing pitch decks?

"Martina and Giorgio . . . your friends. *You*. You guys are different from me. You're . . . rich people. You were born to write like Ferrante and take beautiful pictures and eat figs under a Mediterranean sunset. I'm . . . utilitarian."

Marco pushes himself up suddenly, dusting the sand off his hands. "Are you fucking kidding me?"

I snap my eyes over to Marco. "What?"

"Nadia, you're fucking brilliant—"

"You don't have to say that. I'm not fishing—"

"Yes." He laughs incredulously. "Yes, I do. I've been around you. Every day. For almost a month. You know *so* many things. You read constantly—more than Giorgio ever has. You remember details about people and places you hear one time. You're basically a fucking botanist."

"Please tell Soph that. They'll laugh until they shit."

"Seriously," Marco says. "Why are you so hard on yourself?"

"Why are *you* so hard on yourself?" I counter. "You called yourself a *user*. If this is how you use people, sign me up for life." The sentence flies out of my mouth before I can stop it, but I'm not embarrassed. It's the truth.

"Because I am," he replies quietly. "And I come from a long line of users. But I want to be different—"

"You." I take hold of his face in my hands. "Are. You are different. You *love* me, Marco. And I don't mean that in an emotional way, I mean that in an active verb kind of way. You love me down to my core. You fill me up with goodness, make me feel seen and safe and like I could just—"

My mouth stalls. Suddenly, my eyes prick with tears.

I feel the warm planes of his hands moving up and down my arms. "What?"

"I've been lying to you." I suck down a shaky breath. "I've been lying about who I am, Marco. All of this. This person I'm being for May. It's a lie. The real Nadia is fucking . . ."

I try. I really do. I try to force the word *sick* to my lips, but it just won't come.

Instead I say: "*Depressed*. She lies in bed for weeks on end and eats too much candy and doesn't brush her teeth. She reads books because they take her out of her body. I *hate* my body."

"Hey—it's okay." He brings his hands to my cheeks, now slick with tears.

"The real Nadia is a runner. As soon as things get hard, she runs and hides and cowers."

"Then I guess I'm a liar, too," he says, his voice deep and catching. "I haven't dated a woman for more than three dates in years. I've never lived with a woman, traveled with a woman, woken up next to a woman and not felt shame and anxiety. I've *never* been in love before. And worst of all, I lied to you to get you here—I told you it would only be for May and I knew I'd want more. I looked at you and I thought, *I can be different. I can do this.* And I feel like . . ." He pauses to let out a short, joyful laugh. "Like I am better with you. I don't know what you were like before, but maybe we can keep going, you know? Beyond May."

There is no before, I want to tell him. Instead, I press my forehead to his. "Maybe."

He doesn't push me any further. Instead, he holds me. We stay like this, bowed close together, reverent.

"Why did we do this to ourselves?" he whispers eventually.

"Chaos demons," I reply. "We left our chaos demons chained up for too long."

A chuckle thrums through his chest. I burrow my face into his neck and breathe in the scent of him as he says, "Let's just *stay here,* then"

"Fine, I'll run away to Italy with you."

"Twist my damn arm, Nadia."

Finally, we're laughing again. He tightens his arms around me, then pulls us backward until we're lying flat in the sand, his stubble grazing back and forth across my forehead.

I think back to the moment we first met—I'd been so afraid of becoming some sort of footnote or side quest in Marco's long and fabulous life, discarded after three days like an old rag. Instead, I'd fallen into something bigger. *What are we doing?* I want to ask, desperately. *Why are we doing this?* If there's one thing I know with total certainty, it's that Marco and I seem obsessed with, alarmingly drawn to, hurting ourselves. *Are we good for each other?*

Instead, I ask, "Hey, why did you publish your photographs as Adam West?"

"Adam West's the original Batman. He was a total stud."

"Really?" I lean away to look up at him. "*That's* why?"

"Not everything has to be complicated, Nadia. Not everything is a deep, treacherous metaphor."

"Oh, right," I chuckle. "Silly me."

Thursday, May 18

Our plane lands safely in Philly and, thankfully, nothing changes between us—not yet at least. That's what I'm afraid of the entire time we're in the air; all I can think about is how there are these versions of myself I've layered on so thick, like wallpaper in an old home, that the strata of my fakeness are surely starting to show.

I told him I'm a liar. Now he knows.

I barely took my medicine in Rome. A Meloxicam here and there to keep me going, but I mostly left my organ insurance pills rotting in the bottom of my suitcase underneath a few paperbacks and my dirty clothes pile. I knew he'd never go looking in there.

It's only a matter of time.

I'll be just like Charlize. Marco will find me, sobbing in my apartment, close to death.

Watching Charlize, you can't help but think: *You don't even look sick. Just get up and let yourself be loved.*

Now, I say this to myself. *Just let yourself be loved. You can figure it out. It's not that complicated.*

It's not. Loving a sick person is quite simple. You just have to be selfless and extremely patient and incredibly flexible. You have to be okay with hearing *no* and *I can't* and *not today* over and over, coming home to find that the once-vibrant, formerly brilliant person you thought you were dating is now green-gray and wearing the same ratty, foul pajamas you left her in hours ago. You have to know how to worry about the right things, bracing for the pain before it comes, like, *What triggers her migraines?* And *Will she need one of my kidneys?*

Marco talks about himself like he's something difficult: a societal menace that should be covered in caution tape and framed with stop signs. But Marco's flaws—too honest, too worried he'll fuck up, too thoughtful, too nervous he won't be good enough—are things I can help with. Or at least I could try.

There's no helping me.

When we land, there's no awkward decision-making conversation. We climb into Marco's car and drive back to his uncle's house, on the far side of the bay. We park in the same garage he walked me through the very first night we met and I leave my shoes at the door, no black footprints or forehead blood trailing behind me this time.

I follow him inside as he carries our bags, picking up the mail and the local papers that have accumulated on the porch. Marco's on the phone talking to someone without any worry if I overhear. He talks about a showcase in LA and a gallery in Miami and an investor. While he orders us dinner, I water his uncle's plants and replace the empty rolls of toilet paper.

We've stitched ourselves to each other. And I'm not ready to lose him yet. I'm not ready to rip myself away.

Friday, May 19

Soph: nadia youre back from la citta eterna right????

Allie: Yes babe it's on the calendar

Soph: well sorry, I haven't seen her yet and her cars not here

Allie: That's because she's in loooooooooove jail!

Soph: love jail????

Allie: Love jail! You know, the first three months of any relationship where you disappear off the face of the earth spending all your time, energy, and money on your new lover.

Soph: omg no way

Nadia: Good morning, assholes! I am absolutely not in love jail. I am at Marco's, and I promise everything will be back to normal very soon.

Allie: You're STILL AT HIS PLACE???

Nadia: Yeah, why? Everything ok?

Soph: hahahahahahhaahahah

Allie: Hahahahhahaha

Nadia: What?!

Soph: you are so totally in love jail

Saturday, May 20

My phone has been ringing every few days, and I keep letting it go to voicemail, but today, Liv texts me before she calls.

can you talk?

With Marco, I am so blissful if I wasn't lying down, I would be floating. We are two stars in the galaxy, light-years away from everyone else's bullshit.

I watch him step out of the shower, a white towel hanging heavily around his hips, and comb his hair away from his face. I try to imagine the aftermath of all this. It's foggy, as far off and unbelievable as the days I lived before all of this. So, I decide while lying in his bed that I won't think about what comes after—at least not for another hour.

I delete Liv's text.

"I SHOULD PROBABLY . . ."
I don't want to leave Marco—and I certainly don't want to leave his uncle's house with its impeccably curated coastal decor and eastern-facing sunroom that has become my own personal bayside retreat. But like any good Catholic, I'm suspicious of this happiness—this time slip I've fallen into with Marco.

I need to get ready for my real life—which is approaching faster with every day—and I need to do laundry, and I'm *sick*. I can act like I'm not, but I have a monthly standing doctor's appointment with Marco's cousin next week. What's more real than that?

I'm in a cold war with my sister; shouldn't I be thinking about that?

Not that I've tried to call her—or even thought about answering one of her texts or calls. But I should think about it—how I'll explain all of this to her in a way that gets her to finally apologize.

I jab my thumb toward the front door and click my tongue against the roof of my mouth. "You know, pound sand."

Marco looks up from his phone. He's wearing reading glasses. Big, wire-framed reading glasses. My heart melts in my chest. I almost drop my suitcase handle. "Why?" he asks.

"I don't know, I've just sort of been . . . here. In your hair."

He furrows his brow at me. "By all means, if you need to get going—but you're not in my hair."

I chew at my bottom lip for a moment. *I really don't want to leave.* Why can't he just be an asshole, make this easy on me? "Don't you need to work out or call your wife?"

Marco rolls his eyes at me before spinning his laptop around. "The lab just sent me digital scans of these photos from Rome. I want your thoughts on an arrangement."

What's happening? I can't tear myself away. A sudden pang of anxiety hits me square in the solar plexus. *I can't even leave Marco for a night.*

"I can't help you with that."

I know the sensation in my stomach has reached my face because Marco's standing, crossing the room toward me. "You okay?"

"I just really think I need to do some laundry." This sentence comes out louder, harsher than I want it to.

He freezes, a hand reflexively jumping to pull at his hair. "Sure. Of course."

"Right." I swallow roughly and yank my suitcase back to my side before turning toward the front hall. "I'll see you."

"Nadia . . ." I feel Marco's force field as he comes up behind me, hooking a finger under the strap of my purse and pulling at it lightly until it falls from my shoulder. Then, he slowly spins me, without really using any force, back around to face him. "Can you tell me what's actually going on?"

I drop my eyes to the Persian rug underneath our feet. It's beautiful, ornate. So unlike anything in the house waiting for me on the other side of the island. "I have to get used to this."

"To what?" He sounds genuinely confused.

"Being without you. *Leaving* you."

Marco falls into a respectful stillness, but when I lift my gaze to meet his, there's a bright smile in his eyes. Not mocking me but amused in a way that makes me feel like he's not getting it. "A dry run for when you lace up your running sneakers in ten days?"

"It's not funny," I snap. "This isn't a fucking joke."

Without another word, Marco closes the space between us, pulling me flat against his chest and wrapping his arms around my neck as he presses his lips to my temple.

"You're right," he whispers, lips moving against my hair. "I shouldn't have said that."

Sunday, May 21

I can hardly believe Memorial Day Weekend, and the official start of Shore season, is almost here. Every moment of winter and spring had passed at an excruciatingly slow pace, taunting me with alternating cold snaps and unseasonably warm weekends, punctuated by cherry blossoms that blossomed then wilted, blossomed then wilted, in a never-ending edge toward longer, warmer days.

Why couldn't May pass like that? Why couldn't this entire month stretch on with the same languid drip of February?

Regardless, the start of the busy season means more deliveries, so Soph and I head out before sunrise like the only thing that's changed is the weather. Dawn breaks earlier and brighter behind a heavy layer of fog. I finally only need a flannel to keep me warm. I grab Marco's favorite green one off the back of a dining room chair and scribble a note letting him know my schedule for the day. I sign it with a heart and a capital *N*.

On our way out to the farm, Soph keeps stealing sideways glances at me, probably waiting for me to open up, explain where I've been. It's easy enough to ignore this early in the morning. I bury my face in my thermos of coffee and turn up our favorite morning radio show, knowing that when we get to work everything will move as it always does. Indeed, once we get to work the only sound between Soph and me is the steady crunch of grass and gravel underneath our boots as we load up the flatbed with our deliveries for the day.

I forgot how quick and strong Soph is. The only time they pause is to point out a gopher they spy scurrying through the high grass along the path that leads from the road to the greenhouse and fields.

I'm trying my best to keep up. I can't remember if I ever did, but today it feels like I need to. Soph's bigger than me, both taller and broader, but when they stack three crates and carry them without a dolly, I do the same. I barely make it to the truck before my knees buckle and the crates slip from my quaking fingers, falling with a raucous thud—thankfully—onto the bed of the truck.

"Whoa." Soph jogs over, steadying me with a hand on my back. "You okay?"

"Fine," I grunt, trying to recover, but the way the raw wooden slats slid through my hands, they managed to take a solid slice of flesh with them. The outer side of my hand looks raw and pink, blood just beginning to rush to the surface with a sting. "Fuck. Shoulda worn my damn gloves."

"Hold on, I have a first aid kit." Soph climbs into the cab of the truck, returning with a blue nylon pouch that unzips to reveal all the medical supplies they might need to perform a minor surgery. Soph quickly swipes an alcohol-soaked piece of gauze over my wound.

"Shit," I hiss again, biting down on the inside of my cheek. My already weak hands are locking up from the pain and the sudden chill moving over me, now that my heart isn't thundering from effort in my chest. A cold sweat drags down my skin.

"I can take it from here—"

"No, you can't. You're literally gray right now." The moments play out like a stop-motion film with frames removed: Soph puts both their hands on my shoulders and leads me around to the passenger seat of the truck. Now I'm seated and my hand's bandaged and resting against my chest.

I lean my head back and let my eyes fall shut, taking a series of big, gulping breaths to calm my nerves. "You're worried about me," I say without opening my eyes.

Gravel crunches under their boots as they sway from foot to foot. "You've been pushing yourself a lot lately. I don't want you to overextend yourself." After a moment of quiet, Soph adds: "Allie wants you and Marco to come over for dinner tomorrow night."

I blink my eyes open. "Are you staging some sort of love intervention?"

"No, not yet." Soph laughs, leaning against the open door. "We just want to hang out with you—both of you. It's been a while."

"Then why are you asking me like there's a gun pressed to the back of your head?"

"I-I don't know, I wasn't sure if . . ." Soph takes a moment to gather their thoughts. "It's already the twenty-first."

I look away. It is, isn't it? We have about a week left together, and neither Marco nor I have made any moves to amend our contract. "What can we bring? Lemon squares? Balderdash?"

"I'm sorry, I didn't mean to make you feel bad."

I press a thumb to the center of my forehead, the beginnings of a headache forming. Did I take my medicine last night? I can't remember. It's been so easy to forget. Tonight I'll get back on track. "It's okay. I'm really happy right now, okay? I am, and maybe it's absolutely delusional but I'm just going with it."

"If you open up to him about being sick, maybe you guys could figure something out—"

"What if I don't want to be sick?" I cut Soph off. "What if I just want to be this version of me a little bit longer? Is that okay with you, or have you been in contact with my fucking sister and you're working together on a full reeducation plan?"

"Jesus Christ, Nadia." They sigh, dragging a hand down their face. "Sorry. I'm trying to be here for you." Then, after a pause: "I didn't know about your sister."

I can't bring myself to look at Soph, so I direct all my words at the reed-lined horizon and the empty stretch of highway ahead of me. "If I could be this version of Nadia forever, I would do it in a heartbeat. I can do anything he wants. I can go anywhere. I can get on a plane and show up at an art gallery and eat sushi in New York."

"I hate that I know exactly what you mean," Soph says. "It's like . . . like, even after I came out to my parents. I just wanted to be who I was with you guys with them. But . . ." They pause to drag their teeth over their bottom lip. "I couldn't."

Neither one of us does well with vulnerability, so I send my eyes down to my injured hand resting in my lap. A dark stretch of blood is peeking through the fabric of the Band-Aid. My throat hurts. I feel the soft rot of fatigue in my bones.

"I think I'm feeling better now," I say. "Let's finish this up."

INSTEAD OF STAYING at Marco's, I decide to head home. Alone in his cavernous house on the bay, I pack my bag and leave a note.

I feel it coming. A migraine, a flare-up, a *something*. My body isn't recovering like before; each throb through the injured center of my hand reminds me of this. My thoughts are simultaneously foggy and jagged; each one passes through my head like a thunderbolt, rocking me with a red-hot jolt of pain that travels through the nerves on my face, down my neck, into my bloodstream. The pain colonizes my body.

I'm terrified of Marco catching me in my lie like this: walking into the living room to find me green with nausea, dry vomit on my shirt; crying on the bathroom floor, locked up and disoriented by pain.

I'll tell him tomorrow, I promise myself as I crawl into bed. I need to take my medicine but it's so far away. I actually don't even remember where I left it.

Monday, May 22

"Dinner with the family," Marco jokes, pulling into the carport behind Soph's truck. "I should have brought flowers."

I roll my eyes until they land on his. "Save that stunning sense of humor for inside. We're gonna need it."

"Should I be more nervous? I've met Soph and Allie. They're great—"

"Yeah, but you didn't meet them when you were my . . . you know, an actual boyfriend that I spent time with." I shrug, reapplying a slick coat of lip gloss in the orange light of the car mirror. "You were just some guy with a mullet."

This gives Marco pause. He crosses his arms over his chest. "They're gonna be different?"

"Maybe." I shrug and flip the mirror closed. "They're very protective of me."

"So am I! I'm an alpha."

"Mmmm." I tilt my head from side to side. "But are you misandrist-oceanside-gays level of protective over me?"

"I can be," he defends himself. "Just let me google a few things."

As we make our way around the car and up the front porch steps, Marco laces his fingers with mine and says, "We should stay at your place tonight."

Without thinking, I scoff. "You do not want that, believe me. The whole place smells like middle-class ennui and gardenia potpourri."

"Oh, c'mon." He pulls his hand out of mine. "It can't be that bad. You're being dramatic."

I poke a finger into his chest. "One night in my bed and you'll be crying for your uncle's two-thousand-thread-count organic sheets."

"Hold on." Marco laughs, rubbing a hand over the spot I poked as he leans back against the old creaky railing. His expression changes, the angles of his face softening. "You don't really think I'm some shitty satin-slipper-prince type, do you?"

"Satin slipper?" I laugh. "I would love to see you in a pair of satin slippers. Oh, and a leotard."

"Be serious, Nadia. I know we're from different backgrounds, but—"

"But what? Marco, you own property on the island of Manhattan. You wear cologne and use a leave-in conditioner. I have an hourly wage job and sports asthma. It's not a big deal." I shrug, leaning forward to place my hands on his shoulders. He's wearing a horribly fashionable bomber jacket; I looked the brand up, contemplating snatching the jacket from his closet for myself, and almost puked when I saw how much it cost. "We sleep at your uncle's. I love your uncle's! I love organic sheets!"

He sets his jaw hard, hooking a finger on one of my belt loops and tugging me close. "We're staying at your place tonight."

"Why do I have to suffer in order for you to prove a point?"

"Because I want to see where you live."

I sigh, giving his cheek a swipe before turning back toward the door, but secretly, I feel a rush of new, sparkling emotion in my chest. We'd just had a disagreement that was terrifyingly, thrillingly normal.

I pause before knocking on Soph and Allie's front door. I can't stand the idea of going into Soph and Allie's without seeing Marco one last time—getting in a final word or maybe just pressing my mouth to his and sucking all the good faith out of his soul like a Dementor—so I spin around. To my surprise, Marco is extremely close behind me, mouth hanging open as he, apparently, also had one more thing he needed to say.

But when our eyes connect we both break out into laughter. I lean forward into his arms, letting my forehead fall against his shoulder as his hands slide around my lower back.

"You're not a satin-slipper prince-bitch," I murmur against his skin. He smells delicious and familiar, like bar soap and warm skin. I want to spend the entire night making out with him on this porch.

"Thank you." He presses his lips into the crown of my head, pulsing his hands around me. "I needed to hear that."

ALLIE ANSWERS THE door so quickly, I have no choice but to believe she'd been standing there with her ear pressed against the oiled oak, listening to our entire conversation.

"Soph made Cornish hens!" she announces, flinging a long, lissome arm into the air, nearly launching her empty wineglass into the ceiling.

"Oh, wow." I raise my brows. "And you?"

She waves us into the apartment, giving me a devilish look before holding an empty glass up to one of her icy-blue eyes. "I taste-tested all the wines."

We shed our jackets before following close behind. I'm reminded why I've always preferred to spend time here rather than upstairs; Allie and Soph's apartment is identical to my family's unit, except it's extremely well-decorated and contains exactly zero humiliating photos of me. An eclectic mix of relics from Soph and Allie's separate and shared lives covers the walls, bringing the small, beige space to life. Art from Allie's days traveling across South America; pennant flags from Soph's time on the Jersey City intramural rugby team; an overstuffed couch and a long, wooden table covered in candle wax and water rings. Soph's behind the island in the kitchen area, basting their hens while bossa nova drifts on the fragrant air.

"Yo, yo," they call out to us. Marco and Soph shake hands, exchanging strong and dignified looks of approval, and suddenly it really does feel like Marco's meeting my parents. I blush and twirl my hair while they appraise each other.

"Your home is beautiful," Marco says, handing over the bottle of Sicilian Merlot we chose entirely based on the design merits of the label. "Thank you so much for having us."

"Great choice." Soph palms the bottle. "This will go perfectly with the squash blossom risotto."

"Oh my God, *yum*." Allie sneaks up behind Soph and snags the bottle from their hands. Little wine thief. "It took us way too long to do this. It's so nice to have another couple to hang out with."

"Uh, ouch, hello. I'm the not-couple you're usually hanging out with." I grab a grape off the expansive charcuterie board laid out on the island and pop it into my mouth. "And you're serving produce we didn't even grow. So much betrayal."

"You should feel honored I hand-selected fruit all the way from Chile, just for you," Soph teases, heading back to their workstation. Marco follows behind, doing the man thing where he needs to feel useful. If Soph doesn't give him a potato to peel, he's going to start jimmying loose handles and analyzing all the caulking.

After Allie has another glass and a half of wine, we move to the table and dig in to a meal so well prepared, Marco is stunned into an awe-filled silence. Every few bites of risotto, he looks at Soph like he wants to kiss them directly on the mouth.

"I'm sure you've heard all about Nadia's illustrious career in Super Bowl–commercial writing," Allie says, tossing a wink at me between the stemware and taper candles.

"Her specialty," Soph adds dryly.

"Alright, you two. Don't make me separate you." Thank God the lights are dimmed, because there's a swatch of pink growing up from the neckline of my shirt.

"No, actually." Marco eyes me from across the table, the corner of his mouth twitching. Since we've gotten home from Rome, he hasn't shaved his face bare and there's a dark shadow over his cheeks and jaw that makes my stomach clench pleasantly. "I haven't."

"I wrote like, five spots. Only two of them went. It's not a big deal."

"That's two more than most people! My favorite was the one for the laundry detergent brand. I sobbed."

"And there was the one about travel, right?" Soph says, then catches themselves, immediately turning as red as the capicola drying on the charcuterie board between us.

"That one doesn't count," I quip, trying to sound casual. *As long as Marco doesn't notice the way the air has changed around us,* I tell myself. *That's all that matters.*

"What else should I know about Nadia?" Marco directs this question at Allie, the weaker of the two.

"Careful, now," I warn Allie and Soph. "Remember, we share plumbing. I can make your life really miserable."

"I don't know. What's there to know?" Allie is looking at me with drunken, glassy-eyed wonder. "She looks like a sexy mermaid and Shakira had a baby. She's funny and thoughtful and snores. Her favorite color is pink."

"Favorite cake is carrot," Soph chimes in. "Or anything with cream cheese frosting."

I feel Marco's legs shift closer to mine under the table. He bumps his knee against mine, but I can't look up from my plate. I'm absolutely burning up with the humiliation that usually accompanies genuine praise. "Marco knows plenty now. Thank you all so much."

"What about you?" Allie demands, wagging a fork heavy with salad at Marco. Tiny little droplets of oil fling toward his white T-shirt. "Now it's your turn to talk."

We finish out the meal talking about our favorite viral videos and swapping stories about where we were on 9/11. There's never a moment of silence, and as we clear the table—Marco pulling on a pair of yellow gloves and filling the sink with sudsy, hot water—I'm struck down to my core with how much fun I'm having. It's a warm, safe fun that nestles into my chest like nostalgia. I already miss this moment—Marco laughing while Allie throws herself around, telling a story about one of her students, Soph looking on and chuckling in their nervous way. As it happens, I feel myself pulling away, unable to silence the voice in my head that whispers that soon this will all be gone.

Marco's phone rings and he excuses himself, and I take over at the sink, pulling on the rubber gloves and submerging my arms into the water.

"God, how cute is he? And he's obsessed with you. You two are practically married," Allie swoons, pressing a hand to her heart. "It's fucking adorable."

Soph catches my eye, and I look away as fast as I can. "No, not at all. We just click, you know? It's really easy. We're having fun."

"I don't know, Nadia. He's giving long-term-partner vibes—"

"Allison, enough," Soph cuts in calmly.

"Jeeeeeez, full name. What'd I do?"

"Nothing." I shrug, trying to sound unshaken. "Let's just talk about something else."

"But what happens next?" Allie whines, hopping up onto the counter. "We can't just act like everything goes back to normal—"

"This is the last thing I want to talk about right now, ma'am. You're drunk."

Soph pushes off the island and slips between Allie's legs, wrapping their arms around her waist. "She'll give herself another mental-breakdown haircut, and we'll all move on."

I laugh, even though that joke kind of stings. "See? There you go. Soph always has a solution."

"Ugh, I love the short hair—why do we have to call it a mental-breakdown haircut—?"

The balcony door slides open and Marco steps back inside. "Sorry about that. My brother called and then my stepmom got ahold of the phone."

"You better be." I snap off the rubber gloves. "I haven't worked this hard in years."

"Leave the dishes," Soph says, corralling us back toward the table. "I made us a tiramisu."

AFTER DINNER, I lead Marco up to the second story of the beach house, making a show of our arrival. I Vanna White in front of the pale blue front door with the faded *Welcome* wreath my mom bought from a yard sale approximately fifteen years ago.

"Three bedrooms. Two baths. One skylight. Innumerable bugs. One lazy piece of shit. Three doors that don't work—"

"Okay, I get it." He laughs. "Let me in."

"I'm not done! Three doors that don't work, and tonight? One celebrity." I press my hands to Marco's chest as he rolls his eyes and gently pushes my hands away.

"You're hilarious."

"Aren't I?" I turn the key in the door and, with a shaky breath, push it open. "Ta-daaaaa."

The apartment is exactly as it always has been, exactly as it always will be. The furniture is all slightly too small with faded fabric and scuffed corners from years of use. Our kitchen table is wicker and glass, a real 1980s coke-den special. But moonlight pours in from the skylight, drenching our island—smaller than Soph's—and the countertops, and the space feels clean, pristine, compared to downstairs. There's no art on our walls, just family pictures in heavy frames.

Soph sent us away with an armful of leftovers that I put away while Marco walks around the room. He's moving slowly, almost with reverence. He runs his fingertips over the afghan draped over the back of the couch. He pauses to look at every picture of us on the walls.

My mom's favorite photo is one of me, Liv, and Nicky on the beach in Calabria one summer when we went to visit her family, taken on a Kodak camera and now hanging next to our TV.

We're all standing in the shallow sea tide, deeply tanned and hair unkempt. Nicky's grinning with all his might, Liv's arms tucked protectively around his neck. I'm squatting at their feet, my chin against my knees, eyebrows furrowed in contemplation. We all look so much like ourselves.

Marco squints at our little, dusty faces. "Look at you. Adorable little moppet."

"See, I've always been a mystery."

He lets out a deep laugh. "Your home—your life—it's nice, Nadia. It's really nice."

"Is it?" I ask quietly, crossing my arms over my chest.

He nods. "It feels full, saturated with—I don't know, good things. Your friends, your parents—" He jabs his thumb toward the photo. "I've never had anything like this."

Saturated with good things. I shift awkwardly at his words. I bite at my lower lip and ask, "Does that . . . bother you?"

"No. I mean, yes. But not actively." He furrows his brow, shoving his hands down into his pockets. "You have a lot to be grateful for."

"I know," I say softly. "I've never brought a guy home to meet anyone before. They can be a lot. It's not like a white picket fence type of situation. It's all very messy and loud and someone is always in crisis. I always sort of . . . kept people away, because I was embarrassed. And it can be hard to explain . . ." I gesture around the room. It can be hard to explain something so simple, so traditional, so pretense-less when it always seemed like everyone around me was reaching out for more. When I had always been reaching out for more. How many times had I pushed my mom to replace the brocade couch? How many times had I made fun of the swollen, squeaky doors that wouldn't shut? How many questions had I evaded from Kai—and all the guys like Kai—over the years?

Saturated with good things.

Marco keeps his eyes trained on the photo of me and my siblings as he speaks. "I had the white picket fence situation for fourteen years. And it was dark. A lot of fucked-up things happen behind white picket fences in big beige houses."

His sudden confession stuns me; I stay planted with my back against the island, holding my arms around myself.

Marco felt at home in a world of self-harm masquerading as hedonism and glamour. In a crowded room full of people trying to feel something, Marco could finally shut off the part of him that felt too much. The little boy, scared and lonely on the boardwalk.

The man who stepped behind the camera and wanted to disappear.

How idiotic am I? It'd never occurred to me that Marco's struggles with substances came from something deeper than the vicious speed run through Hollywood he'd endured. I feel stripped down, embarrassed. It's not just that Marco doesn't know I have lupus. Do I really even know him enough to say *I love you*?

Or are we just fucking kidding ourselves?

In the moonlight, he looks older. The boyishness in his eyes is tucked behind a self-affixed blankness, that distance he can so easily create creeping back in. His mouth is settled into a tight, humorless smile, and he looks very, very tired. I want to kiss every part of him, make him feel good and loved. I don't need to know everything about him in order to know I want to love him.

I round the island and cross the room.

"Hey." I push his hair back from his face, letting my fingers glance along the heavy pull of his brow. I want to massage away his frown. "You're okay now. I'm here."

His mouth twitches as he shakes his head, as if he's clearing his mind like an Etch A Sketch. "Sorry. I don't know what my problem is."

"No." I want him to reach out and pull me to his chest, but he's already turning away, toward the hallway.

"I'm exhausted," he says, voice flat. "Show me those sheets you've been talking about."

That *distance*. It's been weeks since I've felt it. And even though Marco waits for me to lead him down the hall, his hands eventually coming down to rest on my hips, there is a heavy, leaden weight dragging through my chest as I realize I'm not the only one who can run away.

Tuesday, May 23

I'm sorry, okay? Please, Nadia, please pick up. I really need to talk."
  I listen to Liv's voicemail over and over while I sit awake on the cold bathroom tile. I try typing a message out to her three, four times but I don't know how to explain any of this. It's all too much, too long.

Where do I start? How do I even begin to explain what's happened since we last spoke? That my silence was only one part righteous anger—another part humiliation?

I press my eyes shut and fat tears roll down my cheeks. I miss my sister so much it hurts. It's like I haven't slept in years and the entirety of what I've done is physically weighing on my brain, pressing it down into my spine so powerfully I feel like my eyes might explode out of my head.

I'm curled around the toilet bowl in the hall bathroom, sweat pouring down my back. Marco's here with me, in my parents' Shore house. He says he likes it. Would he tell me if he didn't? He only has to pretend for eight more days.

I suppress a small whimper, holding back a bigger, heavier, pain-filled sob. What's that old adage—a hit dog will holler? A sick woman sobs.

The last few days have been consumed with *trying*. Trying to keep my pain at bay. Trying to keep Marco from noticing something's wrong. Trying to act like this version of myself I've been isn't a flickering mirage, bound to disappear if he gets any closer.

I force up what's left in my stomach, praying this will relieve some of the leaden dread pulling me toward the center of Earth, collapsing me in on myself. It doesn't.

I rinse out my mouth and then crawl into bed, skating through the freezing sheets until I find Marco's warm body. He's almost always boiling hot. That's something I'll remember about him— about us. I'll see his face on the cover of *Variety*, and I'll remember, decades before, the way his tanned, soft summer skin felt when it met mine.

"What's wrong?" he whispers, turning toward me, his mouth finding my forehead. I breathe in his scent. *Do you really love me?* I want to know, even if it hurts my feelings. I want to know everything he's ever thought; if we had met in a different way, I'd spend a lifetime teasing each thought out, turning over his opinions like precious artifacts. "Hey, tell me what's wrong."

It's happening again. Not like last time. But almost. "I'm sick," I whisper.

A hand replaces his lips on my forehead. "You're okay."

I laugh a little through my tears and he pulls me close, wrapping heavy arms around me. He presses his lips into the salty rivulets on my cheek. "You'll feel better soon."

"What's this?"

I look up from the paperback I'm trying—and failing—to read, my body wrung out and tossed over the love seat. I can't get the letters to stop swimming across the page in a purple-green swirl. I keep blinking hard. That usually does the trick. Not today.

Even the early-morning sunbeam, the one I've loved since I was a child, hurts today.

When I lift my eyes, I find Marco standing in the long, dark hallway that leads to my parents' bedroom holding up a gallon Ziploc bag.

My breathing stalls for a moment. My hearing dims.

The bag is filled with orange pill bottles, and they rattle as he lifts them.

I must have mindlessly left them out when I was looking for . . .

Looking for my medicine. Trying to make up for lost time.

Fucking idiot.

I push myself upright, letting the book fall from my hands. It hits the floor and slaps shut. "My migraine medicine."

Marco looks between me and the bag, his expression unreadable. "How many migraines do you get?"

I grit my teeth, forcing myself upright and across the room to snag the bag out of his hands, maybe a little too forcefully. "To be a woman is to suffer."

He takes this, both my cutting remark and the overly aggressive act, on the chin. But when my back is to him, he asks, "Why'd you cut your hair?"

I freeze, turning toward his voice. "What?"

"At dinner, Soph said something about your hair. Your *mental-breakdown haircut* or something."

"Uh, yeah." I shrug a shoulder, trying to still the storm brewing in my chest. "I just wanted a change."

He's not looking at me. He tangles a hand in his hair, a nervous habit. "That's it?"

I nod. "I promise. I was ready for something new."

He seemingly accepts this answer, this new half lie, with a nod. "I have to get going—I'll see you later. By the way, you left your phone on the bed. You have about eight missed calls from your sister."

"Oh . . . " I'm almost knocked backward. I lower myself back down into my reading chair. He hasn't accepted anything. Instead, I feel like he's collecting evidence. The proverbial monkey's paw curls a finger, and suddenly, our intimacy—this weird cosplay—feels like a weapon. I should say, *Why were you looking at my phone?* But I'm stunned silent.

"You should call her back," he says simply, before pulling his car keys from his pockets and reaching for the front doorknob. He shifts from foot to foot, ready to leave, but I know if he leaves right now, it's with something unsaid. Maybe he can hear my thoughts, feel the anxious thunder of my heart. *Just fucking say it.*

With a final, blank look back at me, he asks: "Did it bother you when I said you should be grateful for your life?"

Yes. "No. It was an emotional moment for you. I . . . I completely understand why." I tighten my hand on the bag of bottles.

He drops his gaze from mine. "Look, I might have to go to LA for a few days. I got an invitation to be a part of this inaugural exhibit," Marco says. "Which makes our situation even more complicated. I'd need to be there for at least a day, plus two days for travel, and I feel like a dick, since I just told you . . . to be grateful."

I try making a joke. "I've been to LA before, it's not anything worth—"

"I mean, we're almost at the end here, Nadia. If I leave today, when I come back we're over."

His words hit me. Square in the chest. And I even make a small, injured noise from the impact. "What a way to put it."

"It's the truth, though, isn't it? In a week, we're breaking up." There's something in the way he says *truth—breaking*. Before I can get my bearings, he blurts out: "I want you to come to LA with me. I want you there with me. I need you there with me."

"Marco," I say slowly, carefully. "I can't do that, you know that. I would love to, but I told you before—before we started dating and before Rome. My life . . . my job. It's all here."

He forces a breath out from between his lips, shoulders rounding forward. My words sink into him like a knife.

"Okay," he says, dragging a hand back and forth over his chin, working at the skin, leaving a path of pink in his wake. Marco abandons leaving, temporarily; he steps over my discarded book and comes toward me, lowering himself down into a squat. Here, we're at eye level. "Quit your job, then." I don't even need to hear the words—I can read it in his eyes, his features that hold in them a strength I can only dream of. *I want you* brims in them, dark and sweet and honest. "I'll support you for now, that way you can travel. Evergreen can still be your home base. Just come to LA, and then we can figure it out."

"What?" An incredulous laugh rips through me. I sit up straight in the chair, dropping my feet to the floor. My calf muscles twitch. "Have you lost your mind? We agreed to date for the month of May and now you want to support me financially?"

His expression crumbles. For the first time ever, Marco looks pissed. Actually *angry*—his features are hard, the heavy, shadowed lines in his face cutting through all his prettiness. "Then what are we doing? Just torturing ourselves?"

"I don't know, Marco," I push back. "This was your idea. You wanted an end date."

"That's not fair, Nadia."

"Why? Because I agreed? You also agreed. I didn't know you were even thinking about keeping me—"

"Of course I am. I'm here with you, giving you as much of myself as I can. I said so in Italy, Nadia."

"You didn't say it directly. I-I wasn't—I didn't think you wanted a serious relationship."

"Okay, fine. Let me say it right now. I know I'm inexperienced, but I want to *try*. Even if I fuck up entirely, please stop pushing me away, because I can feel what you're doing. You're getting ready to run. But I *have to* even if I fuck u—"

"I have lupus." The words tumble out of my mouth so fast they all come out in a jumbled string. My voice bounces off the ceiling.

Marco stills. Everything about him comes to a complete stop. He holds my gaze, unblinking. "What?"

"I have an autoimmune disease. Lupus." I drop my eyes to my feet, my comically jovial pink toenails. "I was diagnosed six months ago. It's . . . not deadly, not at first. But I was really sick back then, and that's when I lost my job. Because I—um, I couldn't do it anymore, and so they fired me. And I was so depressed I . . ." I bite down so hard on my lip I can actually taste blood. "I tried to kill myself." Then, I laugh.

He doesn't say anything.

When I look up at Marco, he swallows hard. "Oh my God."

"This . . ." I hold up the gallon bag. "Is my medicine. I'm supposed to take it every day. But it's been hard the last week so I'm starting to feel *really* bad. And, um, I hurt my hand"— I hold up my bandaged palm—"at work yesterday and it's not healing well. I may need to go to urgent care later. So, yeah. I can't go to LA. Because I'm not well enough and I definitely, *definitely* shouldn't put my body under more stress."

"Stress?" he says. Marco closes his eyes for a moment, bringing his thumb and finger to pinch the soft skin between them, then he casts his gaze to the ceiling. "Sorry. This is a lot."

"It is," I agree. "That's why I didn't want to tell you."

"Are you still . . ." He clears his throat, bringing his gaze, glassy and distant, back to mine. "Contemplating suicide?"

Humiliation burns in the back of my throat, like hot bile. "Not currently."

"And your sister? She's calling because she's worried about you?"

"We got into a huge fight. She thinks I'm fucking my entire life up, every second of every day."

"Because of me?"

"Because of everything, Marco." I flash him a sad smile. I can't hold back anymore; hot tears brim in my eyes. "Because I'm broke and I don't really have a job and I don't really have friends—except Soph and Allie, who almost *have* to like me, because they're scared for me, too—and I don't even really have you. She didn't want me to be with you; she thinks you're using me, that I'm pathetic for agreeing to this. And I can't blame her for thinking that way because . . ." I laugh again as the tears fall, heavy and slow, pulling through the little red rashes beginning to form on my cheeks. "I can't even *actually* have you. I had to lie in order to have you for a *fraction* of a month."

He doesn't move to comfort me, and I don't blame him. Instead, Marco pushes his hands through his hair again and stares wide-eyed up at the skylight as a cloud passes by, stealing away the sunshine.

"Nadia," he says finally. He still won't look at me. "I can handle this."

"Can you?" I ask in a whisper. "I can't come to LA or New York or Rome or wherever your photography takes you. I can stay here, in Evergreen, and I can live a small, manageable life where I'm *healthy enough*. And that's it, Marco."

"But you did—"

"I did," I cut him off sharply. "I did, and I'm suffering for it. My body hurts. I *hurt*." I feel a strange and terrifying—familiar—sense of acceptance. I stand on steady feet, leaving behind my book and medicine. Then, I move around him toward the hallway. *I need to lie down.*

"I know I need to say something," he calls after me. I stop walking and, with my feet quiet, it hits me how utterly still the world has gone around us. No birds chirping. No music from the radio. No noise floating in from the street. "I know I do. Just give me some time. A moment to . . ."

I turn back and Marco's watching me, eyes fixed in a severe look—an *unfamiliar* look. He's a stranger after all, isn't he? *We're strangers.* His full lips have completely disappeared into a straight white line. "You don't have to do anything, we can just do this, as . . ." I pause to inhale as much air as I can. "We can just do this as we planned."

He doesn't meet my gaze. "Were you ever going to tell me the truth?"

"Not if I could help it," I say. Then I add, in a pathetic, small voice, "I really like the version of myself I get to be with you."

He recoils, an unstoppable, biological response to me, physically turning himself toward the door where he now has a white-knuckled grip on the handle. *Go,* I think. *Go now and finish us off.*

Eventually, in a voice barely more than a whisper, he says: "Will you be okay if I leave?"

I reply, "I don't think I have a choice."

Wednesday, May 24

I wake up on the couch, the movie still paused on Keanu standing alone in the park. I always stop right before he takes off the blindfold and realizes he's alone. I rewind to the beginning.

Up until yesterday, I thought I was Charlize. I thought I would get the luxury and privilege of leaving Marco. It felt like something I deserved—the right to walk away unscathed—after everything else I'd gone through. But instead, I'm here—sick and hurting and confused.

And Marco is somewhere else—on a plane, in Los Angeles— living his life.

How could I have been so dumb? Of course it was always going to end this way.

My phone is quiet except for an occasional ding. Allie keeps sending me videos. She doesn't know what happened. I'm too embarrassed to tell her, to gently request that she leave me alone.

I reach for the notepad on the floor, next to the trash can I've had to keep close by.

things i never knew before lupus:

I add one more:

3. you might feel like a Charlize but you are actually a Keanu—advertising asshole who gets laid and thinks he deserves the entire fucking world.

Thursday, May 25

A lone in the quiet of a life and a house that no longer feel like mine, I play Liv's voicemail one more time while every cell in my body throbs and aches.

She doesn't sound desperate, just tired and very, very sad. It doesn't matter what she said to me, why we fought. Her voice comforts me. I can almost smell her vanilla perfume, her spearmint gum, her essential Liv-ness. I can almost feel her head resting on my shoulder, the closest we get to hugging.

Liv has always been vicious and dramatic. And I would always meet her in the afterglow with a joke, a shrug, a peace offering.

I wasn't supposed to walk away. Maybe I'm a runner, but not from Liv. Never from Liv. Even if she deserves it.

I HAVE TO drive to Philly.

I have to talk to Liv in person, and we have to make up. Too much time has passed already, the damage of which I can't even begin to quantify. It makes my pulse race and my throat feel like it's closing up.

I drag myself back into the bedroom to get dressed even though my head feels magnetically drawn to the center of the Earth and my hands are too stiff to button my jeans.

I need my sister.

She's the only person who can help me through this, help me untangle this mess I've made and maybe find a way I can save myself from this situation. I don't want to sink back down into the deepest, darkest place I've ever been—but right now, it doesn't feel like I have any control.

THE RIDE FROM Evergreen to Philly is treacherous, and while sitting in traffic on the Walt Whitman Bridge, I dry heave into an old coffee cup, feeling like someone has lodged an ice pick through my left eye. Nothing comes up. The morning light reflecting off the cars around me is so blinding I spend the last mile driving with partially closed eyes. My throat is as raw and ragged as my dignity when I pull down the narrow side street where Mike and Liv live.

I forgo parking altogether and leave my car running in the middle of the street with the hazard lights on. Each step I take feels like a headfirst collision between a broken, exposed bone and the sidewalk. I'm somehow both sweating and freezing cold. Maybe Liv's sixth sense kicks in—but more likely she can hear my labored breathing when I finally make it halfway up her porch steps.

The front door swings open and she appears, still in her pajamas, frizzy-haired and wide-eyed.

"Nadia, what the hell?"

"Liv," I pant. "I'm sorry."

"You look . . ." She blinks twice, hard.

"I'm sorry I missed all your calls," I say, pressing a hand to my chest to try and calm my heart. "I'm sorry I went away and didn't tell you. I'm sorry I went to college and I'm sorry I missed your twenty-eighth birthday because I had that big meeting in Vegas. I'm sorry—"

"Slow down," she says, reaching out for me as she comes down the steps to meet me. "Are you okay? Your forehead is drenched—"

"I'm fine, please just listen. I have to tell you everything—"

"You can tell me everything, just come inside—"

Our voices crash together, one over the other, but I can't slow down. I have a horrible, horrible feeling. Suddenly, I'm scared. "We don't have time to sit! I really need you—"

"Why don't we have time? What's going on?" Her voice cracks as it reaches a fever pitch. "Are you having an episode?"

"Stop! Stop saying that! I'm not insane." I grab on to the railing for support and start the story, from the beginning, as best I can. "Marco invited me to Italy and I-I didn't think it would be like this. But I'm in love with him or something, and I lied to him and now I just . . . I . . ."

The sound dims in my left ear. Then, it becomes overwhelmed by ringing. I press my hand flat against my ear. *Shit*, that hurts.

Liv grabs ahold of my arm. "Hey, slow down . . ."

"No!" I yank away, out of her grasp.

My throat is dry. *So* dry. I'm thirstier than I've ever been in my entire life. I'm so thirsty that if I don't drink water right now, I'm afraid of what might happen. I just need to tell Liv that I'm thirsty.

"Nadia?"

I can do this. I can say it. But the sun is so bright, it's glaring off her front door, and there's a car alarm going off. I can smell everything, and I hate it. I just need to focus on getting *something* to drink.

"I need water," I try to say, but my teeth snag on the words and my lips are too slow.

"What do you need?" She sounds so panicked. I must have gotten some of the words out. I try again.

I need water.

"Nadia." Her eyes, a stunning shade of green like the Ionian Sea, have doubled in size. She reaches for me, hand trembling. Why is she panicking? She's so ridiculous.

I'm fine!

"Nadia, what's happening?"

I said I'm fine! I'm just thirsty. I need water.

"Michael," Liv yells over her shoulder. She's always yelling, deep from inside her diaphragm. She's so loud, sometimes it feels like she's stolen everyone else's voice so she can take up the whole room. But she never usually sounds like this when she yells. Right now, she sounds scared. No, actually. She sounds terrified.

I can hear Mike, too. His voice is deep and pleasant, and his arms are so steady under me. *Why are you touching me? I'm thirsty,* I try again. I have to say it. I can't give up.

But suddenly, all I want to do is sleep.

December 22

WH EVER YOU GO, THERE Y U ARE
Some of the letters had slid out from the wooden slats meant to keep them in place.

A decorative blackboard with a knotted-pine frame hangs above the watercooler.

Somewhere behind me a noise machine gurgles.

I am meant to feel soothed. In this oasis, self-loathing is only a concept.

I'm in the waiting room alone. Bundled in my winter coat, cold still nipping the tip of my nose. My skin itches underneath all the layers I piled on and the pit that's been festering in my stomach has seemingly grown a heartbeat, like I'm pregnant with dread.

I eye the door.

Still time to just leave.

Forfeit the hundred-fifty bucks I paid to book this appointment online.

But intellectually I know that this is not an option.

I started researching two nights ago. Then, this morning, I stood in the middle of Suburban Station thinking very calmly that I should buy my *supplies*, just in case.

It was a thought that came so naturally. *Time to do the shopping for when I kill myself.*

Then, I wanted it. I wanted it so badly. To end everything—all of it.

The pain in my legs that kept me up at night; the never-ending headaches that made the little sleep I got unproductive and feverish; the shame and terror that gripped my chest and made it impossible to move from my bed. I hadn't eaten in days. All I did was drink coffee and chain-smoke spliffs that made my head feel full of fiberglass.

If I could find a way to go, I would finally feel better.

"Nadia Fabiola?"

Too late.

She smiles at me from the doorway, her eyes shining in the dim waiting room light. It's designed to look like someone's living room. So much care has gone into shielding me from the truth of the matter. I can't imagine what it would be like to sit here with the father of my children or the parent who had systematically broken my spirit.

I'd probably never be able to smell a Palo Santo candle ever again.

Suddenly, I am grateful to be completely and totally alone.

I follow the woman into her office. It's also bleak. The walls are covered in positive affirmations painted brightly over various vistas. A mountain range tells me to *BREATHE IN PEACE.* The floor is littered with tissues.

"Sorry for the mess. I had to run out to grab lunch and didn't have time—Oh, let me grab these!" She has on a pair of blue medical gloves. She smiles at me while plucking up some of the tissues.

"I know, this is about as medical as we'll get. I promise. Sit, Nadia, please."

Without taking off my coat or purse, I perch on the seat. My hair is tucked back under my hood and I am just a big, moon-faced baby with bloodshot eyes and wine breath. I stare out at her from my mass of black fabric.

"Cold out?"

It is, but I can't bring myself to talk. I clear my throat and run my tongue over my bottom lip. It's dry and cracked and tastes like blood and nicotine.

"I can make you a tea," she says brightly, delicate eyebrows shooting up toward her hairline. "Earl Grey?"

Everything about her is delicate. Her hands, small and pale, are crossed over a notebook in her lap, the medical gloves tossed along with the tissues. She watches me with kind green eyes, wet and sort of red-rimmed. Maybe she had been crying with her last patient. Maybe she's allergic to inspirational posters.

My therapist—or this therapist—is my age. How sad for me. She's wearing a hot-pink cardigan over a flowy top, and I suddenly wonder why I never wear flowy tops. Framed degrees pushed to the back of her messy desk say, *Yes, I'm here because it's my job, but let's not dwell on that. Let's talk about you.*

She's watching me, smiling softly. She clicks her pen and opens her notebook.

"You're Audrey Felton?"

"I am. It's great to meet you. Thank you for filling in your intake papers so thoroughly." Was that a dig? Couldn't be, but it sure felt like one. It sounded like the setup to a joke: *How does an unemployed suicidal writer spend their days?*

I find my voice, clearing my throat a few times before I speak the longest sentence I've spoken to another human in weeks. "I've never done this before. I know how that sounds, and I know I should have made an appointment sooner, but I . . . Anyway, I should have come here when I was more . . ." I trail off into silence.

"More what?" she asks gently.

"Willing to . . . be alive."

Audrey doesn't move. *Heal me,* I think. *This is so embarrassing. Please, heal me fast.*

"You don't want to be alive?"

I dig into my pocket and pull out the note.

It's a pathetic mess of a note. I'd written it after drinking all day. I'd been so sick, I wasted four hours just puking up violet, acrid semi-solid mess.

I unfold the paper and hand it to her.

I sort of remember what it says. *I'm sorry you never thought this could happen to someone like me . . . I think I've done this all well enough. I'm sorry if this seems extreme . . .*

A little on the nose. Pathetic for a writer. All clichés. So very hack.

Audrey lips part as she reads it. Then, they come back together in a practiced line.

"Well." She reaches for the tissue box and hands it to me. "Thank you for changing your mind."

Friday, May 26

N adia? Nadia, how are you?"

My ears are still ringing as I blink out of the light sleep I've been drifting in and out of involuntarily for the last day. Through the wash of sound, I can hear her voice. Gentle and deep.

"I'm Dr. Willis. Sorry to wake you up, I know you've had a rough morning. Can you see me okay?" A woman with soft gray waves is sitting beside where I lie in a hospital bed.

"Hi, Doctor." My voice sounds like it's coming from somewhere far off inside my skull.

Dr. Willis pulls a stool up to the edge of my hospital bed and looks at me with genuine, soft concern. "Feeling okay?"

I nod then try to lift a hand to my face but the wires and tubes connected to my arm snag painfully. I let out an anxious squeal of hurt and fear. Dr. Willis jumps up to help me untangle myself. When she settles back onto her stool, she leans folded hands onto the side of my hospital bed.

"Your sister let us know about your diagnosis and correct medication regimen, *and* she put us in contact with your rheumatologist. We discussed the elevated levels of protein in your urine, indicating some potential renal damage due to systemic lupus erythematosus. Does that sound right?"

I nod.

"Okay." Dr. Willis gives my bed a little maternal pat. "Nadia, yesterday you had what's called a tonic-clonic, or grand mal, seizure."

"A seizure?" I repeat. Why couldn't I remember that? Wouldn't I remember that? All I can remember is feeling thirsty and scared; Mike's arms under me and then the back seat of his car.

"This is not uncommon in lupus patients who have very high levels of inflammation."

Very high levels of inflammation. "I've been forgetting to take my medicine."

Dr. Willis bobs her head. "Okay. I'll note that in your chart, thank you. We're going to keep you overnight again and run some tests. I ordered a chest X-ray so we can see if you have any inflammation in your lungs or heart, as well as a brain scan. I'd also like to run another round of blood work, but we can do that tomorrow. For now, let's get you rested, okay?" She watches me for a moment longer, her eyes unreadable. "I know it's a lot. Do you have any questions or concerns?"

"Maybe . . ." I run my tongue, dry and chalky, over my bottom lip. "Where am I?"

Dr. Willis looks startled, then she lets out a small laugh. "God, right. University of Penn hospital, dear." She pats the edge of the bed before getting to her feet. There's a nurse in maroon scrubs standing off to the side, typing at a computer. I hadn't noticed her at all. How long has she been here?

How long have I been here?

Does Marco know?

Marco.

Hot tears burn my eyes. "I did this to myself."

Dr. Willis pauses with her hand on the doorknob. She turns

back to face me. "Regardless of whether or not you've been taking your medicine, you did not *do* this. Sometimes things happen and no one's to blame. Try and get some rest, okay? You don't need to figure out everything right now, and tonight you don't need to focus on anything other than trying to get some food down."

She leaves me alone in the yellow room.

Soon, I fall back asleep.

I WAKE UP an unknowable amount of time later to Liv pacing at the foot of my bed, walking and speed-whispering into her phone. Then, she sees me watching her and quickly hangs up.

"Finally," she says, rushing over to my side. "I was just checking in with everyone. Nicky's on his way."

"What time is it?" My voice comes out hoarse and broken.

"Five-thirty in the afternoon."

"Oh my God—"

"Don't freak. You have to stay calm." She thrusts a paper cup of ice water into my hands.

"Stay clam," I say.

"What? You need to hydrate, right now. You've been in and out of sleep for twenty hours."

I obey. Has water always been this good? I drain the cup, and she brings me another. "I'm sorry," I say when she hands it to me. "I'm so sorry." Why is this the only thing I can say?

"Enough, okay?" She pushes the tears off my cheeks, strong arms encircling my head. I wrap a feeble arm around her waist and pull her to me. Liv shifts her weight away, and I notice she's standing strangely, a fist pressed into her hip, like she's reinforcing her lower back. Her shirt billows slightly, and suddenly everything about her shape seems different.

Without thinking, I reach out and press my other hand against her stomach. It's hard and domed, a strange sensation underneath my fingers, but instead of pulling away, I press into her. Her stomach presses back.

Liv gasps and jolts away from me, grabbing me by the wrist. "What're you doing?"

"Your stomach." I reach out for her again, but she evades my touch.

"*Stop* it."

I blink. Everything is foggy, light. The room feels like it's made of cotton. *Nicky's on the way.* But where's Marco? Why is my sister standing like that, leaning from foot to foot?

"Liv, are you pregnant?"

She turns away, back toward the sink, getting me another cup of water. "Not now, Nadia."

"You are, aren't you?"

Liv leans heavily into the sink before bringing her eyes—her stunning eyes even more aquamarine as they glisten with tears—back up to mine. "That's why I kept calling you. I was nervous—scared, actually—to tell you, but it was getting harder and harder to hide. I wanted us to just *stop fighting*, a-and I couldn't do this without you anymore, Nadia. I just couldn't."

Fuck.

For days, my sister was desperately trying to reach me for the very same reason I'd driven to Philly when I could barely stay vertical: she'd needed her sister.

"You called me," I murmur, tears burning at the corners of my eyes now.

"Of course I did, you fucking moron. Who else would I call?"

"I am *so* sorry, Liv. I am so, so—"

She slams a balled fist down onto the edge of the sink, cutting me off. It's a dramatic action, but it makes only a muffled *thunk*. "When people love you, they need you. They *expect* things of you." Liv makes an irritated swipe at her eyes before pushing off the edge of the sink. "*We* needed you."

I'm MOVED INTO a better room—a bigger room with a perfect view of the Schuylkill River Trail and the lit-up cityscape. Liv takes my phone and promises me she'll handle texting everyone. If I have missed calls or messages from Marco, she doesn't let on, and I'm so grateful.

Just for a little while, I don't think I can be trusted to function as an adult. I entrust myself fully to Liv. She fluffs my pillow, brushes my hair, puts a little bit of Aquaphor on my lips. She talks on the phone nonstop. I hear her describe the way I looked and how I crumbled to the ground about fifteen different ways.

Visiting hours end, but we tell the nurse that Liv's pregnant and she brings us two dinners and promises she won't rat us out. Liv kicks off her shoes, unbuttons her jeans, and climbs into the bed next to me. I want to rest my hand over her stomach so badly. I want to know everything about this magic thing that's happening between us, quietly, while she flips through TV shows.

"Should we watch *Law & Order* or *Bones*?" she asks while I shift to make more room for her.

"*Bones*. Definitely *Bones*."

"David Boreanaz is such a babe."

Without thinking, I say, "I think Marco and I are over."

She dismisses me with a brisk shake of her head. "We'll think about that later."

It's decided, then. The show begins, the theme song playing, the premise set up. There are bones that need to be *Bones*'d.

Liv fiddles absently with the tape on the back of my hand. From the side, she really looks like our mom. Everything's fuzzy again—but a good fuzzy. Fuzzy like sleep after a long day.

"Remember when we used to share a bedroom?" I ask, my voice already fading away. I hope this doesn't scare her. *I'm okay,* I think. *Just tired.*

"Uh huh," she huffs. She doesn't take her eyes off the TV. "That fucking sucked."

Saturday, May 27

There's a soft knock at my door before it clicks open, and a figure—broad and handsome and painfully familiar—darkens the threshold.

I push myself up in the hospital bed. "Doctor."

The door clicks behind Dr. Antoniou and he turns to me with a look of total annoyance. "God, city people. Why would I lie about being your rheumatologist?" He punctuates this by taking two very noisy pumps of hand sanitizer from the dispenser by the door. This feels like a rhetorical question, so I just sit up a little straighter in bed, smoothing a hand over the back of my head. My curls are completely stretched. I haven't brushed my teeth in . . .

Why do I care?

With a shake of his head, he crosses the room and sinks down into the chair that Liv had spent most of the morning occupying while I was transported from the room to various other floors around the hospital where my body was examined, X-rayed, pinched, pricked, and frequently left to wait in really cold hallways. Underneath his long, lean frame, the chair looks cartoonishly small. He slides forward, locking his eyes on mine. "How are you, champ?"

Fucking *hate* that word.

I almost hate him. Almost.

Sebastian and Marco look a lot alike, especially right now with Dr. Antoniou not in any of his usual medical garb. I blink twice to make sure I'm not imagining it. But it's all still there, all the hurt in my chest, when my eyes refocus. "Um, I'm okay? A little better." I point at the IV drip over my shoulder. "They're giving me The Good Stuff."

He laughs. "They better be. You've had one hell of a time. How do your joints feel? Your muscles?"

"Stiff. But not as achy as before."

"And your head?"

"Better." We fall into a tense, awkward silence. I keep my eyes fixed on the thin blue blanket stretched over my legs. He's watching me with a look halfway between concern and pity. Eventually, I ask: "How was your trip?"

"It was nice." He nods. "Wonderful. I heard you've had a very eventful month."

I drop my eyes immediately. "Did he tell you that?"

"Your sister, actually."

"Traitor," I mumble.

Dr. Antoniou laughs softly. "I'm happy you took my advice to get out more."

"Marco is very persuasive."

"He is. He's charming." Sebastian nods, pulling his lips into a sloping frown. "I think your sister has spoken to him—given him an update on your situation."

"I wouldn't know," I say softly. "I relinquished my phone to her."

"I'm really happy you told him," Sebastian says. "I wish you'd been honest from the beginning."

I shake my head. "I knew that would happen—I knew if *he* knew I was sick, we wouldn't have ever spent the last month the way we did— that he would feel different about me, fundamentally, as a person. And then . . . then he wouldn't have ever pulled me out of myself."

Dr. Antoniou makes a noise in the back of his throat. "You didn't want him to see you the way everyone else has started to see you."

I nod. "Weak. Incapable. Stalled."

He draws his brows together, knitting them in a look of gentle admonishment. "Is that how you see yourself?"

I yank my gaze away and direct it toward the window. It's pouring rain out, and I imagine poor Liv fighting against an edgy, soaking crowd on her hunt for a decent hoagie. "I really don't need you to be my therapist right now."

"You're right, I'm sorry." He stands to leave, smoothing his hand down his khaki-clad thighs. He turns back to me, one last time. "By the way, just because you feel something does not mean it's true. Just because Marco thinks everyone sees him as a massive failure and embarrassment doesn't mean he is. Would you agree?"

I nod again.

"Okay. So, when I tell you that just because you feel like your life is over, please consider . . ." He bobs his head side to side. "Please consider that maybe it's not."

January 6

Before everything

"Y ou *will* get better."

I'm beginning to believe I was put on Earth to single-handedly destroy Audrey's patience.

"But I should be able to work by now," I push back. I'm taking today's session with a pillow held tight to my stomach. I've been gaining weight at a remarkably fast pace, and I'm afraid she might notice.

"Nadia." Audrey leans forward, bringing her hands together in a prayer motion. Like she's literally begging me to stop being such a dick. "You're doing a lot of *really* hard things right now. You're in and out of doctor appointments constantly, you're here with me—"

"That doesn't mean anything," I cut her off. "I should be doing all of it. I'm healthy." Except I sleep thirteen hours a night and still wake up feeling like I spent hours treading water.

She reads the room. "Okay, even if there's nothing wrong with you, can you admit that you haven't been feeling like yourself?" Audrey leans back in her chair and takes a protracted sip of tea, giving me a second to think before I lash out. She got her bangs trimmed over the weekend, and I have to keep myself from telling her how pretty she looks. We're at war. There's no time for compliments.

"Why would I want to feel like me? I fucking suck. I'm an absolute embarrassment to what I told myself I would be by now. *Everything* I wanted to be when I was a kid, I'm the exact opposite. We won't even get into the fact that I *had* my dream life. I had it, and I *fucked* it." I pause to take a breath. Then, I start counting off on my fingers: "I'm running out of money. I'm running out of energy. I sleep thirteen hours a day. I don't talk to anyone other than *you*. I'm running out of ways to lie to myself and say that this is all part of some bigger, better plan. It's just . . . I'm nothing. I am a *no one*." I end my rant with a heavy gulp.

Audrey watches me carefully, without any judgment. She watches me like I'm a caterpillar on a leaf. Then, after a moment of silence, she says: "Okay. You're no one."

I watch her, my chest heaving with the effort of expulsing all my trauma "Right."

"If you're no one, then . . . what does that make your work?"

I drop my eyes to the carpet between our feet. Was not expecting that. "I don't know. What did I ever really do? Convince people to buy junk from brands that hated them? Nothing, I did nothing. My work was nothing."

"And if your work was nothing, then what was your job?"

"Nothing," I say quietly.

"And Kai firing you? Saying the terrible things he said to you?"

"Nothing."

"And all that pressure you carry around? That sense of obligation you feel to do and to be? If you're no one and your work is nothing, what is that?"

"Nothing," I say with something that feels an awful lot like confidence. "It's nothing. It's total bullshit. It's a fucking scam. It's . . . it's something I made up."

I look up to find that Audrey is smiling at me. She holds up her hands and does a little razzle-dazzle.

"Nihilism. Kind of fun."

AUDREY HAS CRACKED open a door in my mind, with rusted hinges and moss grown over the frame; a door so long neglected that we spend our entire session just clearing away the debris that keeps me from reaching the handle.

"Let's end with a visualization," she offers. Usually, this is the type of thing I may fight her on.

Instead, I cross my arms over my chest and lean back against the freezing-cold windowpane. Behind me, snow falls for the first time in years over Philadelphia, blanketing everything in a gray-white silence. If cars drive by, we can't hear them all the way up here.

I've moved over to my favorite place in her office—my perch on top of the radiator underneath Audrey's window.

I love the freezing-cold air that rattles the window and the way it feels like I am dangling over the edge of the building. I love looking out past the Delaware River, past Camden, and directly at the tree-lined horizon. It all goes on and on for miles: roads, houses, trees, cars. Up here, I am above the fray. From my perch, it's easier to detach—to observe.

"Close your eyes. Imagine yourself submerged in calm. Let your shoulders melt down your back. Imagine you're someplace that brings you joy. Nadia, where are you?"

The beach. At our Shore house. It's August and the sun is high and hot. I'm lying face down on a towel that smells like suntan lotion and the dried pages of a paperback book. I can hear my brother and sister playing in the tide, shouting over the crash of the ocean. There's a breeze, unobtrusive and kind, caressing my back. Someone lights charcoal in the distance, firing up a grill for lunch. I can feel my heartbeat in my neck.

"Evergreen."

When the exercise is over, my cheeks are wet and my chest feels lighter than it has since November. Maybe sooner.

I don't know anything,

I don't know what any of this means, how healthy I am—if I'm even healthy at all. All I know is that if I get in my car now, in an hour I'll be back to the last place that made me feel really happy.

And when I get there, nothing will have changed but maybe I'll be safe enough to start again.

Tuesday, May 30

On May 28, Liv takes me home with her from the hospital. She helps me into my pajamas and then into bed. She assures me that even if I wanted to do something about my situation, I wouldn't have the energy to tackle it all right now. Instead, I need to take life one moment at a time and in this moment, rest comes first. Then, she stays in bed with me while I shake with quiet tears. Assuring me that there's no way I've ruined the one good thing that's ever happened to me. That Marco will call. He will. And if he doesn't, then that should tell me everything I need to know.

She doesn't see what I've done as the type of emotional betrayal that changes the way Marco sees me forever. She can't—she's my sister. She remembers when I believed in Santa and was afraid of mall escalators. And she doesn't see Marco's face every time she closes her eyes.

On May 29, I manage to take a shower. But underneath the steam, my mind and body are suddenly gripped by a breath-stealing panic.

I'll never see him again, will I?

We'll never kiss again; never point at the sky and name the song on the radio together; we'll never say things we regret and ask for forgiveness and find ourselves willing to give it, fully—no questions asked.

One day, I'll turn on my TV and see him again. A stranger, maybe with salt and pepper freckling his hair. They'll announce he's getting married to a tall woman with narrow hips and perfect bone structure and all her health, an overflowing chalice of energy and vitality. And it'll make perfect sense.

Today, I fight with myself. Liv's home is shining clean, all white and reflective. I am the dark spot, the rain cloud. I move from room to room like a ghost.

I can figure this out, I tell myself. I can be the person he needs; I know I can. Haven't I spent a lifetime *trying?*

But Liv is right. If there was room for forgiveness, wouldn't it have come? Wouldn't he have called? Wouldn't he have known exactly what to say, in the moment, to make me feel okay?

I push myself out of bed and wander downstairs to find my phone, which my sister has sequestered in an effort to help me focus on resting.

I find it on the dining room table. I have more missed calls than I've ever had in my life. My heart hammers as I unlock my phone and scroll. Some are from Marco.

Many are from Marco.

I crawl back into bed, pull the covers over my head, and hit call. "Nadia."

At the sound of my name, I bite as hard as I can into my bottom lip. *"Nadia?"*

I hang up.

Wednesday, May 31

I'm taking you back to Evergreen." Liv makes this declaration while ripping the duvet off me.

I let out an enraged groan in response, rolling over to bury my face in a pillow. It's got to be six o'clock in the morning. The sun is still pale and milky, falling through the blinds in a gray rickrack. "Oh, *now* you want me in Evergreen?"

"Nadia." She pulls on my pajama pant leg until I have to roll over to keep from losing them altogether.

"Stop," I moan. "Go *away.*"

Liv's standing at the foot of the bed, fists pressed into her hips. "Get up, put your shoes on, and get in the car."

I slowly push myself up, narrowing my eyes at her. "What the hell's going on?"

"You're being evicted. Now. Let's get a move on." She's gathering up the few things I've commandeered in the room—her hair spray, an extra deodorant—and throwing them into a plastic bag.

"Why? I thought I was resting—*stop it*, Liv. You're not funny. I'm not leaving."

Mike appears in the doorway, swinging a car key on his index finger. "Car's packed, babe." Then, to me: "Morning, gorgeous."

"Mike." I'm scrambling out of bed toward him. "Tell your wife I can't leave."

Mike immediately lifts his hands in an act of open resignation. "I am absolutely not getting involved in Fabiola drama. Car's packed and I'll be waiting downstairs."

Fucking guy. Liv's moved on to rolling the duvet into a ball so I can't wrestle the length away from her. I make a feeble attempt to fight for the blanket, crawling back across the bed and wrapping my arms around her as she turns away and shouts at me that I smell like shit.

"I would absolutely rough your ass up if you weren't pregnant," I threaten her through gritted teeth, trying to pry a corner out of her titanium grip.

"Oh, yeah? I could still kick your ass, weakling," she grunts.

"You *wish.*" We're moving in slow motion, like two turtles fighting over a single piece of lettuce.

"Look, I'm sorry for what I said before about you and Evergreen and Marco—"

"*Stop,*" I cut her off. "We are not talking about him—"

"Just listen to me, okay? I know things have spiraled and I know it hasn't been perfect, but you can't just give up, Nadia—"

"That's not my decision! He *knows.* I told him and he chose to leave. He said he needed time, and he bolted—"

"You are so much more than the last week!"

"And I'm no*t giving up*, I'm just—"

"No more cloistering!" she yells at me. Like actually *yells.* "The life you've built for yourself is different. It's weird and wild, but it's *better. You* are better."

Stunned, I sit back on my haunches on the bed.

"Forget about Marco for now, okay?" Liv huffs, smoothing down some hairs that came loose in our pathetic little scrap. "Let's just *go.* You need to move."

WE SIT IN the carport, staring up at the second story of our family beach house, sharing a family-size bag of popcorn, Liv's one and only craving.

If I wasn't completely numb, I'd feel sick to my stomach.

"What do you think you're having?" I ask Liv without taking my eyes off the balcony. That balcony was my favorite place when we were kids. I would wake up early so I could be there when my mom fired up the moka pot. She'd make me a cappuccino with extra milk and sugar and let me drink it with her as we watched the sun break through the marine layer. Maybe one day Liv's little one would want to do the same. It would drive her insane to have a child that was as precocious and sensitive as I had been.

"Probably a boy," Liv says, sucking the salt off her fingers. "Just have a feeling."

"Sexist." Then, I look over at Liv. "I'll miss you."

"I'll be back this weekend to make sure you aren't growing mold."

"No, don't do that. You've done so much already. I'll be okay."

Liv nods. "You will be." She reaches over and wipes her wet fingers on my arm. I squirm and grimace at her. "I'm not helping you carry your stuff up."

"Jeez. Lazy."

I don't really have anything to carry upstairs. My purse, a plastic bag filled with medication, and some clothes. I make my way up the old wooden steps that lead to our door and find that, weirdly, it's ajar. I can see into the apartment and all the lights are off. Soph or Allie must have dropped by.

"Soph?" I call out as I push my way into the apartment. "Allie?"

There's a shadow, a figure stirring by the kitchen island. My entire body tenses with pure terror. "Hello?"

The shadow shifts and a gasp sticks in my throat. I reach for the doorknob, fumbling with the metal as I try to backtrack. "Liv?" I call out feebly, but it's too late. She can't hear me now.

Then, the lights flicker on.

The figure before me is frowning, arms folded over his chest, a gentle tumble of wavy hair swept sweetly behind his ears. Wearing his reading glasses. Looking like he stepped out of an episode of *Baywatch*.

"Surprise," he says.

My legs soften and my bags slowly slide from my arms to the floor.

The look on Marco's face transforms from serious to deep concern in a nanosecond, and he moves swiftly toward me, arms opening wide to catch me if I fall forward. And I just might. He looks nervous—beautiful but nervous, eyebrows tented with anxiety. "Easy," he says. "Easy."

I recoil from his open arms, flattening my body against the door. "W-what the fuck are you doing here?"

"Your sister texted me," he says very precisely. "She said she was dropping you off. She told me to get a key from Soph. I figured she hadn't told you, but I didn't mean to scare you."

"Oh my God . . ." My hands make a shaky grab for my hairline. I'm dizzy. I reach out to steady myself against the wall, but instead my hand finds something soft—Marco's chest. He's so close, I can almost hear his ragged breathing.

"Nadia." His lips. They're soft and warm and pressed against my temple. *Kissing me?* "Please sit. You *need* to sit."

"No . . ." I try to pry myself away from him, but his fingers find my elbow and guide me to the couch. He keeps guiding me until the fabric meets the backs of my knees, and I'm able to sit. "Y-you're here. You talked to my sister, and now you're here?"

Marco nods curtly, settling beside me. "She told me everything and she sort of . . . warned me. Told me it may be a little while before you could reach out. She said you were *spooked*."

I clear my throat, but my voice still comes out hoarse. "That's one way to put it."

He looks tired.

"Nadia, I wish you'd told me sooner. I wish I'd had time t-to—to be *better.* I wish I could have—"

"No," I cut in, my voice hoarse and angry. "No, I didn't *want* you to know."

His eyebrows drop together, his mouth twisting into a tight, sideways frown. "I realize how complicated I made this situation between us. I take responsibility for that. But what if you'd had a seizure in Rome? What . . . what if something worse had happened and I didn't know how to help you?"

"This is exactly why I didn't tell you," I manage through clenched teeth. "It would be all you thought about the whole time. It would have been the only me you saw. There wouldn't have been room for any other version of Nadia. Just worry and medicine and exhaustion and *neediness*—"

"Okay, okay. I'm sorry—I don't want to make you upset—"

"See! You just did it, right there." I'm trying to raise my voice, but it just cracks with the effort of my desperation. "I do *not* need to be lectured right now," I continue. "I did what I did because I *wanted to,* okay? We never promised each other anything. We said we'd date for May and that was that. How was I supposed to know I'd fucking fall head over heels for you?"

Marco can't argue with that. Instead, he leans forward and presses the palms of his hands together. "I should have never left things with you the way I did. I should have never left you for a stupid work trip. How do you know this isn't because of the stress I put you under?"

I pull a throw pillow to my chest, and I wipe my nose with the back of my hand. "Because . . . I've been this bad before. Maybe . . . maybe not quite this bad. But I've been really sick. When I met you, my medicine was working. Finally. And *I* was working. So, I faked it. I know that makes me selfish—"

"It doesn't," he cuts in, leaning forward to lay a hand over my knee. The comfort this gesture brings me is instant.

"Yes, it does," I say, trying to keep my voice harsh and steady, but I can feel myself being pulled back to him. *I don't want to be harsh.* "I don't care if I'm selfish. I'm happy I did it, and I'd do it again. This month with you has been the best of my life. It *fixed* me." I spit this at him like it's an insult. "No one has ever treated me the way you do. No one. I lied, and I hurt you, just so I could hold on to that. Don't you think you deserve better? Someone who you can take to Rome without being afraid that they'll fall apart?"

"Hey." Marco flexes his fingers, still around my knee, sliding close to me. *Hold me,* I want to say. *Let's just forget everything for now.* "You just said this was the best month of your life—what do you think it was for me, Nadia? Do you think before May fourth I was just living my fucking dream? I'm not perfect—you saw how imperfect I can be. Don't *you* deserve someone better?"

Tears are prickling at my eyes. I don't cry. I *won't* cry. "Fuck that. I don't *want* better. What's better than you?"

"Exactly, see?" He lets out a soft laugh from the back of his throat, bringing his thumb up to swipe quickly at my cheek. "It *fucking* hurts to hear someone you love ripping themselves apart. I want you, okay? Every version of you, and I am so fucking mad at myself that I had to almost lose you in order to see that. The moment I walked out on you, I knew I should have turned around, but . . . God, there's no excuse. I'm just sorry." He goes quiet for a moment. His thumb paints small circles around my kneecap. "If you don't want me, for whatever reason, okay. But don't just push me away because of that one moment—because I accidentally validated this idea you have of how I see you."

I do. I push his hand away, lumbering to my feet. "You want a version of me that doesn't exist. You want the person I was in Rome."

But Marco's faster than me, rising and following me across the room. "Don't tell me what I want, Nadia."

"Don't tell *me* what *I* want, Marco." I turn and press a quaking finger into my chest. "I know exactly what I want. What I want is *you*. But this is how I am, and what if you decide it's boring? What if next time you see how fragile I am, how really fragile I am, you want to leave?" A single, hot tear falls from my eye, crashing onto the floor between us. "I won't be able to take it."

Marco locks his gaze on mine, chest rising and falling as his breath comes in ragged tears. He steps closer to me, his fingers glancing along my jaw; his lips part as his gaze moves over my features. "God, I am so fucking in love with you."

I squeeze my eyes shut.

"What about what I did?" I whisper. "I am not the woman you've been spending time with, Marco." My voice cracks on his name. I open my eyes. "I-I need a fucking kidney."

My last big reveal. *Ta-da*.

His eyebrows snap together. Marco's mouth opens, then closes. His hands fall back to his sides, and for a second, I'm terrified I *actually* did it—I've completely scared him away. "You need a kidney?"

"Not right now. But one day, yes, I might need a kidney. I may cut off all my hair because I'm too sick to brush it. I'll probably never, *ever* be sexy in Rome again. But you will always be *you*."

Marco chews his lip. Then, he reaches for my crossed arms, for my hands buried underneath. "I'll brush your hair," he says. I want to pull away, but before I can, he curls his fingers around mine and brings our hands to rest over his heart. His hammering heart. "I'll help you out of bed. Fuck, I can give you a kidney. I just want you, Nadia. I don't care about Rome or LA or New York or Evergreen. I'll go wherever you need me. I want to wake up at your side and *know* you—whatever version of you—are going to be there. I *love* you."

I love you, too. For days, it's been my only consistent thought. Instead, I whisper, "You're making this so, *so* hard."

"Good." With his free hand, he finds my lower back and gently eases me to him. "You will not leave me standing alone in the place where I first realized I love you." His eyes are burning into me, holding me. Daring me to keep lying when he knows—I know—all my defenses are down. "That is not how our story ends, okay? So, say it. Tell me what you want."

I pull in a shaky rush of breath. "You." And then, I crumble into his chest. Finally, he holds me.

"Marco?"

It's the first thing I say when I come out of my deep sleep. Through the window I can make out the moon in the dark, cloudless sky. I feel alone in my bed. I'm in a shirt I don't recognize. Fear grabs me in the chest. "Marco?" I say again, louder.

A shadow beside me stirs. "I'm here," he says, rolling toward me.

A heavy, warm arm circles my head. A pair of lips rests against my temple and every part of me relaxes.

"You're real?" I grumble.

"Yes." He laughs, warm breath on my ear, his lips in my hair. "I'm flesh and bones."

"Can we go back to Evergreen?"

"We're already here," he assures me. "You're home now."

"Did I take my medicine?" I ask through a yawn, already falling back into the grip of sleep.

"Mmm-hmm." His fingers trace a lazy pattern over my shoulder. "You took your medicine. We called Liv. You texted your mom. You're all good; go back to sleep."

"You sure?" I manage, words lazy on my tongue. The moon is just a blur now. There's a lightness in my chest, a calmness that has reached my bones.

"Promise," he whispers. I feel the sheet move up around my shoulders, his bare chest against my back. The warmth of his thighs around mine. Then, I fall back asleep.

Thursday, May 32

"Tell me about your dad." This is objectively the least sexy thing someone can say to a person they just had sex with, but I do it anyway.

"Oh boy." Marco stretches his arms, bringing them back down to rest behind his head. "Yorgos Antoniou. What a guy. *He's* where I get all my most charming personality quirks."

I roll up onto my side, propping my head up in my hand. "Like your obsession with minor league baseball?"

Marco considers this, biting anxiously at his lower lip. "Boy, I wish. George only likes sports where he can bet on people like they're dogs. Anything that involves someone getting the shit kicked out of them, really. The less teeth the athletes have, the better." Marco keeps going, very clearly on a roll, completely entertaining himself. "George loves to drink. He loves to gamble. He loves fake breasts—"

"Wait, hold on," I cut in. "Do *you* love fake breasts?"

Marco rolls his eyes. "Not like, explicitly. My dad and I have different vices, but it's really not a mystery where I get my, uh, *appetite* for fun from."

I reach out to Marco and rest a hand against his bare chest. "Was he a good dad?"

"Yeah, he was, actually. My mom is kind of . . ." Marco flutters his eyes shut. A facial expression I know to mean: *Where do I even start?* "He did his best even for a dirty, rotten cheater."

I suppress a grimace. "Okay, so he's generous."

"Right," Marco grunts, giving my hand a squeeze before sitting up straight and swinging his legs out of bed. "When people are watching, he's incredibly giving. You'll never meet someone putting more change in a Salvation Army bucket. Why do you ask?"

I shrug. "The night after Soph and Allie's . . . you kind of mentioned your childhood."

"I did, didn't I?" He tosses me a smile over his shoulder—a wink of that sad guy I met a month ago. "I was jealous of your life that night. *Really* jealous."

"Hey." I poke him in the back. "It can be both of our lives now."

"Speaking of which . . ." He gets up out of bed, even though I try desperately to hold him back while he pulls on his boxers and leaves me behind in a knotted mess of sheets. When he comes back into my room, Marco presents a thin, square package with a flourish. "A gift, madam. Open it."

I carefully tear away the outside paper. "It's a wall calendar?"

"Uh huh." Marco's sporting a very satisfied smirk. "Flip through it."

The first page is a photo he took of the Brooklyn Bridge the day we went for our picnic—I recognize the view right away. The calendar begins with May. I flip the page around to him. "*Adorable.* I love it."

Now he's grinning, rocking from foot to foot. "C'mon. Keep going."

"Jeez, alright."

I turn the page and there's another photo Marco took over the last four weeks. A high-contrast shot of me reaching into a pear tree outside Paola's villa. The leaves look like crosshatching over the sky, and a shadow bruises my exposed shoulders as my fingers break through into the sun, grabbing a piece of fruit. It's a gorgeous photo, one I didn't even know he'd taken.

I'm almost too distracted by the photo to notice—but the month is still May. And the dates keep going. Thirty-second, thirty-third, thirty-fourth . . .

"Wait." I laugh, turning the page. "It's still May."

Then again. Another May.

Another.

And another.

"They're *all* May."

"What did you tell me back when we met?" Marco reaches out, fingers sliding down my neck to my shoulder. "I had until the end of the month, not a day more." He gives me a gentle squeeze. "I figured we'll just have to make sure May never ends."

I lift my eyes to meet his. There's moisture gathering in them again. "Marco, I might actually cry . . ."

"Don't." He laughs, leaning forward, pressing his lips to my forehead, pressing his body into mine. "Today is officially the thirty-second day in May."

I let myself fall back against the sheets, relishing the feeling of his weight on top of me, the tickle of his hair in my face. Marco's been exceedingly gentle with me since yesterday, and I want to tell him to knock it off. *Grab me,* my body begs. I push his hair out of his face and say, "Just like in the movie."

He grins down at me. "You get it."

I bury my face in his neck, breathing in his smell. *You're safe,* I tell myself. *You can cry now. You're safe.* But I'm not ready to.

Maybe one day I'll feel brave enough to let Marco really see how much he means to me. But for now, I just hold on to him.

If yesterday I'd decided I would never run away from Marco again, today I am positive that every moment of the last six months was leading up to this.

"I love you," I say once, then again. Over and over. A brand-new mantra.

Acknowledgments

This book leapt from my heart right onto the page. From the trenches of my own sickness and sadness, I escaped back to Evergreen. When my body ached and my life changed and I contemplated how I would ever do *anything* ever again, Nadia stepped in and guided me toward a new way of life. When July took me to Italy, Marco and Nadia came along; we ate pizza together, we listened to the footsteps on the cobblestoned streets together. They've been the best company. So, first and foremost, I want to thank these fake people that I made up in my own head for everything they've given me. It is with an extremely nervous tummy that I turn them over to you, dear reader.

Dom, thank you for being my, well, everything. Support system, best friend, personal comedian, chihuahua father, accountant, life coach, personal chef. May will always be our month. I hope I have you in every lifetime.

Ariana and Claire—thank you for believing in me and my work, over and over again. Thank you for understanding that I am a very strange woman interested in very strange things. Thank you for being better at talking about my work than I will ever be. I really hope I never do this without you both. Same time next year? <3

To the entire team at Avon—marketer Michelle Lecumberry, publicist Hannah Dirgins, designer Diahann Sturge-Campbell, copyeditor Karen Richardson, and cover designer Yeon Kim. Your care and consideration for my work, the attention to detail and affection you bring to each project blow me away every time. Thank you for making every part of this book better.

Brittani, thank you so much for helping me bring my work to new readers. Your focus and partnership has brought a new spark to this whole process. Our conversations leave me feeling hopeful, buoyant. I can't thank you enough.

Photine, thank you for your big, beautiful brain and *all* of the love and support and encouragement you've given me. I could not have written about Nadia's experience without you. Your ability to exude love is such a wonderful gift.

To my earliest of early readers, Maggie and Natasha, your love and support of Nadia from the very first time she stepped from my brain onto the page has been incredible. I can't believe you first met her in 2020. You've been by my side through a lot of ideas, a lot of hurdles, a lot of words. I hope that never changes.

Audrey, thank you for literally giving me yourself to put into these pages. Is Audrey a good therapist? I think she may be the best in the world. You're wildly full of courage, just like Nadia.

To all of the romance authors who have come into my life as friends and mentors since *Summertime Punchline* debuted—I don't think I would have survived my first few months of being an author without you. Your wisdom, your guidance, your love, your support, your encouragement—all of it has changed this process for me. Being in community with you is everything.

Writing Hell, you already know what it is. You're all insane, and I love you so much. We're riding this thing 'til the wheels fall off.

Hannah, I thought about dedicating this book to you. You're so special to me. You're in every page. I love you so much. Let's be friends forever.

Emily, I could never have done this or, basically, anything without you. You are both an artist and a champion of art. Every time I write a joke, I ask myself, "Would this make Emily laugh?" I admire you so much.

To everyone who purchased, borrowed, read, shared, and celebrated *Summertime Punchline*—thank you, oh my God, thank you. I don't really have words for the way you have made me feel. Please know that I will never stop feeling gratitude for your enthusiasm in those early days when I was certain no one would ever read Del's story. You are special to me, and I hope I made you proud with this one.

Mom and Dad, I love you. Thank you for everything.

About the Author

Betty Corrello is a writer, comedian, and proud Philadelphian. Despite her hardened exterior, she is biologically 95 percent marshmallow. Her greatest passion is writing stories where opposites attract, but love is chosen. When she's not writing, she can be found fretting about niche historical events most have forgotten—or petting her very tiny dog.

Discover more from
Betty Corrello and Avon Books

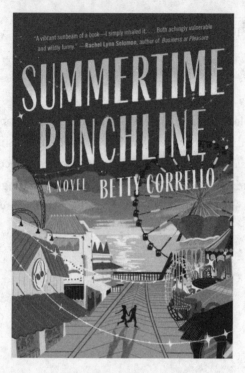

"This is a hilarious and sweeping love story about a comedian forced to return to her Jersey Shore hometown and confront everything she left behind ten summers before. A plucky heroine remaking herself. A beach setting. The meaning of home. Humor. Romance. This one ticks all the boxes."

—Mary Kay Andrews,
New York Times bestselling author

"A wonderfully witty love letter to stand-up comedy, true love, and there being no place like home."

—Georgia Clark,
author of *It Had to Be You*